"Nick."

Their eyes met, a̶n̶... something... Mayb... she'd seen from hi... and vulnerable. It w... put his hand lightly o... ...ng her into the curve of his body and ...ging his mouth down on hers.

For all that she'd wanted him, for as intense as those feelings were, the first brush of his lips against hers was soft.

But the impact...

She felt it all the way to her core, and everything feminine and sensual inside her sprung to life, demanding that she deepen the kiss. She put her hand on the back of his neck, tipped her head to the side and thrust her tongue into his mouth.

He tasted so good. There was no awkwardness to the deepening of their embrace. His tongue rubbed over hers, adding to the fire within her.

This wasn't going to be just one kiss.

Dear Reader,

I'm so excited to bring you this bodyguard story and introduce you to the Price Security team. I love the idea of a team of people who are really good at protecting everyone else and putting themselves second. Luna Urban has never had a family, but growing up in the foster system taught her to protect herself and others. Getting a job as a bodyguard for the elite Price Security team has given her purpose and a found family. She never compromises her clients' safety, so when she starts getting feels for Nicholas DeVere, she tries to shut them down.

Nicholas DeVere has been lucky his entire life, but the people he loves and cares for haven't been. He seems charmed, having escaped death more times than even he can count. But when his look-alike bodyguard is killed, everyone is taking the threat to his life seriously.

He picks Luna as his bodyguard, at first thinking that he might be able to control her and find the killer on his own, but Luna is smarter, faster and tougher than Nick estimated. As they follow the clues and uncover the truth of Nick's past, they soon find themselves in each other's arms.

I had so much fun writing this story and hope you enjoy reading it and meeting the entire team at Price Security.

Until next time!

Happy reading,

Katherine

BODYGUARD MOST WANTED

Katherine Garbera

HARLEQUIN
ROMANTIC
SUSPENSE

Recycling programs
for this product may
not exist in your area.

ISBN-13: 978-1-335-59381-8

Bodyguard Most Wanted

Copyright © 2023 by Katherine Garbera

For questions and comments about the quality of this book,
please contact us at CustomerService@Harlequin.com.

Harlequin Enterprises ULC
22 Adelaide St. West, 41st Floor
Toronto, Ontario M5H 4E3, Canada
www.Harlequin.com

Printed in U.S.A.

Katherine Garbera is the *USA TODAY* bestselling author of more than one hundred and twenty-five novels. She's a small-town Florida girl whose imagination was fired up by long hours spent outside sitting underneath orange trees. She grew up to travel the world and makes her home in the UK with her husband. Her books have garnered numerous awards and are sold around the world. Connect with her at www.katherinegarbera.com and on Facebook, Instagram and Twitter.

Books by Katherine Garbera

Harlequin Romantic Suspense

Price Security

Bodyguard Most Wanted

Harlequin Desire

Destination Wedding

The Wedding Dare
The One from the Wedding
Secrets of a Wedding Crasher

The Image Project

Billionaire Makeover
The Billionaire Plan
Billionaire Fake Out

Visit the Author Profile page at
Harlequin.com for more titles.

This one is for Donna and Scott Scamehorn, who are always living their best lives and helping us to do the same whenever we are with them. Love you!

Acknowledgment:

Sandy Harding and John Jacobson were so supportive of this idea and went above and beyond in helping me place it and sell it. Thank you both for your hard work. I love working with you both.

Chapter 1

Nicholas DeVere was used to seeing his name in the headlines—The Golden Prince Found Dead at Debauched Beachside Party. Not the most flattering of headlines, and the truth was, Nick wasn't used to being proclaimed dead. "Nice to see something can still surprise me."

"Surprise you?" Finnian Walsh asked under his breath. His assistant had close-cropped, thick brown hair and was always perfectly groomed. "Please tell me you have a plan to deal with this. The cops think it was murder," he said.

"Breathe, Finn. It's not a big deal," Nick said, projecting a calmness he was used to faking. His tie felt too tight as he considered the news story. He thought it was murder as well.

The first attempt on his life had happened when he'd been only six months old. Since then he'd been kidnapped, blackmailed, and had his vehicles tampered with—more than once. He'd kind of become nonplussed by attempts on his life. But even he had to admit that having his bodyguard and lookalike Jack Ingram murdered…well, it was giving him pause.

The loss of so many people he'd known in his life was taking a toll. He'd reached his limit. He was going to prove that someone had been trying to kill him and he was going to catch them before someone else died.

Finn threw his hands up and walked out of his office. Only to return a moment later. "I get that you think you can't die, but those of us who love you wish you'd treat your life with more care."

"I know," he said to Finn's back as he paced in front of the desk.

Nick either had to take himself out of the spotlight, renounce his place in the DeVere family and disappear…or put an end to this. The cops were, of course, treating this case like it was their top priority. Given the massive fortune that he was due to inherit when his father died, it made sense. But Nick had never been one to sit and wait. With his resources, he had a better chance of finding the killer before the overworked and understaffed police department. "I'm not as blasé as I seem. The board of DeVere Industries has insisted on a new bodyguard and security team, and I agreed."

"You agreed?" Finn said.

"I thought that would make you happy."

Finn shook his head as he walked over to Nick, putting the back of his hand to Nick's forehead. "You're not running a fever, so we can rule out delusional."

"You know I don't keep you around for your wit," Nick said dryly.

"You wound me," Finn said. "When you get all agreeable, it makes me suspicious. You only tolerated having Jack as your bodyguard because he looked like you and would handle public events you didn't want to attend."

"Which is no longer an option," Nick said. "I intend to find Jack's killer—"

"What are you, Sherlock Holmes now?" Finn asked sardonically.

"Worried you might have to be Watson?"

"No, I'm much more a Mycroft."

To be fair, his assistant was right about Sherlock's older brother, the mastermind. Finn had a way of organizing and manipulating everyone around him to make things happen. Despite the gravity of the day, Nick smiled. "There weren't a lot of people who knew I'd be in Malibu last night. There were even fewer who knew the security code to the mansion. So, the list of possible killers has to be small."

"Aren't the police working the case?" Finn asked, sitting down in the leather guest chair across from him, casually crossing his legs. He'd been with Nick since prep school and balanced him out.

"Yes. But they want to write it off as a drunken accident. It's only the fact that security system had been disarmed and the cameras turned off that are being forced to investigate further. We both know that Jack would never drink too much to stumble and fall off the balcony."

"Indeed. Especially when he had the twins in his bed," Finn said. "So, when are we meeting the new bodyguard?"

"In an hour. I need the conference room set up. The board and I negotiated, and we agreed they'd hire the company who would comprise the new security team, and I'd pick someone from the group to be my new body-guard."

Finn pulled his smartphone from his pocket. "What's the company name?"

"Price Security," Nick said.

He heard Finn's fingers tapping as he did an internet search. Nick had done his own as soon as he'd been informed. DeVere Industries was much more than his family's legacy. He'd taken an active role in running and expanding the company since his father's cancer had returned and the old man had to stay at home. He knew how much this legacy meant to his father, and as contentious as their relationship could be at times, he was determined to keep the company thriving as his father would have.

The Price Security website gave away very little. Just the logo and a contact form. And the tagline *Security is priceless, and your life is worth the price.*

He had no idea what they were dealing with.

"I'll dig deeper. I think I've heard of this Giovanni Price, the owner. An hour isn't a lot of time. I'll have Hazel set up the conference room while I prepare some information for you," Finn said, already walking out of his office.

"Thanks."

Finn waved and closed the door behind him as he left. Nick got up and looked out his penthouse office window toward downtown Los Angeles. The board wasn't a fan of the fact that he'd refused to move to their tech campus in Northern California, but instead had stayed in his offices above his nightclub, Madness. Nick hadn't been willing to compromise on this. He was preserving his family's legacy, not sacrificing his lifestyle.

But now…

He wasn't sure that Jack would have been safer in Silicon Valley. He felt Jack's death deeply, not just because they'd been friends, but also because Jack had died in his place. How many more deaths could he take?

He put his hand against the glass window and lowered his head. He wouldn't ever let anyone see this side of himself. Grief swamped him and he mourned his friend for a moment.

He didn't dwell on it. The only way out of grief was motion. He needed to find out who'd killed Jack so he could bring his own form of justice, and then maybe that mark on his soul wouldn't feel as heavy.

But he knew from the past that it would.

He straightened and looked down at the streets, but in his mind, he wondered who he'd pissed off and why they were coming after him. He dealt in favors now; spread his wealth around him to create the illusion that his life had some higher meaning.

Had someone seen behind the façade? Was that why Jack had been attacked and killed?

He didn't have the answer yet, but he wouldn't stop until the killer was found. Nothing was going to stand in his way. Not the DeVere Industries board, his father, or anyone from Price Security.

Luna Urban was exhausted when she walked out of the international terminal at LAX. She looked for the familiar black Dodge sitting at the curb, blatantly waiting in the no parking zone for her. She would never admit it out loud, but every single time she returned from a trip, she held her breath as she stepped out of the airport. Giovanni—Van—had never let her down, but a part of her…never could quite believe that he'd be there. He was leaning against the passenger's-side door, talking to the airport security guard.

He wore a Dolce & Gabbana suit that had been custom made to fit his large muscly frame. He was bald and had a tattoo on his neck of angel's wings. He took off his sunglasses when he saw her approaching and left the security guard to turn and smile at her.

"Welcome home, Luna. We missed you. I was afraid that Jaz wasn't going to let you come back to us," Van said in his low, gravelly voice as he opened his arms.

Luna stepped closer to hug him. Price Security was more than a business. As Van liked to say, they were family. The group of misfits that no one wanted, but somehow Van had shaped them into a working team.

"Yeah. Me too," she said. She'd been working as the bodyguard to famed teen rap sensation Jaz. His tour in South America had just wrapped up and she'd spent the night partying with him and his entourage before getting on the flight to LA. "It was fun, but the kid knew I'd cramp his style if I stuck around."

"Keeping him alive isn't cramping his style."

She agreed, but Jaz was young and felt like he couldn't die, so he liked to take risks. And now that the tour was over and he was going back home, her contract was up.

"I hate to do this to you, Luna…" Van started. "But we have a new client and I need all hands at his place in less than two hours."

"Even me?"

"Especially you. The contract said everyone on the team, and they are paying us a bonus," he said. "Have you had a chance to catch up on the blast that Lee sent out?"

"No. Don't glare at me. I'm hung over and jet-lagged. Most people wouldn't even be lucid right now. I'll read the blast while you drive. What's the dress code?"

"D&G, like me. The entire team is getting ready at the tower. We'll go over in the Hummer limo."

Who was the new client Van was pulling out the flashy labels and big guns for? She opened her email. The words were blurry at first and she had to force herself to concentrate just to read them. Billionaire playboy whose bodyguard died after falling off a balcony… and, at first, they'd thought it was the billionaire himself who'd died.

"Okay. So why me? If he doesn't want Kenji, he's an idiot."

"I agree, but he didn't hire us, the board of DeVere Industries did. And he made some deal with them that he could meet all of the staff and choose his bodyguard."

"You agreed to that?" Van made the decisions on all assignments. He might be pretending to play nice with this billionaire, but Luna knew in the end Van wouldn't budge if he felt the guy made the wrong choice.

"They are offering an insane amount of money for something that should be a cakewalk. Which is making the back of my neck itchy."

But it couldn't be a cakewalk if they were offering that much dough. "What gives?"

"It's Nicholas DeVere."

Oh.

Superrich. Like probably more than a billionaire. His family was famed for its wealth and tragedy. His mom had died in a car crash when Nicholas was only six months old. His cousins and uncles had died in a yacht bombing somewhere in Asia; Nicholas had been partying on shore at the time. He was infamous for escaping death.

Looked like he'd done it again.

Nick wasn't sure what he was expecting from the brief notes he'd read on each security agent, but walking into the conference room and seeing five people all dressed in black suits standing in a group wasn't it. There was Xander Quentin, tall and menacing, he was a big behemoth of a man and stood at the back. He had thick black hair that curled around his collar. Then there was Kenji Wada the Japanese American bodyguard the board heavily favored. He was tall; not as large as the behemoth, but still big. He was lean and had a thick fall of jet black bangs that dropped over one of his eyes.

Next was the leader—Giovanni Price. Not as tall as the other two, he exuded a strong aura of menace, even with the angel's wings tattoo peeking over the collar of his white dress shirt. He was bald, clean-shaven, and his eyes, when he noticed Nick, seemed to bore straight through him.

None of them would do. He wanted someone whose loyalty would be to him. A bodyguard he could manipulate to go along with whatever he asked. That left Rick Stone, the stoner in the corner, who looked like he was going through withdrawal, and the woman, Luna Urban, the only team member he couldn't see. Where was she?

He finally spotted her in the shadow of the big guy. She wore her brown hair pulled back in a tight ponytail. She had high cheekbones and a pert nose. Her eyes, when she met his stare, were direct, giving nothing away.

He let his gaze drift lower, but the suit gave her an air of androgyny. It was well fitted, and as she stood next to the men, she didn't stand out. In fact, it was almost as if she were trying to blend in and not be seen.

"Thank you all for coming," he said. "I'm Nicholas DeVere, but then you probably recognize me."

"Should we?" the behemoth said in a crisp British accent.

Nick didn't answer, just gestured toward the large conference table. "Have a seat. Can we get you anything to drink?"

They all moved to the big leather chairs that were dotted around table as Hazel entered. His admin assistant was in her sixties but, trim and fit, appeared younger. She had short blond hair that she wore in a pixie cut. She looked at the serious group and then back at him as if she wasn't sure what to do. He nodded slightly toward the beverages and she smiled.

She went around the table, getting drinks for them. Everyone asked for water except the stoner, who wanted a Fanta. Hazel left as Finn joined them.

"I'm Finn Walsh. I believe we spoke on the phone, Mr. Price," Finn said, going over to offer his hand to Giovanni Price.

The man shook it. "We did. Nice to meet in person."

Price's voice was low, with a rough quality to it. Nick had a feeling it was the kind of voice that could be heard through a crowd. But Price knew how to control it. Nick could tell by looking at him that the man could control almost anything if he wanted to.

"Nice to meet you, as well," Finn said, taking a seat next to Nick and setting down his notepad so he could read it.

Rick Stone will be the easiest to manage. The girl seems like trouble.

They were all deadly serious, and Nick had the feeling that it was going to be difficult to manipulate anyone he chose.

Price cracked his knuckles and then put his hands on the table in front of him. "From our perspective, this job would entail twenty-four-seven detail. I think we are looking for four-days-on, three-days-off shifts so we might—"

"No," Nick said. "I want one guard with me all the time. No days off."

Price leaned back in his chair, crossing his massive arms over his chest. "Why don't you tell us a little about yourself?"

"Nicholas DeVere, only son and heir of Emmett DeVere. I own the nightclub Madness and am known for being a generous man."

"If that's the case, then why did someone try to kill you?"

He stopped and looked down the table at the woman. Luna. She met his gaze squarely and didn't blink or move. He had the feeling she was looking for something in his face, but he already knew she'd be disappointed. No one ever found what they wanted with him, other than money.

"Good question. Perhaps I'm not as charming as I like to think I am."

"Fair point," Price said. "Why are we here?"

"The board will force me to go on leave if I don't have a bodyguard," Nick said. "We are at a critical point with the negotiations on some new contracts, and me stepping out of the way would serve certain parties.

I'm not interested in that, so I've agreed to their terms. Also, I won't give the bastard who killed Jack the satisfaction of thinking they have driven me into hiding."

Finn pulled his notepad back and, out of the corner of his eye; Nick noticed his assistant was writing. He ignored it. This was the story he was going with. He wasn't interested in debating the kind of bodyguard he'd accept. Either Price and his team would agree to his terms or Nick would go it alone.

And he really wanted to go it alone. He wasn't about to risk any more lives or waste any more time.

Chapter 2

Something wasn't right here, but Luna wasn't sure what. Spoiled rich men didn't usually try to keep her from doing her job. Normally they were all bravado and then cowered as she took control. But Nick wasn't fitting the profile she'd expected. She had to admit she was dog-tired and not as sharp as usual, but something was off. She ran over the information she'd been given in the car on the ride over. Nick DeVere's doppelganger victim—Jack Ingram—had been his bodyguard for almost three years.

That was a long time. And as much as they were supposed to buy into his whole "rich guy with no real cares" persona, she could sense there was more at play here. She stood while Van let Nick sweat under the weight of his stare—but Nick wasn't sweating. He was cool. Like someone who wanted something and had nothing to lose.

It was a dangerous combination. She knew it, and she suspected that Van knew it too. It might help if DeVere knew that Van had known Ingram. But there hadn't been an opportunity to talk.

Luna wanted to shake her head as she realized the problem. There was too much testosterone in this room. Those two were both used to being the alpha, and neither was going to back down.

There was more to DeVere than met the eye. The file she'd read had mentioned his preference for providing favors to everyday people who crossed his path. He was known as Midas or the Golden Prince in the media. But he wasn't greedy. He spread his fortune around wherever he went.

What was she missing?

She walked over to the large plate-glass windows that overlooked the other buildings in this area of downtown LA. There were a few Art Deco buildings and then some newer less distinct ones. The neighborhood wasn't gentrified yet, but she could see it slowly happening.

There was a glint as she scanned the rooftops. She double-checked it and then launched herself across the table at Nick DeVere just as he stood to say something to Van.

A second later, a bullet hit the glass with a loud sound. Kenji responded to her movements and turned into a shooter's stance, pulling his SIG from his coat pocket. Then he noted the bulletproof glass.

Rick was on his feet and out the door in a flash.

Luna knew the glass wouldn't shatter, but with the rush of adrenaline going through her, she barely registered it. Hitting Nick with her full body weight and knocking him to the floor, she used the momentum to roll him underneath her.

He put his arms around her and tried to roll to cover her, which she countered by staying on top of him. She felt the coiled energy; he was going to try again.

"Stay," she said, forcefully pushing his shoulder as he made to move.

"You're exposed."

"That's my job," she reminded him.

His assistant hit the floor and crawled over to where they were as more shots hit the glass. She wondered if the shooter intended to shatter it, but it would take at least fifty rounds to do that. Luna glanced up into DeVere's icy blue eyes. His strong jaw was locked, and he looked angry. She glanced over at his assistant and saw a mélange of emotions moving across the other man's face. Finn was in love, or at least in deep affection, with his boss.

Luna wanted to get back into the mix, to help the team, but she knew she couldn't leave DeVere until the shooting stopped.

"Someone really wants you dead," she said.

"Or maybe they don't like my windows," he retorted.

"Perhaps. But two tries in as many days…who'd you piss off?"

"I told you, people like me."

There was a humph from his assistant and Luna turned to look at the other man. "He's got enemies?"

"Well, there's—"

"Finn."

Finn arched both eyebrows and sort of shrugged his head. "Not everyone is happy. That's all I'm saying."

Luna put her hand in the middle of DeVere's chest, lifting her head so they were more eye to eye. "It's easier if we have a list of suspects. The cops will run it, but they are always understaffed. Any ideas who might be coming for you? You mentioned—"

"There's a firefight going on. Shouldn't you be concerned with that?"

"I'm guarding you," she said. "And gathering intel. Trust me, DeVere. I'm good at my job."

The bullets stopped.

"Get off of me," Nick said, sitting up with her on his chest and setting her aside. He stood and turned to face the room. "What the hell is going on?"

"Someone is trying to kill you," Luna said.

"Well, they aren't very good, are they?" he sneered. She could tell he was rattled, but only because of the sharp way he'd straightened his tie despite being so at ease earlier.

"They missed on purpose. That was just to rattle you," Van said.

"They'll have to try harder."

"That's not the right reaction," Luna said.

"If I cowered every time someone threatened me, I'd have never left my childhood home. Finn, have Hazel get in touch with that detective who's investigating Jack's death. Tell her what happened."

Finn just nodded and left the room, his fingers flying over the screen of his smartphone. Luna started to follow, so she could speak to the cop herself, but Van stopped her.

"Stay here. I want you on DeVere. Xander and Kenji, go check out the rooftop and see if he left any traces. Lee reported that Rick was on foot chasing someone through the garment district."

Lee was their eyes in the sky, she stayed in the office as a rule in the command center and kept in touch with everyone. The woman was more comfortable in front of her bank of computers than she was in the field. Though she had some solid skills there as well. Van always had his earpiece in and he and Lee were always monitoring everything.

The other men left and she turned to DeVere. "You okay?"

He seemed surprised by her question as he pulled at his tie. She couldn't help but remember how solid he'd felt beneath her. "Of course."

"There's no *of course*. Despite what you said, being shot at isn't normal."

"No, it's not," he said. "After Jack's death and the media claiming it was me…well, I did suspect someone might be gunning for me, which is why I agreed to a new security team."

"Good, I'm glad to hear that." At least he had some sense that he wasn't invincible. "I'd also like to know if there are people who might want to kill you," she said.

Luna was still trying to build a profile for this client in her head. He was polished and smooth, and as the time passed from the incident, he was recovering. Actually, pretty quickly, she had to admit. She was still a bit shaken. She felt like her instincts were a little slow but put that down to the lack of sleep. It couldn't have been something she felt when her body was over Nick's.

"Do you have any rooms where you won't be a target?" Van asked, shuffling them into the hallway.

She should have gotten them out of the exposed room. She glanced at Van, but he just shook his head, which she took to mean it was not a big deal.

"I'm not sure what you mean?" Nick asked. "I doubt that the shooter will come back."

"You never know. Do you have any space without windows, and possibly only one door?" she asked. Van knew she was tired from the last gig, but she didn't want him to start coddling her or having to make excuses.

"Yes. I have a panic room up in the penthouse," Nick said.

"Okay, go up there," Van said. "Will she have a phone signal in there?"

"Yes, of course," Nick said.

"I'll ping you when you can come out."

Luna put her hand on Nick's arm and it was surprisingly muscular for a playboy. "Come on."

"Wait a minute. I'm not sure who you think is in charge here—"

"We are. We were hired to keep you alive and that's what I'm going to do. Luna, don't let him out of your sight until I say otherwise."

"No problem, boss. Mr. DeVere, lead on," she said, urging him to move. He resisted for a moment, and she thought he was going to try to go toe-to-toe with Van, but then he shrugged.

"I want to talk to the cop when she arrives. We can wait in Hazel's office. There's only one window and I'll stay back from it. I'm not a damsel who needs to cower."

"That works for me," Van said.

This job was full of twists and turns. More than she'd expected, especially with Nick's reluctance to speak… but there was a glint in DeVere's eyes that made her believe he knew more than he was telling.

Finn and Hazel were both standing in the far corner of her office when he walked in. Nick doubted that the shooter was still anywhere around, but he could appreciate the Price Security team's caution. The board had really done a good job in selecting them.

His phone rang and he answered it without a thought. He wasn't under lockdown even though Van seemed to think he was in charge.

"DeVere."

"Nicky! Thank God. I just saw the news," Verity Vaughn said. She was his ex-wife, but they'd always been on friendly terms. "I'm so sorry about Jack."

"Thank you, Verity. I'll let you know when the funeral is."

"Oh, of course, also where to send flowers...actually, do you want me to take care of all of that for you?" she asked.

"Um, why?" he countered. Verity wasn't normally one to volunteer to do anything for anyone else.

"I need a favor," she said, that pouty note in her voice.

Nick could picture her sitting at her writing desk, dressed in white and making a list of possible things she could offer to get him to help her out.

"What kind of favor?"

"Just a teensy one. Have you heard that Hugh is leaving me?"

"No, I heard that you're leaving him," Nick said. Verity was on her third husband, and she did have a hard time sticking with one man. Rumor in their circle was that she'd found a new lover in the Caribbean and was anxious to move down there to be near him. So anything that helped Verity on her way, he was willing to do. "What do you need?"

"Thanks, Nicky, I knew you'd come through. He's insisting that we stick to the prenup and that means I can't take any of the gifts he's given me. I am sure that if you spoke to him, he'd see reason."

"Send me the list of what you want and I'll talk to him," he said. He had no doubt that Hugh wasn't heartbroken, but the man didn't like to lose.

"Thanks, darling, that's all I wanted. I'll get to work on Jack's funeral arrangements. Should I use Finn as my contact? I assume he's still by your side," she said.

"Yes."

"Great. 'Bye."

She hung up and he pocketed his phone. Turned to see Finn shaking his head. "If you want to know someone who I don't trust...then it's her."

"Her?" Luna asked.

"Verity Vaughn. His ex. She's shady AF," Finn said.

Everyone was looking at him except Van, who was on the landline. Nick was frustrated with Luna. She was already poking into things that went beyond bodyguard duties. For his entire life everyone—from his father, to the board, to investigators he'd hired—had written off the deaths that happened around him as accidents. He'd always sensed there was more to it. Jack's death would be the last one to happen to someone he knew and cared about.

So he didn't have time for Luna Urban and her list of suspects and theories. Nick was taking action and no one, not even his hotter than expected bodyguard was going to get in his way.

He just ignored Luna; he wasn't ready to deal with everything that had been stirred up since the moment she'd launched herself across the table at him. Turning to Finn he said, "Verity will be in touch regarding Jack's funeral. She's not shady."

"Whatever you say, boss."

Finn and Verity had always had a contentious relationship, which had struck Nick as odd since they were both very similar.

He just clapped his hand on Finn's shoulder. "Thank you for dealing with this and with her."

"Of course," Finn said with a smile.

"Does she have access to your Malibu mansion?" Luna asked.

"What? Yes, but she wouldn't try to kill me," Nick said. "I'm worth more to her alive."

Luna just nodded and wrote something on her smartphone keypad.

Hazel's phone rang and she answered it before glancing at Nick. "Sir, I have security downstairs, there's a Rick Stone and Detective Miller here to see you."

"I'll go and get them," Van said. "Luna is in charge while I'm gone. Give her anything she asks for."

The other man left and Luna pocketed her cell phone. "I'm going to need access to your files and anyone he came in contact within the last month." She directed this toward Hazel.

Hazel didn't move, just looked over at him.

He smiled at his admin assistant. She only took orders from him. "I'll approve it on an as-needed basis."

He turned to Luna and gestured for her to follow him into the hallway, where they could speak privately.

"Yes?"

"Thank you for everything you are doing, and I know you are very good at your job, but you work for me. At the end of the day, I will consider your advice for my safety but never forget that you have been hired and can be fired," Nick said.

Luna crossed her arms under her chest, pulling the expensive fabric of her suit taut against her breasts, distracting him because it contrasted with her toughness.

"Okay. As long as you remember that dead guys can't pay their bills, so I'll do whatever I deem necessary to keep you alive. And if you don't like it, then you can discuss it with E. DeVere, as he's the one who called and personally hired us."

That was something Nick hadn't realized. His father had hired this team personally? Did his dad know more about Jack's death than he'd let on? He was going to have to take a drive out to Malibu and visit the old man, but not until he got the windows replaced and dealt with Price.

"We can discuss that later. Not in front of the detective," Nick said. "That's nonnegotiable."

"Works for me," Luna said just as the elevator arrived on their floor.

Detective Miller, Van and the stoner were chatting. Seeing the other man with the security team chief and the female cop, it suddenly made sense. The stoner, aka Rick Stone, was an ex-cop. They all stopped talking as they approached.

"Mr. DeVere, are you okay?" Detective Miller asked. She was around five-five but held herself in a way that made her seem taller. She had dark curly hair that she'd pulled back into a ponytail, but a tendril had escaped to twist against her cheek. Her eyes were green and there were bags under them, as if she didn't get enough sleep.

"I'm fine. Luna and the Price team had the situation well in hand."

"Is there somewhere we can talk?" she asked.

"All of my offices have plate glass," he said. "We

could talk in the nightclub. As you can guess, there're no windows and lots of seating."

"Great. Where is it exactly?" Luna asked.

"Third floor," he said. "I'll take the detective down there while you gather your troops."

Nick led the detective to the elevator. He wasn't about to allow Luna or anyone from Price to be in charge. That wasn't his way, and the further he got from the bullet incident, the angrier he was becoming. It felt like someone was toying with him. He really needed to take the time to figure out who and put an end to it.

Luna had started to follow Nick and Detective Miller, but Van had asked her to stay. So, she was half listening to Stone's report. It was funny how being on a case changed Rick's energy. The edgy, nervousness that had been dominant before had faded away and he radiated a calmness that came from doing what he did best.

It forced her to acknowledge that, honestly, none of them was good in interpersonal relationships as much as they tried to make them work. Each member of Price Security seemed more comfortable protecting others than they did connecting to regular people.

She didn't delve too deeply into it, bringing herself back to the job at hand. Jack Ingram's death was starting to seem to her like the opening move in a very-well-thought-out plan.

"I tailed someone with blond hair who ducked out of the building where I think the shot came from, but lost him once we got into the garment district. Not sure if he was our guy. He was carrying a gym bag and had on a baseball hat. I couldn't get close enough to stop him," Stone said.

"You're saying 'him.' Are you sure it was a man?" Luna asked, thinking of Finn's suspicions of Verity.

"No, I'm not," Rick said.

"Do you think they knew someone in the district? Did they duck into one of the stalls or shops?" Van asked.

"Probably," Stone replied. "The detective said they think this is a fluke, maybe someone who had been following the case about DeVere and wanted some notoriety. She said DeVere is insisting his bodyguard was murdered. She didn't sound like she believed it."

"Why not?" Luna asked.

"I guess there's some history there. He's been close to tragedy a lot. Detective Miller thinks it's his way of coping. This shooter might just be someone who wants to ride on the coattails of Nick's near-death experiences."

Van shook his head. "I don't like the way Ingram died either. It was too calculated for a minor copycat criminal. Keep on it. Did you work with her beyond that?"

"No," Stone said. "I just speak cop, and they know I'm one of their kind."

Luna smiled. "That's good news for us. What do you think, Van? Is Nick making too much of the death?"

"No clue. I've asked Lee to look into it, but it might help if we had the police report too," Van said.

"I can talk to some buddies, see what I can get for us," Rick said. "Want me to skip the confab and head to the station instead?"

"Yeah. Do that. Report back to the Tower when you're done."

Stone left and Van turned to her. "DeVere is going to be difficult. There's something he's not telling us. I can feel it."

"Me too," she said. "I'm just tired and not making the right connections. Sorry I was slow in the room."

"Your slow is still faster than everyone else. I promise you'll get a solid eight hours' sleep as soon as we get out of here."

"I'll hold you to it," she said. They got on the elevator and went down to the nightclub. "When are you going to tell him you're here because of Ingram?"

"Maybe never," Van said.

She let it lie for now, but she didn't like secrets. They always led to mistrust, and DeVere was edgy as it was. But it wasn't her call. And, right now, she was happy enough to leave it be.

It was a large space with an Art Deco statue over the bar that looked like some sort of burly imposing figure. There were sconces on the walls and DeVere and his people were all sitting at a high table in the middle of the club. The detective stood next to them, taking notes on her notepad.

Luna had to smile. Rick had mentioned that the department had been going more high tech, but a lot of the detectives preferred pen and paper. Luna did too. Her brain worked better when she had written stuff down.

"My man followed someone who might have been the shooter into the garment district."

"He told me," the detective said. "We'll look into it. We definitely want to catch whoever took the shot at you, Mr. DeVere. I think hiring Price is the right move. Just listen to them and stay quiet for the next few days."

"Quiet?" Nick asked. "I don't live a quiet life. I have a contract I'm in the middle of negotiating in Silicon Valley and a VIP event Friday night here at the club."

"You should try to postpone everything you can.

Maybe have the Silicon Valley people come here and cancel the party," she said. "That will give us a chance to find the guy."

"I can move the meeting, but the VIP event is on," he said. "It's a launch party for a friend's new album and I'm hosting, so definitely not. But I'm sure Price and his team can handle it."

"Of course," Van said. "It's here?"

"Yes," Nick said, turning to Xander and Kenji as they returned.

"What did you two find?" Van asked as they approached.

"Nothing. No trace of the shooter," Xander said. "I talked to a woman who thought she saw a guy with a baseball cap go down the fire escape, but she admitted it could have been her neighbor or one of his friends."

"Same. No one saw anything, and the roof was clean on the building I checked," Kenji said.

"Who did you talk to?" Detective Miller asked.

"Just the people out front," Kenji said. "I'm not a cop, ma'am. Didn't go door-to-door or anything like that."

"I guess that's all I need for now," Detective Miller said. "I'll let you know if we find anything and vice versa, Price?"

"Sure thing. Here's my card," he said, handing it to her.

Detective Miller said her goodbyes and left. Van was talking to the team as Nick went over to Finn and Hazel. Luna followed, not liking how independent their new client was.

"Coordinate with them. Let me know if they have any demands that won't work," Nick said to his people.

He headed to the elevator.

"Hey, wait up," Luna said, catching him by the arm.

"I need to see my father; you can come with me."

He didn't wait for her to answer, just started walking toward the elevator in the back, which she realized must be his private one. Xander noticed her and tilted his head to the side in question.

"Let Van know I'm going with Mr. DeVere and I'll have my tracking app turned on so he can find me. I'll check in when we get to the senior DeVere."

"I will," Xander said.

This job was getting more out of control by the minute, and a big part of that was Nick DeVere. It was time for him to learn who was in charge. And, frankly, she was tired of him treating them like his staff. Her original impression that there was more to him than met the eye was clearly deceiving. He was coming across as a spoiled man-child who hadn't ever heard the word no.

Now he was rushing to his daddy, no doubt to complain about his new bodyguard. She wasn't going to give him a chance to throw another tantrum. As soon as they were alone in the elevator and the car started its descent, she reached around him and pushed the stop button, turning and cornering him.

"Let's talk."

Chapter 3

Being cornered by a woman in an elevator wasn't unusual. But Luna wasn't putting the moves on him. She held him where he was with a grip that would be hard even for him to break.

"What's up?" he asked dryly.

"Enough of acting like I am an inconvenience. Unless you want to die, it's time to start appreciating why I'm here. I'm sure it escaped your notice, but everyone on my team is working damned hard to keep you alive. Start cooperating or I'm going to make your life very difficult."

For a minute, all the rage and grief he felt boiled to the surface, and he lifted her off her feet, turning so she was pinned in the corner. He stepped in close, leaving her no room to attack him or to force him back out of her way.

Up this close, Nick noticed that her brown eyes were

actually hazel and had flecks of gold in them. She had a small scar over her left eyebrow and her breath smelled like mint.

"I saw what you did," he said carefully. He really needed to get away on his own. In this mood, he was dangerous, and the last time he'd felt this way was three damned days ago when Jack had died.

He wanted to behave in a way that he knew the De-Vere heir couldn't. He wanted to punch someone or something. Drive way too fast and see if his luck held.

He felt trapped by everything that happened in the last few days and it seemed as if the future was going to be more of the same. He had questions. He wanted answers. He had no time for Luna Urban's interrogation.

"I appreciate everything you have done for me, but at the same time, it's useless. I'm not sure if you've heard about me, but I'm bulletproof. I can't die, but that doesn't mean that people around me don't. Excuse me if I don't fall all over you and suddenly decide you and your team are my new best friends, I think we both know I'll be alive long after—"

"Stop. You're not bulletproof. You've been lucky so far. Today wasn't luck, by the way. That was me doing my job, and if I hadn't been distracted, I would have had you out of the room before that bullet hit the glass."

Distracted? He wasn't going to argue with her about his seeming good fortune when it came to dodging death. The facts spoke for themselves. But she'd been *distracted*?

"What distracted you?"

"You," she said as if she were reprimanding him. She put her hand on his chest and shoved.

He held his ground, arching one eyebrow at her. Ignoring the feel of her hand on his chest. "Was it my handsome good looks?"

"I'm being polite, but the next time I won't be."

She ignored his gibe, which he noted. He had to figure this new bodyguard out and then determine how to ditch her.

He almost smiled. Something about her was different from everyone else who had been around him. She didn't brownnose or pretend to be awed by him. She treated him…well, like he was a regular guy.

"I'd love to see that," he said, stepping aside and hitting the button to resume the motion of the elevator car. "We can talk later. I have to go and see my father."

"Why now? Are you thinking of having him fire us?"

"No. He rarely does what I tell him, but he hasn't responded like this to my other near misses… I want to know why. It might be the board footing the bill, but the old man made the call," Nick said.

"That's not odd. He is part of the board and you're his only son and heir."

She grabbed his arm as they stepped into the parking area, pulling him to a stop and positioning herself between him and the darkened garage. She put one hand under her jacket—no doubt on her gun—as she surveyed the space before she nudged him forward.

"Which car is yours?"

"All of them," he said.

"All?"

"You know they call me Midas."

"So? Midas wasn't foolish. Rushing off when someone just shot at you is. And honestly who owns this many cars?"

He almost smiled again, but then reminded himself

he wasn't keeping her around. There was a keen intelligence to her that he'd almost missed earlier when she'd been in the conference room. "I like fast cars. Let's take the Bugatti."

He walked to it, and she dropped to the floor to look under the car before standing again.

"What are you doing?"

"Looking for obvious devices," she said. "Someone killed your bodyguard three days ago and just took a shot at you. I'd feel safer if Xander looked over the car before we took it. Would you agree to that?"

"No," he said.

But then the sentiment behind her words echoed in his mind. *Someone killed your bodyguard.* As urgently as he wanted to speak to his father, he wasn't sure he could handle another person dying for him. Not today. "But if it will make you feel safer, sure."

She didn't question him, just pulled out her phone and sent a text. Five minutes later, Xander, the behemoth, walked toward them. He smiled at Luna and nodded at him as Nick tossed the keys.

He caught them one-handed. "This won't take but a minute. If you don't mind, I'll check out the rest of your vehicles after I do this one."

"No problem. I'm sure Price will bill me for it," Nick said.

"He definitely will," Xander said. "No such thing as a free ride, according to the boss."

"Well, everything I touch turns to gold," Nick said.

Luna stood off to the side, watching the big guy work.

Nick wondered at her relationship with all the men on the team. They seemed to be a close-knit group, but she didn't exactly look like she belonged. "How'd you end up in this business?" he asked while they waited.

"I was making a living doing some mixed martial arts fighting and Van saw me one night. He needed a woman to guard a client. Someone who was good at hand-to-hand combat. I turned him down flat. But he offered me a lot of money, promised to train me, and I gave it a go. Turned out I was good at it," she said with a slight shrug.

She was downplaying it. Making it seem like Price's training would have worked with anyone, but he knew it wouldn't have. He also got a clear picture that her loyalty would always be to Price.

"How long ago was that?" he asked. She looked like she was in her late twenties, but something in her eyes almost made her seem older.

"Ten years," she said.

"You don't look old enough to have done this for ten years," he said, trying flattery to see if that had any effect on her.

"Thanks," she said, kind of looking down and away. "But I am plenty old."

He wanted to ask more questions but cautioned himself. He didn't want to get to know this bodyguard. He hadn't even meant to let Jack get as close as he had. He should have stuck to his routine of rotating bodyguards, of changing his habits, but he'd started to feel like the curse had been lifted. It had been almost three years since the last similar incident.

Three years, and he'd thought that maybe he was on the other side of the bad karma that had been following him around since his birth. But he knew that had been a misjudgment and one he wouldn't allow himself to make again.

"You're good," Xander said, tossing the keys back to Nick.

He caught them in one hand and then walked to the car. He heard the sound of Luna's heels on the concrete as she walked beside him. He didn't look at her. She was his bodyguard. Not someone he was getting to know, and he was determined to remember that.

Luna wasn't entirely sure why Nick thought he was bulletproof, but she watched him carefully as he drove through the LA traffic. It wasn't too heavy, and he hit the community lane and didn't look back. He drove over the speed limit, but she felt safe. He had the music blaring and she could tell that conversation was the last thing he was interested in, which suited her. But she had to keep herself busy, otherwise she was going to drift off to sleep.

She reached over, turning the volume down. "About those enemies…"

"I don't have any," he reminded her.

"Finn mentioned Verity Vaughn," she prompted him. Luna didn't know much about his ex-wife. In fact, she pulled out her phone and sent an info request to Lee.

"Finn and Verity don't get along, that was just him acting out."

"You said you're worth more to her alive," Luna continued. She wasn't going to just write this off. Former partners often turned killers.

"She's got her own money," he said. "Verity can be very demanding, and she usually turns to me to smooth things out for her."

"Why do you do that?"

"It's easier to give in than to try to fight with her," he said. "She's difficult, but she's not a killer."

"We'll see. Anyone else like that?"

"No."

"You've only had one lover?" she asked because he was being a pain. He wanted to ignore the fact that someone had shot at him.

"Not quite."

"Anyone else who's *demanding*?" she asked.

"I'm sure *you* are," he said. "Most people I know just want to make their own life easier."

"And you help them with that?"

"When I can," he said.

"Do you say no sometimes?"

"On occasion."

"Recently?"

"I see where you are going with this—" he started.

"Listen," she said, cutting him off. "You don't want to believe that someone you know, someone you've talked to, would try to kill you, but honestly, that's probably who it is."

Luna had read the articles and knew his reputation as a tragic wealthy figure. The public knowledge of the incidents that he'd been close to had been written off as accidents and from what she'd read that seemed to truly be the case. But Nick believed there was something more.

"Nothing is ever that simple. And there are only a handful of people who have been in my life for all of the…incidents."

"I thought the only times you were intentionally targeted were in the recent death of your bodyguard and today's attempted shooting." Van had mentioned that

Nick thought he was bulletproof, but the other near-death experiences had all been ruled as accidental. Did Nick know something more he wasn't sharing?

"Yeah, never mind," he said, turning the radio back up and driving a bit faster.

She watched the cars around them, looking for anyone who might be following them. She kept herself alert, going over everything he'd said and she'd seen while they'd been at his office. The impression she'd had of a shallow playboy was gone.

Their conversation in the garage had revealed more than he'd probably expected it to. But he wasn't a frivolous man, and unless she missed her guess, he felt more about his bodyguard being killed than he wanted the world to see.

They arrived at his father's mansion in Santa Barbara before she knew it. She watched for any vehicles that might be tailing them but didn't see any. It was odd in her book that someone would have tried to shoot him and then disappear, but she knew Van would figure that part out. She pinged Lee with her location to make sure the team knew where she was.

"This place looks nice," she said wryly as they were waved through the guard gates.

"Understated isn't something that we DeVeres do," he said.

"Yeah, I got that. What are you hoping to find here?" she asked.

"Answers," he said. "You'll have to wait while I go and speak to him."

"I'm not doing that."

The place had enough guards and active and passive security, but she wasn't leaving her client. His life was in her hands. She'd never known her father or, for that matter, her mother, but she imagined that Nick might need his father after everything that had happened today.

"I'm not budging on this. My father is ill and I don't know you."

"Sure, I'll give you privacy while you talk to him. But I'm not staying out here with the car," she warned him.

"I wouldn't expect you to since it's hot today," he said, a hint of unease in his eyes. "The agreement that your agency signed has an NDA attached to it."

"Yes. The moment I left with you, I was on the clock. I won't be discussing anything that happens in your life with anyone but the team."

"Good," he said, getting out of the car.

As they walked up the steps, the front door to the mansion opened to reveal an older man with thin, close-cropped gray hair. He wore a suit and stood tall and easy in it. He nodded at Nick as they got closer.

"Your father will be pleased to see you again, Nicholas."

"I'm sure. Aldo, this is Ms. Urban, she's my new bodyguard. This is Aldo Barsotti, my father's butler."

"A pleasure to meet you, Ms. Urban, please call me Aldo. As we weren't expecting you, I'll need a moment to make sure your father is ready."

"Don't bother. I'm not bringing Ms. Urban in with me," Nick said, striding past the butler and up the large spiral staircase.

Luna sighed, moving quickly to stay on his heels. Nick acted like he wasn't in danger here.

The butler closed the door behind her and Luna started

up the stairs after Nick. She called back over her shoulder, "I need to be outside of the room he's in."

"Of course, Mr. Nicholas has always just done what he wanted," Aldo said, keeping pace with her.

"I've noticed. Have you worked for Mr. DeVere for long?" she asked. Remembering what Nick had said about only a handful of people being around for all of the "incidents."

"Almost forty-five years," Aldo said. "Follow me. Can I offer you a drink?"

"I'm good," she said, following the butler up the stairs and down another wide hallway. As they got closer to the closed door at the end, she heard Nick's voice on the other side. "Is there another entrance to the room?"

"Only a balcony," Aldo said.

"Can I see the balcony?" she asked.

"You can through that large window," he said gesturing to the one at the end of the hall. She walked to the window. For a large house, it was quiet, and it was clear to her that there weren't many people here. She opened the window, looked out at the balcony, and then down at the landscaped garden below.

She was going to need to speak to Nick about his impulsiveness. This was the kind of behavior she wouldn't tolerate. Even Jaz, the teenaged rap star, had heeded her warnings and allowed her to secure locations for him. She should have been able to secure the area before Nick had gone in to speak to his father. That was something she would put in place after they left.

She soon found the best position to keep an eye on both exits from the room.

Aldo stood outside the door to the bedroom. Luna

would have liked to talk to him further to try to get more information on Nick. The fatigue she'd carried with her since she'd landed was still there, but she had found her second wind. Things were starting to make more sense now.

Putting the pieces together, she had the feeling that Nick thought his bodyguard had been killed because of him, which was odd if it truly was a freak accident. But Van suspected there was more to Ingram's death than just an accident too. Also why was Nick so determined to take the blame for it? Was there something else she was missing? Before she could make more sense of it, there was a loud crash from Nick's father's room.

She ran for the door, which was now open because Aldo had rushed in at the sound. She found a lamp smashed on the floor and an older version of Nick standing over it. She scanned the room, looking for her client, found him not too far from his father, but in the shadows.

"See. I told you I had a bodyguard. And she's very good at her job."

She went to Nick's side, pocketing her gun. "What's going on?"

"Just seeing how good you are, my dear," the older man said.

"How *good* I am?"

"At keeping my son safe. After all, you weren't by his side," he said.

"I agree, sir. That was an error in judgment. We still haven't hammered out all the details of my employment yet," she said.

"She had the balcony and this door covered," Aldo added.

"For pete's sake," Nick said. "She's great. I want to know why you didn't tell me about that the threat you received."

"What threat?" she asked.

Chapter 4

Nick wasn't pleased at all with his father. The old man was being cagey about some letters he'd been receiving for thirty-two years. The exact amount of time that Nick had been alive, in fact. His father was supposed to be taking it easy after his latest chemo treatment, but instead he was hurling lamps to the floor to check the reaction time of his bodyguard.

Though why his father hadn't mentioned it before, Nick wasn't about to get into. Their family kept secrets close and didn't share them, and Nick could even understand that his father might have been reluctant to worry Nick when he was younger. But now, when his father was terminal and Nick's life was on the line, he'd finally had no choice but to come clean.

"It's nothing for you to worry about. Nicholas, we can discuss it—"

"No, Father, we can't. She signed a NDA, you're good to talk in front of her. Aldo, I need a drink."

"Of course, Mr. Nicholas," Aldo said. "Emmett?"

"I'll have one too. Bring it to my study if you don't mind," he said.

"Father." His dad was acting like they were going to have a social visit. After he'd dropped the bomb of receiving the letters every year, he seemed to want to move on. But there was no moving on from that. Nick deserved to know the details.

"Son, you asked for a drink. And I have kept all of the letters in a file in my study," his father said, following Aldo out of the room.

"Where are we going? I would like to secure the room and the area before you two go inside," Luna said, walking between him and his father.

"Just down the hall there. The next door on the right," Nick said, gesturing to it.

"Wait here," she said, walking into his father's study.

Nick turned to the old man. "You're being a little bit dicey with the information, and that's not like you. And you slipped up by hiring Price yourself instead of going through the board. Just level with me."

His father sighed and then reached over to touch the side of Nick's face. Something he hadn't done since Nick had been a little boy. "When your mother died, I promised myself I wouldn't allow that to happen to you."

"And you haven't. But was there a chance it could have?" he asked. The police thought he had survivor guilt in the extreme, but Nick had always sensed that the incidents in his life were connected. He just hadn't wanted to admit it.

"Yes. There was. It will make more sense when you

see the letters," he said and then sighed. "There's no easy way to put this. Before I met your mom, I played the field."

He rolled his eyes. "Dad, I didn't think you were saint. Is there really a reason for me to hear this now?"

"When you were born, I got the first letter saying that I had another son and that he should be my heir," Emmett said.

"Do you? Dad, do I have a half brother?"

"No," he said. "Aldo and I have researched every lead and gone back to every woman I slept with. There is no child of mine out there. I thought it was just a blackmail attempt and ignored it," his father said.

"But the letters kept coming?"

"Yes. Right after your mother died in that horrible crash, I got another one. It was vaguely threatening. Stating that if I didn't want to lose you in the same way, I'd recognize my true heir."

Nick's heart beat faster as he listened to his father's words. What was the old man saying? "Was Mom murdered?"

"I don't know. The police never found any evidence of vehicle tampering and there were skid marks as if the car skidded on the road and slid off the edge of the cliff."

But his father hadn't been sure. Aldo came up the stairs at the same time as Luna called all-clear. He put his hand on his father's arm to steady the old man as they walked to the study.

This changed everything. Who was this heir that someone was speaking of? He would have Finn start looking into it. He couldn't help but wonder how his father had kept this a secret all these years and why. Why not just tell him, so they could work together?

Entering his father's study, Luna stayed by his side. And it was odd, but for a moment, he felt like he knew her—knew this stranger—better than he knew his father or Aldo.

What else about his father's life was he hiding?

Aldo handed him his drink and Nick downed the whiskey and soda in one long swallow. His father opened a drawer in his desk with a key and then leaned down for a retinal scan. Nick set his empty glass on the side table and walked over to his father's desk just as the old man took out a large file and set it on the surface.

"This is everything. The last letter came the day that Jack was killed. It said specifically that they were tired of waiting and they were going to kill you and then come for me," his father said, pushing the file toward him.

"Sir, we need to let Detective Miller know about this," Luna said.

Nick glared at her. "I will."

He opened the file and looked down at the letter, which had been printed. He'd have Finn run diagnostics on the paper and ink and start narrowing things down. But Luna was right, the police should have been notified from the beginning about this.

"Why didn't you go to the cops?"

"I wasn't sure the threat was real. Jack's death is the first time any of these letters has been tied to us," his father said.

"But you knew they were threatening me?" he asked.

Emmett didn't answer. Nick just moved away to look out the window. Luna followed him wanting to offer comfort but that wasn't why she was here. She forced herself instead to scan the yard to make sure it was clear. She noticed that Aldo moved next to the older man, urging him back from the exposed position.

She turned to Nick, who just shook his head, walking over to the desktop where all the letters were. His expression wasn't readable. But she didn't have to be Nancy Drew to figure out he was pissed and, she suspected, hurt.

She walked over to him.

"What do you want to do?" Luna asked.

"Take these letters home," he said. "But I suspect Detective Miller will want copies too."

"I can take photos of them and send copies to you and Miller. Sound good?"

"Yeah. Make it quick."

She could tell he wanted to leave; he paced the room like a caged lion. He wanted to attack, she could see that clearly, but he didn't have a good target for his rage. His father, though strong and lucid, was a weak man.

Aldo was supporting Emmett and urging him to the desk and the tall leather chair. Luna stopped scanning the documents with an encoded app on her phone and pushed the leather chair closer to Aldo and Emmett.

Aldo smiled his thanks. Luna just went back to what she'd been doing. The early letters had been printed on a dot matrix printer. Wow. Emmett really had been receiving these threats since Nick's birth.

When she finished, she emailed a copy to Lee back at Price Tower, asking her to inform Detective Miller about them and to see if she wanted to talk to Emmett DeVere.

"I'm good here," she said to Nick.

He looked…well, gorgeous and moody, as he always

did, but something had changed in her client the moment his father had revealed he'd been keeping the threat to himself all these years.

Aldo was watching Nick and Emmett both, his gaze flickering, and Luna felt the tension between the two of them and realized their complicated relationship might have something to do with her current assignment. Emmett seemed to make Nick even more arrogant and impulsive and risky. Why? She'd read the cursory file about the DeVere family and knew that father and son had seemingly had a strained relationship for years, but this was something else. This was different.

"My boss has informed Detective Miller. She'll be in touch with you."

"I'm not sure I want to discuss these with her," Emmett said.

"As it's evidence in an ongoing case, I don't think you have a choice. You can do it when she comes or she'll get a warrant, and if that happens, there's a chance the press will pick up on it," Luna said.

The old man had had her sympathy when she'd first seen him. He was old and frail-looking, but his eyes revealed a wily intelligence. She'd always hoped for a better parent-child dynamic than life had showed her and was usually disappointed.

"Yeah, Dad," Nick said, coming back over. "You might not get your own way with this. Don't think of it as doing something for me, but instead doing something for Jack. You always liked him."

"Of course, your father will cooperate with the police. This matter has gotten too serious not to," Aldo said. "When do you think they will be contacting us?"

"I'm not sure," Luna said.

"Thank you. Do you need anything else?" Aldo asked.

Luna glanced over at Nick. He'd rushed here to make sure his father was okay. Somehow, she had a feeling that the fact that his father had kept this a secret for all these years was something he hadn't been prepared for.

"No," Nick said. "Luna, will someone from Price be with the detective?"

"Yes," she said, knowing that Lee would have Rick make contact with Detective Miller. He was really good at this type of thing since he'd spent all those years as a DEA agent. "We can leave whenever you are ready."

His father turned away to face the large bay window. Nick didn't even look over at his father, instead he spun on his heel and left.

She moved to follow him, but Aldo stopped her with a hand on her arm. "Thank you for everything you've done this afternoon. It's never easy with these two."

She smiled at the older man. "You're very welcome."

She found that Nick was waiting for her at the top of the stairs. "Didn't want to give you any more reason to grump at me."

"I don't grump, I protect," she said, hiding a smile. He wasn't as blasé about the attempt on his life now. The letters had changed something for him.

She'd glanced at them herself and couldn't shake the feeling that something was off. The letters weren't concrete and didn't really seem to relate to any events—no incriminating details or information that tied the letters to specific crimes or attempts on Nick's life. They were just vaguely threatening.

"It feels like badgering," he said of her commands.

"Great, if that makes you listen. I plan to keep you alive…and now we know that I've seen the letters, I think this might be even more serious than we thought," she said.

"The shooter didn't have you convinced?" he asked with a teasing grin on his face.

He was practically flirting with her. Odd, but not unexpected. She was pretty sure this was his defense mechanism, his way of making sure he still had the upper hand. She'd seen a chink in the façade he liked to project to the world. It made sense that he'd want to steer her back to her first image of him. But it wasn't going to work. She finally felt like she was glimpsing the real man behind Nick DeVere.

She'd wanted to make Nick into the spoiled playboy. But she'd seen his real fear for his father, and then his true disappointment in him. She'd never forget that. He was starting to be more man than client. These little pieces of the person that made him seem more real to her. And that was dangerous for her and for him. The threat to Nick was real. She had to stay sharp.

No matter how much she might long for something else.

"I mean he could have been aiming at someone else," she said. "It's not always all about you."

He threw his head back and laughed. "Darling, it's always about me, which you will learn quickly. Let's go. I have to get out of this place."

"Did you grow up here?" she asked, because he seemed restless like he wanted to talk. Glancing over at Nick she noticed how comfortable he was in this place. He walked thorough the rooms as if he knew them well.

"Until I was eight, and then it was boarding school," he said. "But Father traveled a lot back then. So, it was usually me and a nanny."

"A nanny?"

"We didn't keep them for long. Usually six months," he said.

That felt odd to her, but given that Emmett had been receiving threatening letters about his son, maybe not so odd. She followed Nick down the stairs, carefully watching the interior for any signs she might have missed on the way in, but saw nothing untoward.

She snapped a photo of a portrait she hadn't really had time to study. It was of Emmet, a woman and a child. She supposed it must be Nick and mother, but she wanted to verify it before making an assumption.

Nick noticed she had the camera app on her smartphone open and then shook his head. "My mother. I don't have any memories of her, so this image is what I usually see when I think of her."

Luna nodded. "I didn't know my mom either. I always think of the mom from *Boy Meets World* when I picture mine."

He looked at her. "I don't know what that is."

"It was a TV show in the '90s. One of the group homes I lived in had a poster on the bedroom wall of the family," she said, remembering the clean but old, tired room she'd been put in. She'd shared it with Mazie.

"I didn't take you for an orphan," he said.

"What did you take me as?" she asked as they walked outside. She did a quick visual check of the Bugatti, but since they'd parked in a gated driveway, she felt like the car was probably safe to drive.

"Tomboy with a close relationship with your dad. Maybe someone who was trying to be the son he never had," Nick said.

"Nope."

Interesting. She'd noticed most men clients she'd had over the years often thought that. Or they'd thought she'd been victimized as an orphan. Her background wasn't sad or extraordinary. Just a girl who'd had to raise herself, and figure out what she wanted to do, when fate stepped in. Or rather, Van stepped in.

When they were both in the car, he looked over at her. The setting sun cast a shadow on his cheekbones, making her very aware of how good-looking he was.

"Am I what you expected?" he asked.

"Hmm." A nice noncommittal sound so she didn't have to risk letting him know that she was intrigued by the man, not just her client.

Nick shook off the vestiges of disappointment the further they drove away from his father's house. He didn't know why he'd been surprised that his father had kept something so important a secret for so many years. That was sort of the old man's MO. He tried to control every detail of Nick's life while staying aloof and distant.

When he'd been younger, Nick had allowed himself to believe that had been for his own protection. The letters that they'd seen today…those went back to the time of his birth.

Well, hell.

"So?"

"I'm not sure what I expected. As you know, this was sort of a last-minute assignment for me. I didn't have time to really do as much research on you as I would have liked."

"First impressions then," he said.

"Asshole."

He looked over at her, arching one eyebrow. She didn't give much away, which wasn't surprising. Most of the bodyguards he'd hired had kept to themselves. They didn't get involved because once a relationship become personal, mistakes could happen. Had Luna made one in her past?

"Sorry. Rich asshole," she said.

He hid a smile as he turned his attention back to the road. They were getting closer to downtown and his club, so he needed to be alert as the traffic was heavier here.

"Fair enough. It's kind of my vibe."

"Ha. That's a lie. Your vibe is someone who is very spoiled but also very generous. For as much as you want me to believe it's all about you, I don't think it always is."

He didn't like that. "It is about me. Sometimes I have to make it about someone else to get what I want, but in the end, it's all me."

"Good to know. I won't be flattered if you do something nice for me."

"Oh, you should be flattered," he said.

He liked her. But that was all it could ever be. He'd linked the tragedies that always seemed to happen around him to something else a long time ago. He thought he'd just been lucky, sort of like Midas. Everything he touched worked out for him. But sometimes the tradeoff was that other people got hurt.

He'd tried to limit his close relationships because of that. Finn had said he was paranoid because of the way the events unfolded and that it was probably survivor's guilt. But Nick had always thought it odd the way the incidents had been staged.

He intended to get to the bottom of it, and now with his father's letters, which he'd had Luna send him a copy of.

He'd have to be careful with Luna and the rest of the Price Security team. He wasn't about to put another person's life in danger. He'd always been the invincible one. His last nanny had said that, like Harry Potter, his mom's death had given him a sort of magical protection. And he knew that she'd meant it to soothe a small boy who'd lost his mother,

But her words had always been oddly true. He felt untouchable.

Luna wasn't. .

And as clever and funny as she was, he knew that she could be killed just like Jack, his cousins and his mom had been.

"For the party, I'll need you in evening wear."

"Great. I look really good in a black suit and tie, as I'm sure you've already noticed," she quipped.

"That won't do. You'll have to dress like a woman who I'd be dating. I don't want anyone to know I have a new bodyguard."

"The shooter will know. Rick chased someone through the garment district," Luna pointed out.

"The world doesn't know."

Luna drew in a breath, like she was going to argue with him.

"Don't bother. This is a nonnegotiable for me. You either wear a dress and act like you're my latest fling or I get rid of the team altogether."

"You know you can't do that. But, fine, I don't really mind a dress. What else?" she said.

"No weapons. I don't want my guests to feel anything other than a good time," he said.

"How am I supposed to protect you without my weapon?" she asked.

"You said that Van hired you because you were good at hand-to-hand combat. I think the biggest threat at the party will be men hitting on you."

"I doubt that. The risk is yours, not mine," she said. "Why won't you take this seriously?"

"You saw the letters," he said. "Someone has been threatening me for decades and I'm still alive."

"By chance," she said.

"Not chance. Fate," he retorted.

"Fate? Isn't that the same thing?"

He shrugged. He wasn't going to get into his complex relationship with karma and fate. But he knew that he was untouchable. Luna Urban, who grew up in a group home and worked as a bodyguard for the rich and famous...well, not so much.

"Trust me on this," he said as he hit the button to open the armored doors of the underground garage at his club and penthouse. He parked the Bugatti and then turned off the engine, turning to face her.

"You can go home and get your stuff. I'll have a room ready for you in the penthouse when you get back," he said.

"Again, I can't leave you alone."

"You can. I'm going to be upstairs. Leave the behemoth to watch over me. You said you needed sleep. I want you alert and ready," he said.

"We can check with Van. Normally, I'd work—"

"This isn't normal, Luna. None of it."

"As I said, we'll check with Van."

He got out of the car and she followed him, close by his side, always scanning the area around them for threats. She was very good at her job and he liked that. But it also made it more important that he find a way to get her and all of Price Security off the case.

He knew that Jack's killer was going to come for him again and this time he wanted the murderer to get close. Close enough for Nick to confront him and then kill him. It was time for Nick to stop letting fate decide.

Chapter 5

Van agreed with Nick. Luna arrived at Price Tower and knew she should sleep, but she'd caught a second wind. Lee was waiting for her with a no-nonsense look on her face. The older woman was the communications hub for their team and their unofficial mother. She made sure that everyone stayed in line.

"Hey, girl. Good to have you back in Cali," Lee said, hugging her. "The boss wants you to sleep, and we'll catch you up later on everything. The letters you sent are interesting. But I haven't had a chance to really dig into it. Rick and Detective Miller are with the older De-Vere. I want a full rundown on that house. Was it like the Rich Wives shows that we watch?"

"It was. Why are you telling me all this?"

"Because you won't sleep if I don't. And this case looks like it's going to be a quick one. You need to grab all the rest you can right now," Lee said.

"I agree. Did Xander stay with Nick?"

"Yeah. He's safe for now. I'm surprised you guys didn't have any trouble at the father's house," Lee said.

"I was, too, but I think whoever is behind this knows that Nick and his dad have a strained relationship."

"You think it's an insider?"

"That's my gut. What about yours?"

"Not sure yet. I want to finish analyzing the letters, and Rick mentioned that Nick told the detective that there had been other incidents before Jack's death. I'm cross-referencing them," Lee said. "You get some rest and I'll have it ready for you when you wake up."

Lee left her at the door to her apartment. She was tired but also, as she'd said, wired. She wanted to be doing something, not sleeping, and as much as she knew that later she might regret it; she just couldn't force herself to nap. She packed her stuff for the job, including the one evening dress she had. She got out her laptop and started doing some research. Just putting Nick's name into the internet search engine pulled up pages and pages of stories.

She rolled her shoulders and took out a regular spiral notebook and Bic pen. She started at the beginning with the car crash that had killed his mother and left him unscathed.

There had been five other accidents that had been close to Nick, but he'd survived. Always someone close to him had been killed. Yet the accidents weren't similar and, she had to admit, looked like accidents on the surface.

She heard footsteps outside her apartment door and then someone knocked. She closed her laptop quickly and glanced at the perfectly made bed, tempted to ruffle the sheets, but she wasn't good at petty deceit. Seemed pointless to her.

She went to open the door, unsurprised to see Van there.

"No sleep?"

"Couldn't," she said. "I did some internet searching."

"Me too. I'm not sure about this case," he said. "At first, I thought that DeVere might have set up Jack, but I don't think that's the case."

"Me either. It's odd," she admitted. "Nick is definitely in some kind of danger."

"Is he? Or is he just trying to stir up something?" Van said.

"What did you see that makes you think that?" she asked. "I didn't get that vibe. He seemed shocked when his father showed him the letters."

"I'll trust your gut. His assistant is guarded. Plays his cards close the chest. Not sure what's going on there. Lee's running him through the databases to find out everything she can."

"I will watch him and the woman—Hazel too."

"Good. Grab your notes and let's have a debrief in ten minutes."

She and Van met up with Lee and the others in the communications room, which was really just a big room that sort of resembled the family room in one of the group homes she'd lived in—except everything was new and clean, and everyone had their own space. Luna's spot was a large chair big enough for two people to sit in. She liked to curl her legs up under her while in the team meetings.

Lee had some sort of massive recliner and Van sat on a leather armchair. Kenji was slouched on the long couch, playing a game on his phone. When they'd walked in, he'd sat up and put it away.

"Lee, give us the rundown," Van said.

Lee ran through all the information they'd collected so far. Nothing new from what she'd told Luna earlier, at first. Then she mentioned that she'd found out the last three accidents had been at events where Nick's inner circle were participants.

"Who?"

"The ex—Verity Vaughn, some heiress. His assistant—Finn. And then another name kept popping up— Thom Newton. They will all be at the event on Friday. I think that we should divide up and try to speak to them. Who wants who?"

"I'll take the heiress," Kenji said.

"I can try to do Finn," Lee said. "Since you already rubbed him the wrong way, Van."

"Good that leaves me with Newton," Van said.

"I'll have Xander on the door and, of course, Luna will be with Nick. The cops had pretty much written off his theory that Jack was killed in his place until the letters were found."

"What do you think?" Kenji asked.

"He's definitely been close to a lot of tragedy. But Luna doesn't think he's the kind of man who'd set this all up for attention, and she's spent the most time with him. But the accidents are too far apart to make sense. I mean why try at random times over years only to stop, and then why do it again now? Has something happened to change it?" Van asked.

She knew that Van was just putting these things out there so they'd all keep looking for the connection. She planned to get to the bottom of it. Tonight, she'd have a chance to start finding out about the other accidents from Nick. She was very good at getting information out of their clients, and she had a feeling that on this job, it was what she'd need to do to protect him.

Processing everything that had happened to him today wasn't that hard. He shoved it down and then poured himself a Jack and Coke. He set it on his desk next to the printout of the letters his father had received. The behemoth—Xander—sat in one of the guest chairs facing both the door and the windows. Though why he was watching the window was beyond Nick.

They'd moved his desk into the small alcove where his dressing area was. The walls were closing in around him; he hated this feeling. It reminded him of the time he'd been kidnapped. They'd left him in a locked closet in an abandoned house while negotiating with his father.

He did a deep breathing technique and then forced his attention on the letters. The sooner he figured this out, the sooner he could get back to living his life. At least he had something solid to look at.

The door to his office opened. Xander was on his feet and at the door before it cracked more than a few inches. He looked at whomever was on the other side and then nodded and stepped back.

Hazel stepped in after giving Xander a stern look. "I've just got the mail."

"Of course," Xander said. "Apologies."

She ignored Xander as he moved back to his chair and turned to Nick. "I've had a few inquiries about Friday's event and directed them to Finn. Also, the DeVere board agreed to come here for the contract discussions.

Mr. Price is insisting on metal detectors at the doors and a screening process."

"I'll discuss it with him," Nick said.

"I thought so. I told him we'd have to wait for your approval," she said.

"I'll speak to Price and then let you know. Anything else?"

"Ms. Vaughn called again. I tried to put her through to Finn, but she hung up. She will probably try your cell."

She had tried his cell about eighteen times, and he'd kept hitting Ignore. He'd spoke to her once today and he wasn't up for another chat. "Thanks. Is that all?"

"Um, no there is one more thing. My son is back from his latest tour overseas and I'd like to take a few weeks off," she said. "I know my timing isn't—"

"It's fine. Take as much leave as you need," he said. Hazel had never taken a sick day and had rolled her vacation over for the last three years. "I think it's safe to say it won't be business as usual for the next few weeks. Do you have a temp lined up?"

"Yes. The agency is sending her over tomorrow. I'll go over everything then and have the security team give her a background check."

"Great. Thank you, Hazel," he said.

She just smiled and nodded at him as she turned to go.

"Did you know your boss was trying to install metal detectors?" Nick asked Xander.

"Your life is being—"

"Stop. You guys can't use that justification for everything. My invited guests aren't going to be screened like criminals."

"It's as much for their safety as it is for yours," Xander said. "You're the one who claims to be bulletproof."

Nick squared his shoulders. He was a man used to having the final say and these people from Price Security were wearing on him. "What are the other alternatives?"

"I'd say metal detectors are the easiest and everyone is familiar with them. We could do infrared scans, but Van thought you'd balk at that," Xander said.

He was right. "Does it have to be an obvious scanner or is there a way to have it be more subtle, like mounted in the foyer but not a small walkway?"

"It's not as effective," Xander said. "Let me see what I can work up. We'll need to get someone else in here to watch you if you want me to work with the security installation team."

"Have them come up here to you," Nick said, turning his attention back to the letters.

The event might not be the best idea right now. He'd cancel it, except the detective and Price had both told him to. Nick felt it would be like a signal to whoever had shot at him this afternoon that he was running scared. And he did not like being told what to do.

Xander had been right. He wasn't about to put his guests in danger. He needed the venue as safe as it could be. He messaged Finn to hire some extra bouncers for Friday's event. He then messaged Price to tell him he'd have some extra bouncers under his command during the evening.

Nick didn't like living his life like this. But if it meant getting to the bottom of these incidents, then he'd do it. He pulled the letters back over to him. He could have read them on the screen, but his brain found patterns better when he was looking at paper instead of a computer monitor.

The most astounding thing was how ordinary the notes all looked. Just typed up on a word processing program and printed out in the generic font that loaded with the program. Some had been printed in the late '80s, so they were from a dot matrix printer. Glancing down at the single-spaced printouts, he realized he would have dismissed them at first glance.

It was only when he started to read them that the menace came through. Something so small. Just words on the page. They couldn't hurt him. They weren't meant to hurt him. They were meant to steal his father's peace of mind and to make him afraid.

And as much as Nick wanted to pretend that his father had kept this from him to protect him, that wasn't the reason. His father had kept silent because he had a deeper secret.

Nick wasn't sure what that secret was, but a part of him had always wondered if his father had been having an affair when his mother had died. Aldo had made a comment when Verity and he had gotten married, about fidelity and the DeVere men. Was the real reason for his father's silence that he *knew* he had another son? Possibly another heir?

Nick wasn't going to let this go until he got to the bottom of it. The door opened and, once again, Xander was there before the door swung fully open.

"Wasn't expecting to you this early," the behemoth said, stepping back as Luna walked in.

Luna hadn't wanted to be back this early, either, but the job *was* Nick DeVere. And he was here, not at Price

Tower, so she needed to be here too. There were questions she wanted to ask, and she needed to see his reactions. Van asking her if she trusted Nick had made her realize that she needed to be doubly sure.

She wasn't going to pretend she hadn't been shaken when she'd been pressed on top of him after he'd been shot at. But it would take a colossal ego for him to set up a hit and then act like he was surprised. She wasn't ruling it out. Not yet.

The family dynamic she'd observed between him and his father had set off warning bells. Those two men were playing a dangerous game with each other. It seemed to her that they both had hidden agendas. That was fine in normal family dynamics, but people were getting killed.

"I was ready early and thought I'd come and give you a break."

"Perfect," he said then turned to Nick. "Later."

Xander left, closing the door behind him, and Luna turned to face Nick. He looked massive behind his desk, which had been wedged into a corner with only the smallest amount of space left on one side for him to walk around it.

"Missed me?" he asked drolly.

"You know it," she said. "I had a feeling you'd be going over those letters. I've always found two brains are better than one."

"Depends on the brain," he said.

"Fair enough." Something was different about him from the time she'd left. She couldn't put her finger on it just yet, but he'd changed in some way. "Anything new?"

"Nope," he said. "It always surprises me how dark the soul can be."

She moved closer to see which letter he was reading. Glancing down, she read, and realize it was the one sent after his mother's death.

Guess forever wasn't as long as she hoped. Better luck next time.

That was harsh. Who sent a letter like that? There was no threat in it per se, just malice. "Yeah. I think love can do that to people."

"Whoa, what?" he asked. "Love? Love is supposed to be hearts and flowers."

"Has it ever been that way for you?"

"No," he said, shaking his head. "But…"

"But?"

He just shrugged, but she didn't let it go. "I'm a girl. That's what you were going to say, wasn't it?"

"Maybe. I would have said woman, it's not correct to call you a girl."

She shook her head. "Love isn't bound by gender, you know."

"I do know," he said. "Still, love? These letters seem…"

"Like obsession. I think love is so tightly linked to dark fascination, and that always leads to the shadiest places." She'd seen it so many times. Like her latest client who had been threatened by a fan turned stalker turned obsessive if-I-can't-have-you-no-one-will.

"I am obsessed with cold-brewed coffee, but I've never felt the need to threaten someone for it," he said.

"Nick."

"I know. I'm being glib. But only because that's easier than having to admit that someone out there might have been trying to kill me my entire charmed life."

She got it. She'd worked around enough high-profile clients to know that the whole silver-spoon lifestyle came at a cost. "At least you're not alone."

He didn't respond, just pushed his chair back and stood. "I'm always alone. No matter how close you might be to me, you're paid to be here."

Wow. She understood the sentiment, but surely he had friends who weren't paid to be around him. "I wasn't talking about me."

"Who then? Finn? Hazel?" he asked. "I just don't form those kinds of attachments."

But he did, she thought. She'd seen the brief glimpse of guilt and loss in him when he'd spoke of his previous bodyguard. And no matter how they'd left his father's house, on the way there, Nick DeVere—Mr. I Don't Form Attachments—had been worried. But he had somehow shoved all of that aside.

"It's not a bad thing to form attachments."

"Says you. I'm reading a letter that proves otherwise. My father must have had an affair, it's right here. And even if his lover didn't kill my mother…well, she certainly took a morbid pleasure in rubbing the fact that he'd lost her in his face."

She agreed. "I noticed a later letter that was similar. The one from when your yacht was blown up."

Nick didn't say anything. Just riffled through the papers on his desk until he found it.

"'Goodbye to your heir. Guess it's time to do the right thing by your bastard,'" Nick read aloud. He dropped the paper onto his desktop and moved around his desk toward the main part of the room.

She stopped him.

"I need to pace. I can't just stand here in the corner," he said.

"You can't. It's not safe."

"I'm not safe for you, either," he said, using his body to try to overwhelm her and push her into the corner. The wall was at her back and she could feel the rage coming off him. But it wasn't directed at her.

He needed an outlet for that anger, and she was the only one available at this moment. She had two choices here. Let him think he had the upper hand and let this play out, or take control and force him to calm down.

Luna wasn't sure that either of those was a good option. "Do you have a gym here?"

"Why?"

"Sparring might help you, and it will be a lot safer than if you insist on forcing me into a corner. Which I thought you'd have learned by now."

"What makes you think I didn't let you overpower me?"

She just quirked her head to the side, trying to see the truth in him. But it was hard. Trying to sleep hadn't helped her. There was something about Nick DeVere that was shrouded in mystery. What was he hiding?

"Let's take this to the mat."

"Yes, let's do that," he said. "It's in my penthouse."

"Let me guess, all glass windows?"

"No. It's a closed room. I think you'll like it," he said, reaching for the door and opening it. "I'll show you your room too."

She pushed in front of him. "You have to learn to let me take the lead."

"I've never been a follower."

Chapter 6

Nick's first martial arts teacher had been Risa Young, when he was fourteen. He'd been kidnapped a month earlier and his father had sent in some highly paid ex-military types to rescue him. He'd been saved, but there had been a lot of blood shed on the way out. Nick hadn't been able to sleep for a few months afterward.

He'd gone to Aldo and asked for self-defense lessons. And Aldo had hired Risa. Her lessons had been succinct and to the point. In combat, there was no place for gender roles or for pulled punches. Spar and fight to win—otherwise what was the point.

Over the years, he'd had more bodyguards than many realized. He'd lost a few of them to "accidents" and each of their faces was deeply embedded in his mind. Just another name on a list of those he was responsible for and had lost. He wouldn't let Luna or anyone from Price be added to it.

That was pretty much the ethos by which Nick had lived his life since that moment. But as he'd changed into his Gi and put on his black belt, he wondered how well-trained Luna was. She had said she was more of a street fighter, and while Nick knew he needed to work out his rage in a constructive way, he'd never liked beating up on someone who wasn't his equal.

When he came out of the changing area, Luna was waiting for him. She'd changed into a pair of black high-waisted leggings and a matching black sports bra.

"Do you have any formal martial arts training?"

"Some. I did judo for a while and kick boxing," she said.

Of course, she had. "So, mostly all kicking?"

"I can punch too. I mean mixed martial arts is my specialty," she said.

He rolled his neck. "That works for me. I don't know how intense we want this to get."

"As intense as you need it to be," she said. "You had the look of a man about to do something stupid earlier."

"Some would say that's my usual look," he said.

Luna shook her head as she took up a position across from him. "I know better than that. It's been a while for me, so give me a chance to warm up before you go too hard."

He just bowed to her and then fell into a ready stance. She did the same. He hadn't sparred with anyone in a long time. He preferred to come down here and do forms, and try to keep his center when Finn and Hazel were coming at him with the demands of running a multinational corporation along with his nightclub and social events.

He liked his life, staying busy for him equaled staying sane, but there were times when the noise he used to drone out the emptiness was too much, and he had to come down here and find center again.

As they danced around one another, each making feints and moves, Nick realized that he wasn't going to find peace while she was here. Luna Urban...she was the focus for him.

He groaned inwardly. He knew the feeling that was swelling him. Sex was always a nice distraction, but she was bodyguard. His bodyguard. He knew that if he made a move on her, she'd have to rebuke him. Maybe that was what he wanted. Some fake reason to fire her. To get her away from him. But as he watched her ponytail swing with each move she made, he knew that wasn't it.

Her neck was long and slender, but there was power behind her forward punches when she connected with him. He moved in closer, watching the way she moved. She was feminine, there was no missing that, but there was a strength that intrigued him.

Nick had no doubt he was physically stronger than she was, but the way she moved and cannily watched him made it clear that overpowering her wasn't the way to win. It was the combo of that knockout body and the keen intelligence in her eyes that was making it impossible for him to stop thinking about tackling her and pinning her to the ground.

His body stirred as he remembered the feel of her pressed against him when she'd tackled him in the conference room earlier. It had been there in the back of his mind all day. He wanted to know if it was just adrenaline turning him on or the woman. And did it matter?

Not really. He wasn't going to pursue her. He slept

with women who were one and done. It was safer and neater that way. But at the same time…she was more than a distraction; she was the kind of puzzle that he wanted to solve.

"You're not really into this," she said after a minute, stopping and dropping her arms to her sides. "Did you think of something about your father's letters?"

He should say yes. Instead, he shook his head.

"You have had a tough day," she said. "Getting shot at and learning that someone has been threatening you all of your life. That would be enough to rattle me."

Her voice was melodic and soothing. She was being reasonable, giving all these logical things to blame his distraction on. And he was being a man. Just a full-on masculine, chest-thumping guy, staring at her mouth as she spoke and wondering what she would taste like, what her kiss would be like. She was used to being in control, yet she was cautious. Would she be different in intimacy?

"Nick?"

"Hmm?"

"Is that it? What can I do to help?"

He looked at her for a long moment, sizing up the desire in him, just to take what he wanted—the way he always did. Kiss her. And to somewhat see if she wanted him too.

"Something that I don't think you'll agree to," he said.

She put her hand on her hip, thrusting her chest out and making him very aware of all of the curves of her body, which he'd been trying to ignore. He groaned out loud this time.

"Try me."

Chapter 7

Try me.

She could tell from the tension coming off him that what he had in mind wasn't a no-holds-barred sparring session but something more intimate. It had happened before, an attraction when she was protecting someone, but usually it took more than a few hours. And it was never this powerful.

Then again, nothing about Nick DeVere was normal.

He watched her with that intense gaze. There was something so acute in the way he examined her. His eyes moving over the length of her neck and then down to the scooped neck of her sports bra. That awareness that she'd first felt when she'd been on top of him in the boardroom was back. This time it felt more like a slow, low throbbing that originated from deep inside her body. She felt her breath starting to quicken.

He hadn't moved. Hadn't done anything but stand

there in his Gi and observed her with that space between them. He was waiting. He wasn't pushing, and he certainly wasn't a man who was going to try to take anything from her.

Luna knew that. Had seen his careful control in every situation they'd been in. Even when someone had tried to shoot him. This need for control was part of the puzzle she was trying to solve when it came to who Nick DeVere really was.

And this was important, but her heart was beating faster and, really, all she could do was look at his mouth and wonder how it would feel against hers.

Not smart.

And she always had to be smart.

A girl on her own was vulnerable in ways that many wouldn't realize. She always looked out for herself, and taking a kiss from Nick, a kiss that she wasn't about to deny she wanted, would be dumb.

It could compromise her on the job. That would compromise her place at Price Security, and that would cost her the only family she'd ever known.

That was a price she wasn't willing to pay, but one kiss…

Surely she could have one kiss without losing control.

"I want to do more than try you," Nick said. "But I'll settle for one taste of your lips. I know—" He put his hands up by his shoulders. "I'm your client and I shouldn't be asking, but you did ask what I needed."

"I did," she said. Hearing him say that he wanted her wasn't a shock, but what did surprise her was how those words had seemed to intensify the feelings slowly building inside her. She usually thought of herself as one of the guys, as a bodyguard. But suddenly, with Nick in this workout room, she felt like a woman.

She was aware of every part of her body. Her breasts felt fuller and she was standing taller, shoulders back, watching his gaze move further down her chest, lingering over her average-sized breasts. Luna didn't lack confidence in her body, she knew that she was enough for Nick. That he was seeing a woman he wanted.

"This can't happen," she said, vaguely aware that her voice had dropped to a huskier timbre. Her body didn't seem to understand the assignment. One kiss was what he'd asked for, but she was moist and her breasts were full...and she wanted more than a kiss.

A hot coupling against the wall would be a nice starter. Luna shook her head. It had been a long time since she'd had a lover, but the truth was sex was complicated for her. Why was she suddenly look at tall, dark, and arrogant over there and wanting him?

That wasn't her.

"Why not? Are you afraid to kiss me?" he asked.

"I'm not afraid of anything," she said.

Another lie.

She'd been afraid of a lot of things, but most of them weren't physical. Afraid of being alone. Afraid to lose the family she'd found and cherished. Afraid to let Van down.

But for the first time in a very long one, she was afraid to touch someone. She wasn't sure what it was about Nick DeVere that was causing this sensation, but it was definitely there. And she'd be an idiot to ignore it.

She'd never been one to throw caution to the wind. The only time she had was when she'd joined Van and Price Security. So...

What did that mean?

"Luna."

Just her name from his lips in that deep resonant tone of his voice and she knew that, no matter how many arguments her mind might throw up, she was going to kiss Nick.

So she exhaled, stepping forward, closing the gap between the two of them. She put her hand on his chest, feeling the heat of him through the fabric of his Gi. Spreading her fingers, she reached the naked skin at the open in the vee of the uniform and looked up at him from under her eyelashes.

"Nick."

Their eyes met and, for a moment, she saw something…maybe it was the only real emotion she'd seen from him since they'd met. It was naked and vulnerable. It was raw and sensual. Then he put his hand lightly on her waist, pulling her into the curve of his body and bringing his mouth down on hers.

For all that she'd wanted him, for as intense as those feelings were, the first brush of his lips against hers was soft.

But the impact…

She felt it all the way to her core, and everything feminine and sensual inside her sprung to life, demanding that she deepen the kiss. She put her hand on the back of his neck, tipped her head to the side and thrust her tongue into his mouth.

He tasted so good. There was no awkwardness to the deepening of their embrace. He tasted good as she sucked his tongue deeper into his mouth. Sending shivers of sensual heat through her body. This was what she'd been craving since the moment she'd held him underneath her even though she hadn't wanted to admit it.

This wasn't going to be just one kiss.

And this risk might not yield the results she'd wanted because, honestly, she had no idea what was going to happen next. Something she hadn't felt since she'd left that MMA ring with Van all those years ago.

This.

This was exactly what he'd needed. It was odd that the woman providing it wasn't blonde and busty. Or maybe not. Blonde and busty wasn't really his type. It was what he knew that certain audiences expected of him.

She tasted better than he'd hoped, and those curves, which had been on display in the leggings and sports bra, felt even better pressed against him. Well, almost pressed against him. He kept his hand on her waist and his mouth moved over hers with a surety that came from practice. But with Luna, it felt more like instinct. His mind wasn't working, and he wasn't doing this to have some leverage later, as much as he might have wished that were the case.

He kissed her because she was providing the distraction that he needed from the bombshell his father had dropped.

He heard the door open a split second after Luna did, and she had already stepped away from him and moved into a fighting stance as he realized they weren't alone.

"Xander, what's up?"

"Boss is here. He wants to talk to DeVere about Thom Newton."

Nick was used to jumping from one thing to the next, but his body wasn't done with Luna and there was a part of him that wanted to ignore Xander and get Luna back in his arms. Except the behemoth was going to take more effort to avoid, and Nick was pretty sure Luna had compartmentalized him back into the client category.

"What about Newton?" Nick asked as he walked toward the door. Thom was always coming up with ideas that were going to be the next big thing and asking Nick to invest in them. The only trouble was the ideas rarely panned out and often ended up being not all that well thought out. But the man had gone to prep school with Nick and Finn before his family had lost their fortune in the dot com bust...so Nick kept taking meetings with him and inviting him to parties.

"Just a few things that Van thinks Luna should be aware of," Xander said. "I can spar with you if you want while she's gone."

"Thanks, Xander," Luna said.

She gave Nick a long glance before she turned toward the dressing room. Again, he felt very much like he had as a child being passed between his father, Aldo and a nanny.

He wasn't a child. "She can spar with you, Xander, and I'll go talk to Price. We need to get some ground rules in place."

"I'm not staying here," Luna said. "And going up against Van with that kind of—"

"You. Work. For. Me."

"I know," she said. "But the truth is, this is personal."

Xander quietly left, which Nick was only aware of on a peripheral level.

"I get how it's personal for me. How's it personal for you?"

"Damn. I knew the lack of sleep was going to catch up with me at the wrong time," she said.

Interesting. What was she hiding? It hadn't occurred to him that the threat could come from someone who had manipulated the board into hiring them. Was there someone on the board who wanted control of DeVere enough to threaten his father and try to kill him?

He used his leg to kick Luna's out from under her and brought her down beneath him. His body pressed to hers in an unbreakable hold. Unlike in the boardroom earlier, he was ready for her counter moves and kept her pinned down.

He was turned on, but the threat to his life took precedence and he shoved his lust away. "Talk."

"About?"

"Don't be clever. This isn't the time for that. Why is it personal?"

She licked her lips and groaned as his cock jumped and he knew she could feel it pressed between their bodies.

"It's been a very long time since my dick overruled my brain. Now, I'm not saying you're not tempting me, but I need answers."

She shook her head, her cheek brushing against his shoulder. "I wasn't trying to distract you. I'm just… damn. Van knew Jack Ingram."

"The hell you say."

Nick rolled to his back, next to Luna. That wasn't what he'd been expecting. "Does he think I set Jack up?"

"I'm not sure. But I know he wants to find whoever killed Jack, and he's not sure what you are hiding."

"Hiding? I'm the one who's life is being threatened," he reminded her.

"You're also the one who said you were untouchable and that others die around you," she said in a low, quiet tone that made him question if he'd actually held her underneath him or if she'd simply let him.

She rolled to her side, putting her hand under her cheek and looking down at him. Now that he didn't feel the threat from her, lust was making a play for control. It would be a distraction, but he wasn't sure he wanted one just now.

"I didn't kill Jack. He was a friend," Nick said quietly. "If I'd thought that there was any chance of him being in harm's way, I wouldn't have…"

"Wouldn't have what?"

"Let him go in my place," Nick said.

He remembered all the good times with Jack. The close calls where Jack had been his bodyguard and saved his life, and the fun times when they'd partied through more than one forgotten weekend. Now the man was gone.

And no matter that Nick hadn't intended for Jack to die in his place, there was no question it was exactly what had happened.

Maybe talking to Van would help him see things, form another angle, and finally figure out who wanted him dead.

Luna had never felt this deep a longing to say screw it and just give in to her own desires, but the cost was way too high for her to indulge herself. Nick watched her with that level gaze, and her mind was trying to run calculations and figure out the risks, but her body was wanting a kiss. A real kiss. One that wouldn't stop until they were both naked and he was buried deep inside her.

But the risks.

She would be compromised, and that meant she wouldn't be able to continue acting as his bodyguard.

Let's face it, she thought, that was the only reason she had to be by Nick's side.

And there was another risk. She'd compromise herself on the job and let down the only family she'd ever had or known.

She had to get up, but seeing Nick this vulnerable, seeing him for what might likely be the first time since they'd met, just letting her in and being totally honest with her, was another kind of aphrodisiac.

He made her want to take the risk; except she knew it would have to be this one time. That was it.

She'd never be this close to him again.

She didn't make sense in his world, she had to remember that.

Luna forced down the need coursing through her body and tried to get her brain back in the game.

"What do you mean—go in your place?" she asked.

He sighed, a deep heavy one that she'd never heard from him before. Putting the heels of his hands on his eyes, he stayed still for a minute. Luna did the same.

"I threw a private party at the beach house. At the last minute, I had an email from the DeVere board that needed to be dealt with. I thought about canceling. Jack and I look very similar, and more than once he's enabled me to 'be' in two places at once. This time, while I was dealing with the board, he went to the party."

"So you feel responsible for sending him in your place? You know you didn't make him go," she said, her mind going to the rational place that his guilt-ridden one couldn't allow.

"I didn't stop him."

"Did either of you see a threat coming? Did you deliberately stay safe, knowing he'd die?" she continued.

"No. What kind of asshole do you think I am?" he asked, getting to his feet.

Luna stood. "I don't. You do."

He looked at her for a second and then nodded. "I get your point. But if you've ever had anyone die in your place, you'd understand that being logical isn't easy."

She reached out to squeeze his shoulder in a gesture of comfort, but the electric tingle that went up her hand and arm and straight through her body wasn't comforting. She was still turned on, still wanted his naked body against hers, still in a place that was very dangerous.

She dropped her hand. "I get it. To be honest, that's why I can't just let my guard down with you."

"Are you tempted to?" he asked.

She could almost see him changing gears. She noticed he still had an erection and his body was tense. He stood close to her, and it seemed as if he were poised and ready to pounce if she gave him the least bit of encouragement.

"More than you know," she admitted.

"Do it. I'm not going to rat you out to Price."

"I can't."

"Why not?" he asked.

"I wouldn't be effective as your bodyguard. I might screw up and get you killed," she said.

"You are too highly trained for that to happen," he said.

She shook her head, feeling her ponytail slap against her neck and wishing it would help her snap out of this mood she was in. For the first time in her adult life, she wanted something that she knew—*knew*—she couldn't have. Nicholas DeVere. The charming, billionaire playboy who she made no sense with.

"I'd be compromised. I'd make a mistake. And that's not why I was hired. So, as much as I want to know how you feel moving inside me, I'm going to keep my distance from now on. And I'm going to ask you to do the same," she said. "I like you, Nick. I want you to find out who is threatening you and your father, and keep you alive."

"You can't say things like that to me and expect me to keep my distance."

"You have to," she said. "I won't say it again."

"Can you really just decide to stop wanting me?" he asked. "You don't seem that emotionally cold to me."

She wasn't, but sensibly stopped herself from admitting it to him. She needed to stop letting him push her buttons and she had to go back to being his bodyguard. Sparring with him might have been the dumbest idea she'd ever had.

"I have to. I'm not willing to take the risk."

"To my life?"

Luna nodded.

"I think there's more to it than that," he said, moving closer to her.

It took all of her willpower to stay where she was and not lean in to him. Not touch him and, conversely, also not run away. She was in that fight-or-flight mode, but the fighting had channeled into something different. She noticed his Gi was mussed and she could see his chest underneath it, she remembered each time her body had brushed his.

"What else could there be?" she asked, distracted.

"Price and the boys. You don't want to let them down, do you?"

She tightened her lips and chided herself for being so transparent. "No."

"I thought so. I'm pretty sure you're denying yourself and making having sex with me into some kind of hair shirt so you can prove your worth to your boss," he said.

"You're wrong. Yes, Van and everyone at Price Security mean a lot to me. But you do, too, Nick, and keeping you alive is the only reason I'm in your life. There aren't a lot of places in the world where I make sense, but Price Security is one of them. Being your bodyguard is another."

He looked as if he were going to argue further. But she wasn't ready to go another round with his probing questions that made her face uncomfortable emotions and facts about herself.

"We should get down to Van. I'll meet you in the hallway after you shower," she said.

"Not coming in with me?"

"Definitely not."

"Are you sure that's wise? What if I'm threatened in there?" he asked.

"Xander is outside waiting for us," she said. "He'll be in the change room with you."

"The hell he will," Nick said. "How do you know he's there?"

"He saw us together…"

She knew Xander wouldn't say anything to the others, but she had to get herself under control. She wasn't about to ruin this job just because she wanted Nick.

He opened his mouth as if to say more but simply closed it and shook his head before heading for the changing room he'd used earlier. She went and notified Xander before going to shower and change herself.

Chapter 8

Nick walked into his penthouse not really in the mood to be nice or charming. He had masturbated in the shower to get rid of his hard-on. But his emotions—the ones Luna had stirred in him—were harder to assuage, although somehow easier to focus on than the fact that his father had spent all of his life hiding this mess from him.

The behemoth followed quietly behind him, and Nick was surprised at how silent the other man was.

Nick stopped at the bar, looking at the bottle of Maker's Mark, more tempted than he wanted to admit to get drunk so he'd have an excuse for doing whatever the hell he wanted. But the truth was that had never been his style.

"You good?" Xander asked.

"Why wouldn't I be?"

"I can think of several reasons," Xander said. "The

boss will be up in a minute. You mentioned you had a room without windows."

Nick gestured to a large room he used for parties when his guests needed more privacy than an open area could afford. He stepped into the room, remembering the debauched, three-day drunken orgy that he'd hosted for Jack's last birthday. It had been a weekend to remember. But the place had been cleaned and long couches and chairs had been brought in to make it resemble nothing more than a sitting room. And Jack was gone.

Losing Jack had been the catalyst to finally getting his father to level with him. But Nick couldn't help feeling that if his father had been honest earlier, maybe his bodyguard would still be alive.

"Nice room," Xander said.

The door opened and Nick didn't have to turn his head to know that Luna had entered. His body seemed to have some kind of radar that sensed her presence. His blood felt heavier in his veins and, even though he'd just jacked off, he felt his cock stirring again.

That somehow almost made him smile.

Sure, someone had been threatening him since his birth, the very thing that Nick had always suspected, but he still wanted Luna. He knew he wasn't going to be able to rest until he had her. It wasn't that he couldn't have sex with someone else. He could find a partner easily. It was that he wanted *her*. He needed Luna Urban.

He didn't know why or how she'd become this throbbing need in his soul, but she was.

"Should we bring a table in here?" Luna asked. "Lee likes to have one for her laptop."

"I'll get it. Why don't you catch Nick up on the latest?" Xander said as he turned to go.

Finally, Nick turned to Luna and noticed that she had the buttons on her jacket done up and that her hair, which had been in a ponytail since he'd met her, was down, curling around her shoulders and framing her face. The change in hairstyle should have made her look softer but, if anything, it seemed to emphasize the steel core that was so much a part of her.

Was that why he wanted Luna and not just sex? He'd always been drawn to strength, but had rarely indulged himself there. He'd always chosen the role of someone who indulged others.

"What update?" he asked, trying to match her professionalism, determined to have her but to not let her know how badly he wanted her.

"A name keeps coming up in your schedule. Thom Newton."

"Thom is harmless."

"Finn thought so, too, but once we started comparing the dates on the letters that were sent to your father and the timing of Newton coming into your life, a pattern is emerging."

Nick rubbed the back of his neck. He'd known Thom from boarding school and, though his family's fortunes ebbed and flowed, Nick didn't really think the other man could be the killer. Most of the time Thom came to him with get-rich-quick schemes. Some of them seemed to have potential while others…were a ridiculous waste of time. Nick had lent Thom money more than once over the course of their acquaintance.

"Honestly, I'm worth more to Thom alive than dead. He doesn't know my father or anyone on the board. Or does he?"

Luna pulled out her smartphone and scrolled through

her notes. "There is one vague connection to one of the board member's daughters. But otherwise, no."

"Sheree Caster? He hooked up with her once. I don't think he's a threat," Nick reiterated.

"Why not?"

"He doesn't have the personality to kill anyone. And he certainly wasn't sending threatening notes when I was a baby."

"True, but his mother might have," Luna said. "The notes all mention him as an heir. Did you father have an affair with Newton's mom?"

"Aldo will know," Nick said, glad to have a reason to walk away from Luna. Up close, he was having a hard time keeping his eyes off her lips and mouth.

He called Aldo.

"Nicholas?" Aldo asked as he answered the phone.

"Yes. Aldo, we need a list of all the women my father had affairs with. I think we should start from before I was born," Nick said.

"I'm not sure your father will agree to that."

"I'm not asking out of morbid curiosity. Someone thinks their child is the DeVere heir, remember?" he asked. "We both want to keep him safe. We need to rule out suspects."

Aldo cleared his throat. "Indeed, sir."

"He trusts you and so do I," Nick said, knowing that Aldo would do anything for his father.

"Of course. I'll get the list over to you shortly."

"Thank you, Aldo."

Nick hung up the phone and turned back to Luna. "Aldo will send it."

She simply nodded at him but looked as if she wanted to say something more. He walked over to her, ignoring the fact that even though she wasn't wearing any perfume, she smelled so damned good.

"Do you need anything else from me?" he asked.

For a second, her gaze flickered to his mouth and then she licked her bottom lip and he knew what she wanted. He wanted it too. That kiss that wasn't going to let them escape. The one that had whetted their appetites and made being near her a form of torture he wasn't sure he could endure.

But the door opened before she answered, and he found himself surrounded by the Price Security team. When he glanced at Luna, she was still watching him.

It took all of Luna's control to stay focused on the meeting Van conducted and not on Nick. As soon as it was over, she was going to have to talk to her boss and let him know…she wasn't the right woman for this job. She still wasn't sure why, but she was struggling to be objective about Nick.

It was one thing to say that maybe it had been too long since she'd had sex, but it was more than that. She normally wasn't that sexual, and ignoring her desires had never been this hard before. But as she'd sat across the room from Nick, watching him, she'd seen how the pressure of every moment of his life being analyzed was affecting him.

Though he had always lived his life in the spotlight, this was different. They were delving into a very private part of his existence, and as much as he was willing to discuss it to possibly find the person trying to kill him, he definitely didn't like it.

The team filed out and Luna glanced at Xander, who had to have observed the fact that she'd been feeling more than protective toward their client. He just nodded as she got to her feet and followed Van out the door.

"Van, got a second?"

She watched as the rest of the team trailed Lee to the elevator and, when they were alone, Van turned to her. She almost told him to never mind, but the truth was that this man had saved her and put her on a path she was meant to be on. A path she'd almost compromised in Nick's workout dojo earlier today. A path that, she suddenly realized, had a fork in the road.

"I do. What's up?" he asked, his voice that low rumble she knew could go from comforting to threatening in a nanosecond.

"I told Nick you knew Jack. He is eaten up with guilt over the fact that Jack died in his place. I think you should come clean with him. Nick had nothing to do with Jack's death other than the fact that someone wants him dead."

Van gave her that slow head nod he did when he processed information. "What else?"

"I want him. I haven't given in to it, but there's a chance I will. Maybe you should reassign me."

Van raised both eyebrows at her and then gave her that slow smile of his. "You would never compromise his safety."

Van's faith in her was reassuring, but Luna wasn't as sure as he was. It only took one distraction to lose a client.

"What if—"

"Don't go down that route. The fact that you are even talking to me about your feelings tells me I can trust you to do the right thing," Van said. "If things change, let me know."

"Change?"

"If it becomes more than want," he said.

"I…won't let that happen."

Van reached over and squeezed her shoulder. "You're human, kid. This is the first time in all the years you've worked for me that this has come up. I have to think there is a reason for that."

"What's the reason?" she asked because, like Van, she knew Nick was different, or sensed that he could be. But she hadn't been able to figure out why.

"Only you will be able to figure that out. But I'm not going to blame you for catching feels for the man. The heart wants what it wants."

"I'm not sure it's my heart doing the wanting," she admitted.

That surprised a chuckle out of Van. "Whatever it is. For now, we're good. I'll talk to DeVere about Jack. Might be good to compare notes and see if anything shakes out."

"Okay," she said. What else was there to say? Van trusted her to do the right thing, not only on the job and for the company but for herself. Luna knew her past made her complicated when it came to commitment, and it was hard to ignore the fact that she craved a man who wouldn't be in her life after the job was over.

Was that why she was into him? Even though these feelings were strong and something she'd never expected to experience, maybe they were temporary. Temporary had always been where she felt the most at home. She couldn't deny that about herself.

Luna wondered if it was the same for Nick as she followed Van back into the room. Nick and Xander were talking quietly. Nick's eyes flicked over to her and, for a moment, she couldn't look away. She just stared across the room at him, her pulse racing and her mind indulging in what it had felt like to have him under her on the sparring mat.

He raised one eyebrow at her and she shook her head before looking away. She noticed that Finn stood off to the side, watching the two men. The emotions on his face were hard to read, but she could see that they were complicated. Of all of his entourage, Finn was the one who was closest to Nick. Maybe there was more to be learned from him.

Luna knew he'd been talking to the team, but it was time for her to have a one-on-one. She might not be able to control her emotions for Nick, but she could protect him, and that meant talking to everyone, ruling out every possible person who could do him harm, and keeping him alive until the person trying to kill him was caught.

Price and the rest of his team left, with Finn following them out, and Nick was alone again with Luna. Hearing the Price Security team and Finn discussing his life hadn't been his favorite thing. He hated dissecting every traumatic moment down to the last detail. Though a part of him was relieved he had concrete proof after all these years that it wasn't some ego-driven mania that had made him think someone had been trying to kill him.

"Now what?" he asked Luna.

"I'd like you to reconsider my wearing a gun at the VIP party on Friday," she said.

"No."

He didn't care how many times she asked, he wasn't backing down on that. They'd come to arrangement about the metal detectors for his guests and the list was being vetted by Price Security. Luna had been quiet during the meeting.

"Fine. What do you usually do during the afternoon?" she asked.

"Work, take calls, that sort of thing. Why?"

"It's probably for the best that you pretend to be back to 'normal' so whomever is after you thinks you've relaxed your guard."

He wasn't sure anyone was going to believe that given the way Price Security was all over his building and his life. But at the moment he was ready to do something that felt normal.

"I'll have to be in my office with all the windows," he said dryly.

"That's fine. They are bulletproof and I'll be in there with you. What did Jack do usually?"

"Stayed in the office, went over security footage, vetted my schedule," he said.

"Great. I'll do that. Did he have a desk in your office or just sit at that little table?" she asked.

"Just sat at the table," Nick said as he gestured for her to lead the way out of the sitting room.

"Why are you being so cooperative?"

"I did hire you and, as you pointed out, it would be foolish to ignore your advice. Plus… I need something that I feel like I'm in control of and work is the one area this hasn't touched," he said.

She stopped and turned to him. "Control is an illusion."

"No one knows that better than I."

"Are you sure about that? It still feels like you are playing a game with me."

"Maybe that's because you are," he said.

"What game?"

He shook his head. "Seriously?"

She breathed in deeply through her nose and then licked her lips again. "It's not a game, Nick. I don't get the feelings you stir up in me. They don't make sense. I don't like it. My world is normally very neatly ordered and you are…not."

He almost smiled because hearing that she was as confused by their attraction as he was reassured him. Also, it gave him an excuse to not think about the fact that there were too many moving pieces in his life right now.

His father wasn't who Nick had believed him to be. He was now suspicious of people he'd known for most of his life. And his new bodyguard had him tied in knots.

"Glad to hear that."

"Well, I'm not. I can't do this. You weren't wrong when you said I don't want to let down Van. And yet…"

He took a step closer to her. She was the one thing he wanted that he couldn't have. He knew it. Rationally, it made no sense to place either of them in jeopardy, and sleeping with her would do that. But at the same time, he couldn't resist her.

"Yet?"

"Please. Just let me pretend that I'm in control of this," she said quietly. "I've always been very good at not wanting what I can't have."

"But not this time?"

"No."

He saw the struggle on her face, knew that he was making it harder for her, and there was a part of him that wanted to keep it going, but he couldn't. "What did you want that you couldn't have?"

Her arms came up, wrapping around her waist. She tipped her head to the side, seeming to study him, and he had the feeling she was trying to decide if she could trust him with the truth. "You know everything about me, Luna. You can trust me."

"Just normal orphan kid things," she said.

He had almost forgotten she'd been raised in the foster care system because of the way she held herself and moved.

He had filed the information away. That was his habit. Tucking little bits of things people told him away so he could use them later. He never knew what would be of the most value, but everything a person said had some weight to it.

"Like wanting a family?"

"Sometimes, or just siblings, or a new car, or someone to worry about me," she said. "But I had somehow gotten used to telling myself that I was better alone. And I think I believe it most of the time."

"But not now?" he asked.

She didn't answer him for a long moment and then dropped her arms to her sides. "I have Price, so I know that I'm not alone, but part of me always believes that it's only temporary. That one day soon, he will leave or I will let him down. That's why I'm trying so hard to resist you, Nick."

"Because of Price?"

"No, because I know that anything that happens between us would be temporary, and I'm not sure I would be able to believe myself if I had to pretend like that was enough."

Temporary.

His entire life had been that—of course, on a grander

scale than Luna's had been. Her words resonated, and he knew that, deep inside he feared the same thing. That he collected information about people so he could use it as leverage to keep them in his life.

Luna protected those she cared about for the same reason.

Chapter 9

Luna didn't spend too much time dwelling on the past. If she'd learned anything in her life, it was that regret had no place in it.

Instead of regretting her lapse of judgment from the day before, she woke early and worked out in her room, feeling restless despite the fact she'd finally slept. She'd been given the room next to Nick's and entered the main living area of the penthouse, finding a woman sitting on his couch, holding a to-go cup of coffee and looking a bit put out when she realized that Luna wasn't Nick.

"How did you get in here?"

"I have a key. Who are you?"

"Who are *you*?" Luna countered.

"Verity Vaughn."

The ex. The one who was supposedly planning Jack's funeral, and not a threat.

"Luna Urban, Price Security."

Verity got to her feet, tossing her long blond hair as she did so. She passed the to-go cup of coffee back and forth between her hands. Luna suspected the other woman was nervous. Because her energy made it seem that way.

"The bodyguard? Seriously, Nicky needs someone big and tough like the dude who was downstairs. You look like I could take you."

"You can't. Why are you here?"

"To talk to Nicky," Verity said slowly. "I'm planning his last bodyguard's funeral. And just so you know, he was way tougher than you."

"Are you threatening me?"

"No," Verity said, walking closer to Luna, her high heels clicking on the tiled floors. "Warning you."

"Verity, leave her alone," Nick said, coming into the room.

Luna glanced over her shoulder, noting that Nick hadn't gotten less attractive overnight. He adjusted his tie as he walked toward his ex-wife. He bent to give her a kiss on the cheek and then turned away.

Luna wasn't jealous of Verity Vaughn. Not in the least. But there was something fierce and elemental that went through her as she watched Nick kiss the other woman. As if her body and soul had claimed Nick for herself. But he wasn't hers. He was only hers to protect. Hers to guard. Hers to keep safe.

She repeated it to herself, trying to make herself remember it.

"Why are you here?"

"Jack's funeral, which I almost have totally planned. I would be done, but I'm still dealing with Hugh."

Nick glanced over at Luna for the first time that morning. Their eyes met and held for a moment. As much as he was charming and affable, and seeming to indulge Verity, Nick was clearly annoyed with the other woman. Luna gave him a slight smile before turning away from the two ex-lovers and doing a perimeter sweep of the room.

The sun had risen and the streets below the Art Deco penthouse were busy with cars and pedestrians. Luna wasn't worried about Verity's presence in the penthouse, knowing that Xander would have cleared her to come up. But she was determined not to walk into any more surprises until they caught the person threatening Jack.

She texted Xander, who just thumbs-upped her message. She wanted to ignore the conversation, which involved a favor that Nick owed Verity, but Luna's mind was busy putting together the puzzle pieces. What kind of favor did Verity have in mind, and why did Nick's ex-wife think he owed her anything?

Finn had said that she might be a threat, but Nick had dismissed her as harmless.

As Luna watched them interact, she leaned heavily into the body language training she'd had last year. There was palpable tension between the two of them when they thought the other wasn't watching. But when they looked at each other, it was all big, toothy grins and easy conversation.

There was definitely more there than met the eye. But what? Murder? Why would the woman responsible for killing Jack then plan his funeral? Though, from what Rick had said, killers were complex and needed attention despite not wanting to get caught.

This was the first time Luna had been this close to a murder. Normally, she spotted threats and kept her clients safe. She had been part of routine team investigations because, as Van always said, they each brought unique skills and viewpoints, so he liked having everyone's perspective.

This was different. Luna was on the front lines of danger. The right information could crack the case and save Nick.

But no matter how professional she felt this morning, she couldn't forget yesterday in his workout dojo. She was trying to be the person she always was. A sexless, bionic woman who did her job. But reality was more complex. She wasn't sexless or bionic. She was just a woman who was more jealous of the ease that Verity had in Nick's house than she wanted to admit.

Nick glanced over at her and she realized that she wasn't even close to knowing how to stop feeling turned on when he did that. Like, right now, she was struggling to keep her pulse steady and to control the need in every fiber of her being to touch him. That, she wasn't going to do.

"Luna, I'm going to text you an address I need to visit this morning. Will you clear it for me?"

"I will," she said. "Where are we going?"

"Is she going, too, Nicky? I thought we'd do it together," Verity said.

"I'm definitely going," Luna said. "I am his bodyguard."

Verity just tossed her hair and took a sip of her coffee. Luna had to admit she really didn't like the other woman. But Nick ignored his ex and came over to her.

"We are going to Verity's current husband's house to see if I can get some of her stuff back," he said. "I owe her a favor. It shouldn't take long, and when we get back, the dresses I ordered for you should be here."

"Dresses?"

"That one you have won't do. We want the world to think that I've let my guard down. That means showing up with a date on my arm, not a soldier," he said.

"I don't think that's what we want," she said pointedly.

"It's what I want," he said.

Damn. The word *want* echoed in her mind. She definitely didn't need to be thinking about what he'd wanted yesterday or how his mouth would feel against hers if she finally gave in.

Nick hadn't slept well. He hadn't been able to stop thinking about Luna, and what she had said, all night. She only made sense in his world if he was in danger. That was a hard truth to face, and he knew that he should man up and shove his feelings down as he always did. But seeing her and Verity together made that so much harder.

Verity was beautiful and always had been, but next to Luna, all he could see was the artificial layers his ex used to protect herself from the world. They were a barrier she wore to manipulate the people around her, like her volunteering to plan Jack's funeral just to get Nick to go and negotiate with her husband.

Luna didn't need any of that. She was real and honest, and there was nothing artificial about her. And as much as he knew that she really had no place in his life, that wasn't enough to stop him from thinking about her. To try to create a spot for her.

He was looking forward to seeing her in the dresses he'd picked out for the upcoming VIP event. He could tell she wasn't pleased with the fact he had done that, but he didn't care. He wasn't a man who lived his life by anyone else's rules, and now that everything in his life had been upended, he felt even more determined to do what he wanted.

The door to his penthouse opened and Van walked in. "Great, you're both awake. We need to talk. I just found something in one of the letters."

Nick felt a tingle go down his spine. The letters. He'd been over them himself several times and nothing had stood out.

"Which one?" Nick asked.

"What letters?" Verity asked at the same time.

"Verity Vaughn, right?" Van asked her.

"Yes," she said in that haughty tone she reserved for staff.

"You need to leave."

"I'm not—"

The piercing sound of an alarm rang out. Luna was next to Nick in a flash, one hand on his arm, the other pulling her weapon from her shoulder holster.

"Fire alarm," Van said. "I'll take Ms. Vaughn. You get Nick out of the building."

"Wait a minute—"

"You don't have a minute," Luna said, urging him with her as she moved through the penthouse. She stopped as she opened the door, using her body as a shield as she scanned the hallway for threats before she reached back to take his arm again. He shrugged free of her.

He appreciated she was trying to keep him safe, but he wasn't about to watch her be attacked—or worse, take a bullet for him. "I'll go first."

"You'll do what you're told," she said. "Stay to my

right and just slightly behind me while I check the stair-well."

"I've got him covered," Van said.

"What about me?" Verity asked.

"You're fine," Van said.

Nick didn't like this at all. But he'd been wanting someone to believe him for years when he'd said he thought someone was trying to kill him. He just hadn't envisioned it going down like this. Everything was slip-ping out of his control.

"Clear...but I'm not sure we should use the stairs," Luna said. "It's too quiet. I don't like it."

Van came up next to her and together they formed a protective area around Nick and Verity. He was the damned damsel in distress as far as Price Security was concerned.

"I agree. If the alarm was tripped, then it's a trap," Van said, turning to Nick. "Is there another way down?"

"There are two sets of stairs," Nick said.

"I'll take Verity and go to the right. You take Nick and go left," Van instructed Luna.

"I'd feel safer with Nicky," Verity said.

"You don't get a vote. Get him downstairs and out of the building," Van said.

Luna nodded and her face tightened. Nick saw a still-ness in her that he'd seen when she'd launched herself across the boardroom a split second before the bullet had hit the glass.

In this split second, Van and Verity had left and Luna had turned to him. "This isn't the time to be the boss. I need you to follow my every instruction," she said.

"I will."

He wanted the person threatening him caught. He

wanted Luna safe. So, for just this once, he was willing to take orders.

They entered the stairwell she'd quickly glanced into and cleared. He followed her closely, watching for directions. She motioned for him to stand in the corner while she partially descended the first flight of stairs, glancing both above and below as she did so.

She'd looked over her shoulder and started to motion him forward when a gunshot rang out. A bullet hit the wall just next to Luna's head and she returned fire. Motioning for him to get down, a second bullet set debris ricocheting off the wall, cutting Luna's face. He saw the blood dripping down her cheek.

Fear and anger gripped him and, though he knew he'd hired her to keep him safe, he couldn't stand by while she got injured. He let out a primal yell of anger and rage, and stormed the stairs in the direction of the shooter. He heard footsteps pounding in front of him as the assailant ran down the stairs.

Nick pushed harder, using the handrail and skipping several steps, trying to catch the person fleeing. He was vaguely aware that Luna was behind him, keeping pace with him, but he didn't slow his steps. He didn't stop.

It was time to put an end to this. He was ready to get his life back and to protect Luna. As he'd told her yesterday, he wasn't prepared to let another person die in his place. Not even the woman who'd been hired to protect him.

Luna was pissed. She followed Nick down the stairs as bullets flew by. Now that Nick was exposed, she knew she wasn't in any danger. He was. Making ground catching up to him, when she was close enough, she tensed her body and launched herself at him. She caught him by the waist and used the force of her body to push him to the ground.

He struggled underneath her, but she used all of her strength to hold him down and was tempted to pinch the nerve in his neck to knock him out. She was so mad at him right now. She knew that she needed to be clear-headed, but he kept putting his life in jeopardy. Kept acting like his life didn't matter and that he didn't respect her skills. She looked down into his blue eyes and the barely contained anger within them.

She was so angry, she couldn't speak. On the verge of losing control, which she couldn't allow to happen, she got off of Nick's body and stayed in a shooter's pose until she heard the outer door at the bottom of the stairs open and someone escape out of it. She grabbed her phone, alerting her team that the suspect was in the alley, and then turned back to Nick. He had moved to sit, his back against the wall, watching her.

"What the hell were you thinking?" she demanded.

"That I'm not letting you get injured to protect me," he said.

"That's literally my job, Nick. You aren't going to do that again," she said.

"I'll do whatever I have to," he said through his teeth. "I can't sit still and watch you get injured."

Before she could respond, he pulled a handkerchief from his pocket and pressed it gently to her face. Her cheek had burned when the debris had first hit her, but she'd ignored the rest of the pain. Pain was easy to ignore. His touch on her face wasn't.

"You could have been killed," he said as he moved to his knees so that they were facing each other. His body heat wrapped around her and she felt the exhalation of his breath on her uninjured cheek.

"So you thought it would be better if *you* were?" she whispered. She reached up to touch his face, knowing that no matter what she'd said yesterday, she was already compromised.

Luna closed her eyes. She was going to have to quit. There was no way she could be objective where Nick was concerned.

She felt the brush of his lips against hers and her eyes opened, their gazes met, and she let go. He was alive and safe, despite the fact that he hadn't listened to her, and for just this one moment she wanted to celebrate that. She moved her mouth against his, her tongue thrusting deep into his as she leaned forward until his chest was against her breasts. His free arm wrapped around her waist, pulling her against him as he ravaged her mouth, kissing her deeply and with more passion than she expected.

She shouldn't have been surprised. Whatever else she thought about the attraction between them, it was mutual. She'd realized that yesterday in the dojo and today on the stairwell as they'd both been trying to save each other. But she knew this had to end.

Except, right now that didn't matter. All that mattered was the way his mouth felt on hers. The sensations and feelings spurred by his heat flowed through her body, turning the adrenaline from the chase into something more sexual.

Her center was moist and aching. She craved him. Wanted him right here in the stairwell, even though her smartwatch was vibrating—she was pretty sure Van the rest of the team were waiting for her to check in.

Luna put her hand on his face as she sucked his tongue deeper into her mouth and then reluctantly broke the kiss.

His mouth was wet and swollen from their kiss and she licked her own lips as she got to her feet and then offered him a hand to help him stand. He got up and looked as if he wanted to say something, but she shook her head. She wasn't going to talk about any of this.

She glanced at her watch. The latest message told her to meet in the club in Nick's building. That area had been secured.

She put her hand on the small of Nick's back and felt an electric tingle go up her arm as she directed him through the building to the club. He stopped her before they could enter.

"I want to talk to you alone," he said.

"Boss. Oh, my freakin' God, Nick. Are you okay?" Finn asked, coming toward them before Nick could continue. The other man looked pale and scared. He noticed the blood from Luna's face that had splattered onto Nick's collar.

And went even paler.

"I'm fine," Nick said. "Luna is the only one who was injured."

"Are you okay?" Finn asked.

"I'm good."

"Well, okay. The board is here in the conference room. Kenji wouldn't let any of them leave during the alarm, which freaked them out. So you're going to have to get up there and calm them down."

"Not yet," Luna said. "We need to go into the club and talk to Van."

"Why?" Nick asked.

"The alarm wasn't triggered by smoke or a fire, it was deliberately set. The building is being locked down until we can talk to everyone."

"I thought the shooter got away," Nick said.

"We don't know that they were working alone," Luna said.

"You could still be in danger," Nick said, looking directly into her eyes.

She felt the heat in his gaze and it did little to cool her down. It was only her fear that he could have been shot and killed that tempered her desire. His wanting her made it harder for her to ignore her own feelings. But her wanting him could cost him his life. She had to stop this now.

"No. You could. Finn, come with us. I want to know the names of each of the board members and when they arrived," Luna said, directing both men into the club area where Van waited.

Chapter 10

Nick felt edgy and not really in the mood to listen to interviews conducted by the Price Security team. But Luna wouldn't let him out of her sight and also wasn't up to talking to him alone, so he went to the grand piano he kept in the VIP section of the club and sat down.

Finn followed him over, bringing rocks glasses with whiskey for both of them and sitting next to him.

"So far, this whole 'find who killed Jack' thing is wearing my nerves down," Finn said as he took a healthy swallow of his drink.

Nick straightened his tie before doing the same with his own whiskey. "It is. I could do with a lot less being shot at."

"Me too. So who do you think it is? Price said he has a lead based on one of the letters, but wouldn't share any more information. That man plays his cards very close to the chest," Finn said.

Nick cracked his knuckles and then ran his fingers over the keys, finding solace in the familiar. His mind was whirring with possibilities, fears, and a little bit of anger toward Luna for endangering herself. He soon found himself playing the classicized version of "Dancing On My Own" made popular by a TV show. Finn stayed close to him as he played. His friend was worried about him.

But he had no words to reassure Finn. That was probably why he was playing the piano instead of talking to the board of directors, several of them people he'd known most of his life.

Luna had advanced the theory that maybe someone on the board was colluding with Thom Newton to threaten him. Was that possible? Nick started to go over every interaction he'd had with the different board members. But he knew he had to go further back than the last ten years, when he'd been running DeVere Industries.

He had to go all the way back to when he was a child.

There were five board members who had been there then. There were three more who were children of previous board members, so they would have a connection to his family. His father had handpicked most of them. DeVere wasn't publicly held; it was a shared investment group with Nick and his father holding the lion's share of the power.

He heard the low irascible rumble of Mitch Dumfries voice, a big bear of a man who his father had met after the Mitch had left the army. He'd been instrumental in bringing in government contracts when DeVere had started out.

Nick found himself switching to a Chopin étude,

which helped him to think better. Mitch had apparently known Nick's mom. Had Mitch had a crush on his mom? Or maybe they'd dated before she met his dad? Something that Nick had never really thought about until now. Until he'd read the letter that had gloated about Nick's mother's death.

But if Mitch had known her and had wanted her for himself, killing her would have made no sense.

"Enough with études. I can't deal with this angsty music right now. Play something upbeat," Finn said.

Nick lifted his hands and stopped playing, turning to the other man. "Like what? I'm not sure of the right music for post-someone-tried-to-kill-me."

Finn put his arm around Nick and hugged him tight, whispering, "Stop scaring me."

Nick hugged Finn back. "I'll try."

"Should we try to get back to normal?" Finn asked after he finished his glass of whiskey.

"Yes, but I'm not sure what normal is anymore. It's only been, like—what?—three days since Jack's death. But it feels like a lifetime."

"Nicky! Tell them to let me leave," Verity called from across the room.

Nick sighed. He had forgotten that Verity was there and still needed him to go and talk to her soon-to-be ex-husband.

"I'll deal with her if you want," Finn said, turning and standing up from the piano bench.

"You're just looking for a fight," Nick pointed out. Those two would never get along.

"I am. I suspect she is too. As much as I'm not Verity's biggest fan, we do both love you, and seeing you shot at isn't the easiest thing to deal with."

"For me either. I've always felt unbreakable…" he trailed off. What was he going to say? That he knew those around him weren't? Was he being selfish by keeping Price on the job and by letting Finn, Hazel and Verity stay close to him?

"Don't stop feeling that way. I suspect that's part of what's kept you safe all these years. I'll take care of Verity. You do what you need to. The board is here for the negotiations, and Loni Peters has some new business. She wouldn't elaborate."

"Thanks," Nick said as Finn walked away. He looked down at the keys and thought of how everything made sense when he had a focus. Sometimes it was music. Others, business. Or a woman.

Luna danced through his mind.

What was he going to do about her? That kiss. Hell, if they hadn't been interupted, he wouldn't have stopped kissing and touching her until he'd buried himself inside her body, taking her until they both screamed.

Another distraction, but part of him believed it was more than that.

He should be coming up with a strategy for the board meeting and whatever new business Loni was going to spring on him. It was something he could control. In the boardroom, no one second-guessed him for long.

But he knew that control was an illusion. If he'd had any doubts, that alarm had put them to rest. Price had been bringing the board members down one at a time for questioning. Nick ignored them while he sat at the piano.

In the background, he heard Price questioning the board. Some of them sounded bored and annoyed, others sounded worried.

Nick wasn't sure what to make of that.

"We are almost done with the questioning," Luna said, coming over to him. "Xander swept the boardroom, so you are cleared to go up there when you are ready."

He looked over his shoulder at her. "Thanks. I want to talk about what happened in the stairwell."

"I don't."

"Well, we don't always get what we want, do we?"

"No."

She stood there, holding his gaze in that steady unflappable way she had, and then she exhaled and moved to sit next to him on the bench in the same spot that Finn had vacated.

"Okay. Talk."

Luna had tried to stay away. But her job was to protect him. They were interviewing everyone who had access to the building and the codes needed to bypass security. Price and the rest of the team had that handled. Being close to Nick seemed the smartest place for her to be.

She was still edgy. She should have anticipated he'd run after the assailant. He was too determined in his belief that he couldn't be killed. But she knew that he could be. That, more than likely, someone he knew was the culprit. She had pretty much ruled out Verity as the killer; she'd been in the room with them when the alarm had gone off.

But that didn't mean Verity wasn't working with someone else.

"I could have caught the gunman if you hadn't brought me down," he said.

"What? No, you couldn't have. He had a gun, and if we hadn't been giving pursuit, he probably would have stopped and aimed and hit you," she said.

"Or you," he said.

"We've been over this already, but it's my job to keep you safe. And I wanted to wait until later to have this discussion. But you need to stay behind me. Let me do what I'm good at."

His fingers moved over the piano keys. The music wasn't familiar to her but it stirred her, fanning the flames of restlessness in her soul.

"Who else have you protected?" he asked. "Tell me more about you so maybe I can stop from trying to interfere."

She smiled to herself, he wasn't looking at her, just moving his fingers over the keys, and she couldn't help but keep watching as he did so. His fingers were long and nimble, and he played with the same expertise that he seemed to bring to everything he did. She wasn't surprised by that.

"Well, I just came off tour with Jaz, a pop star. He was being threatened by a major fan," she said, remembering the six months she'd spent in South America with Jaz. "Unlike you, Jaz listened to me. I didn't get in the way of his concerts or parties, but I still kept him alive."

Nick stopped playing. He didn't turn to face her, but as she looked at his profile, that strong jaw and the sharp blade of his nose, she knew he wanted to. He was good at controlling his impulses. That meant that he hadn't dashed around her without thinking. He'd deliberately put himself between her and the gunman.

"You're not bulletproof," she said. "I need you to understand that."

He did turn then, and she saw passion on his face. It was dark and angry, fueled no doubt by the shooting and being trapped in this room. This place where he'd always been the demigod in charge of his world. But the power had shifted with the threat to his life and it didn't take a genius to realize that Nick would rather risk his life than accept it.

"I understand more than you. Those letters only confirmed what I already knew. Someone has been trying to kill me since I was born. I'm still here, but my mother, cousins, friends, bodyguards aren't. What exactly do you think I'm missing?"

He had a point. She saw the events from his perspective, but at the same time she knew his impulses could be a death sentence. "You're getting reckless. That is changing things. Also, these attempts aren't even trying to look like accidents, as they did in the past. There is a new urgency in the attacks that wasn't there before."

Nick reached for his whiskey and took a swallow of it. "So where does that leave me?"

"Under my protection," Luna said. Trapped in her throat were the words she longed to say to him. Promises that she knew better than to make. That no one else would die. That she believed she could keep Nick safe. But he had to want to be safe. "Putting yourself in danger won't bring those you lost back."

He turned to her then, looking down his nose at her, and she shivered at the expression on his face. It was fierce and determined. "I realize that. But watching others get hurt...you're still bleeding, Luna. You won't let me help you, you won't let me try to keep you safe, you won't—"

"You're right. I won't. You hired me for this reason."

"I hired you because I thought you'd provide cover while I investigated Jack's death. But that's not working," he said.

Slightly shocked that he'd thought of conducting his own investigation and that he'd thought she would be malleable. "I can't provide cover if you duck around me."

She just kept hammering away at his lack of self-preservation. She had a thick skin when it came to men who thought she wasn't up to the job of protecting them. It did hurt a bit, though, to think Nick had viewed her that way.

"Going to ignore the personal part?" he asked.

"I am. We're not doing personal."

"I want to," he said. "I need the distraction from all of this."

"That's not my job."

"And you're all about the job, right? Is that why you kissed me in the stairwell?" he asked.

She heard the taunting note in his voice. She suspected he had the same chaotic energy coursing through him that she did at this moment. A fight or a kiss... something physical was the only way to channel it.

"Perhaps. Is that why you're playing the piano?"

He rubbed his jaw and then nodded. "It is. Shall we go up to the boardroom?"

She knew he was frustrated that she wouldn't discuss kissing him, but she still didn't know why she had. She'd been scared for him and angry and scared for herself. And it had been too long since she'd felt anything like that for one person. She'd given into her desires, and while she didn't exactly regret it, she knew it couldn't happen again.

Nick was glad to have DeVere business to concentrate on. He conducted the meeting and ignored Luna sitting in the corner taking notes. Remembering what

Finn had said, it was hard not to look at the board with different eyes. Was there someone who wanted to be the chairman enough to kill him?

Honestly, he thought it would be easier to try to get the other members on that person's side and vote him out. Killing went beyond a need for power and to a certain malice that he wasn't sure anyone on the board harbored toward him and his father. That didn't mean he was right, but as he looked around the table, he determined that most of those in the room didn't have the time to hatch a plot to hurt him.

For a good third of the board, this was one of many companies in which they had a large share. He knew that most of them were more concerned with making money, and as long as the bottom line stayed in the black, they were happy.

"So the latest employee contracts were negotiated almost fifteen years ago and the workplace has changed," Nick said. "Some of the benefits and working conditions that we are being asked to accommodate are pretty much standard in other companies. We've been doing the expanded family leave unofficially, but I think it's time we get it into the contract."

Mitch raised his hand. "That's fine. But this work-from-home thing, I'm not sure it will work."

"What are your concerns with it? Finn will share the study we conducted that showed worker efficiency is up when they are at home."

Nick heard Finn's fingers tapping on his tablet and knew his assistant was sending the study to the board as he spoke.

"My main concern is infrastructure," Mitch said. "A

lot of our remote workers are in rural areas without the capability of high-speed internet connection."

Nick nodded and smiled at Mitch. "I want to shift the office costs in the budget to providing that to our remote workers. We can reduce the size of the office space we are currently using. I have two proposals to finish evaluating that were put together by the workers group, but they are suggesting taking the unused office space and renting it out and using those funds to upgrade remote workers' internet and home offices."

"That might work," Mitch said.

"I don't think it will," Loni piped up. "I mean how do we know they will use the upgraded equipment and services for work only. I'm not sure we want to be providing all of that to our workers' homes."

"We should trust them," Nick said.

"Well, yeah, but that doesn't mean they will be honest," Loni said. "We've seen that they can't be with that entire coffee bar service we provided. The security footage showed more than one worker taking snacks and coffee home."

"We dealt with that six months ago, and there have been no incidents since then. I think this is the time for us to show that we value our workers. They can easily find work that pays close to what we do that will allow them to work from home. I'm putting this forward for a vote."

Nick wanted to make DeVere a place where people wanted to come and work. More than just a job. Something the older board members tended to resist so he kept pushing them.

They voted and everyone but Loni agreed, and it passed. Loni then raised her hand to discuss new business.

"I'm sorry to have to be the one to bring this up, but with Everett's health declining, we need to talk about a succession plan. I know that Nick is next in line, but given that someone is trying to kill him, we might need to have someone else standing by."

Nick leaned back in his chair and crossed his arms over his chest. She had a point. "We need someone who knows the business inside and out."

"I agree," Loni said.

"Do you have a name?"

"I do. Finn Walsh. He's been by your side since you took over from your father and, frankly, his availability is better than yours. I think he's a solid choice to succeed you."

Nick glanced over at Finn and saw his assistant looked flushed and seemed unnerved by Loni's comments.

"I agree. Finn would make a good chairman," Nick said. "He already knows our systems. Any other names?"

Mitch, David and Rochelle all had other suggestions but agreed Finn was their first choice.

Nick conducted the rest of the meeting and asked the succession team to get the paperwork ready for Finn should something happen to himself. Nick then closed the meeting and the board all trickled out. Finn stayed and, for one of the few times since Nick had known him, seemed at a loss for words.

"So…"

"So?"

"This is just so unexpected. I mean I had no idea that anyone saw me as anything other than your assistant."

"Finn, you're my right-hand man and they all know how intelligent and capable you are. I'm glad Loni suggested it. I've been so focused on other things, I didn't even think of putting a plan in place for you."

"Are you okay with that?"

He was. There was no one he trusted more than Finn to run DeVere Industries if he wasn't around. He knew his friend would stick to their code of ethics and continue growing the business for decades. "I am."

"Great. Well, then, I guess I better get back to my desk," Finn said.

Luna came over to him when the boardroom was empty. She'd been taking notes the entire time and put her notepad on the table next to him.

"What did you think?"

"That you're more than just a pretty face," she said. "I had no idea you could be that…"

"Smart?"

"Ha. No, not that. You always carry yourself with arrogance, and I guess I expected you to rule over the board, but you listen and put your employees first. Not exactly what I expected from a self-proclaimed playboy."

Her words touched him and he shook it off. He had more money and luck than one person should be gifted with and he'd always tried to put it to good use. But there was something about knowing Luna saw the good him that made him…well, not think about her as only his bodyguard.

"Glad to hear that."

Chapter 11

The boardroom seemed to suit him as much as being in the club or sitting at the piano. Each facet of this man was more intriguing than the one she'd seen before. She'd already decided to keep things professional between them, so Luna tucked this new revelation deep inside and knew she'd pull it out years later when this job was over, and Nick had moved on and forgotten about her.

She didn't dwell on the memories tucked in there. He'd asked her about the meeting and her impression of him, but she'd seen on his face that he'd wanted to take things personal. There was even a part of her that understood his motivation. They'd both been shot at. One of them could have died. And they were bonded now by that. She was the only person other than Nick who understood what it had been like in the stairwell.

"What now?" he asked. "I know Price has some theories on one of the letters. Is he still here?"

"I'm not sure. I've sent a message to him, but Xander was the only one to see it. And he's not leaving his post downstairs. I suspect that Van is going over the security footage and analyzing it," Luna said, sensing that her coworker felt guilty that the alarm had been triggered while he was on watch.

Heck, she still felt slightly guilty about kissing Nick. There was a part of her that wanted to be the perfect bodyguard, which she knew she could never be because she was human. She couldn't take her emotions out of the equation. But seeking perfection was part of her makeup. Perfection meant that she could work for Price forever, that they could never abandon her.

She had to remind herself that none of them was perfect. The same went for Xander. He'd been downstairs watching the door and screening all entrants to the building. She knew he'd add watching the security footage as well.

"So it's just you and me for now?"

She hesitated to say yes because "you and me" had conjured up an image of him in her arms. "We are."

"You're so wary now. Why?"

"Being alone with you… I know you want to talk about the kiss."

"And you don't," he pointed out dryly. "Do I seem like the type of man who forces a woman to do something she doesn't want to?"

"Definitely not. You're the type of man who seduces her into thinking it was her idea," she said.

He winked at her. "You do see me."

"I do," she said. If only he was the man he tried so hard to convince the world he was. Instead she saw the complexities that went beyond the billionaire CEO playboy. And *that* man…he was harder to resist. She saw the similarities between them despite the disparity in their backgrounds. He understood her.

"So if we can't get physical—"

"We definitely cannot."

"Tell me about yourself, Luna Urban. You grew up in a group home and had an image of your parents from a 1990's TV show," he said. "What else?"

"I'm a kickass woman who doesn't let emotions get in the way of doing my job," she said. As if saying the words out loud would make them true. But in a sense, it did. She had cared for all of her clients. Most of the people she'd been hired to guard were decent, and scared, and going through a tough time in their lives. And Luna had to admit that helping someone when they were vulnerable was important to her.

It was as if she sometimes thought she was protecting the vulnerable girl she'd been. She knew that what was in the past couldn't be changed, but by taking care of someone else, she comforted that girl who'd had no one.

"You are pretty kickass," he said then straightened his tie, something she realized he did when he was… *Nervous* wasn't the right word, but it had to do with an emotion he didn't want to express.

"You're not too bad either."

He gave her a distracted nod. "I'm sorry. I shouldn't have run after the shooter."

She smiled over at him. "It's okay. Just don't do it again."

"I can't promise that," he said. "My mind knows you're capable and that I hired you to keep me safe, but when bullets are flying, I can't cower. I need to do something."

That made perfect sense to her. He was a man of action. Even conducting the board meeting, she'd noticed that he'd had a hard time being still. He moved always.

"I can see that. You really aren't someone who can wait, are you?"

He tipped his head to the side. "Are you seeing me?"

"It's kind of my job to read people," she admitted.

"Am I that easy?"

"Not at all. I'm guessing, based on twenty-four hours of knowing you. I think that you're very used to adapting and changing yourself to be whatever someone needs you to be."

"How do you mean?" he asked.

She might be a little too real for him right now. But this was who she was. She couldn't just pretend. Not with Nick after that kiss. Since she was definitely going to be lying to him and herself about how deeply it affected her, she had to balance that with the truth.

"Well, when you're with Finn, you're his boss and his bro, and then with Verity, you're all charm and generosity. With the board, you were forceful but fair, listening to everyone's point, even the ones you didn't agree with, before making a decision."

He turned so that they faced each other, barely an inch between the two of them.

"What about with you?"

Luna thought about it but had no easy answer. Because she was his shadow, she was seeing parts of Nick that she was pretty sure he hadn't meant for her to. He wanted her to see him as a man who didn't need her protection, yet at the same time, he needed her to stay alive.

She shrugged as he lifted one eyebrow at her as if to say, *I'm waiting.*

"With me, you are cocky and arrogant, and then a

flash of vulnerability comes through," she said. "That's when you are most like yourself."

Normally, Nick always had a planned outcome for every conversation or interaction he started, but with Luna, he didn't. He hated that, because with everyone else, he always got a read that let him know who they expected him to be. If he could anticipate that, he stayed in control. Luna was shattering all of it.

"Cocky and arrogant, I'll own, but vulnerable? I told you. I'm unbreakable."

Raising both eyebrows, she just matched him with that level stare. And he wondered what it was she was looking for in his face. Part of him knew that it was only the juggling act and the different façades that kept him ahead of everyone else. Yet, somehow, she was trying to see past it.

"I scare you," he said as the realization dawned.

That was the only thing that made sense to him. She had thrown him off kilter, and he'd done the same to her. It was why she had put that barrier of her job between them. Why she was busy picking him apart. That was exactly what he did when he was unsure. He looked to the other person and found their weakness.

"You do," she admitted. She brought one arm around her waist and then seemed to realize what she'd done and dropped it. She turned and walked to the plate-glass windows, looking down at the street.

He remembered yesterday when she'd done that and seen the glint of a scope. Was he reading her wrong? Was she just doing what she had to, to protect him? Was she determined to not let her control break again because he'd been shot at?

She took her job very seriously.

"I'm sorry," he said again. He wasn't one of those guys who had a problem apologizing. He screwed up from time to time, owning it wasn't an issue for him.

"For what?"

"Making this harder for you than it should be," he said. "Maybe I should text Jaz and get some tips."

She gave an ironic laugh. "Uh, don't do that. I'm not sure late-night parties are what you need."

"You partied with him?"

"That's what he does to wind down after a concert," she said.

"Then why the objection to my party on Friday?"

"Jaz wasn't being threatened by an unknown assailant. We knew who the stalker was, I was just there to make sure that Jaz was safe."

"Was that easier?" Nick asked.

"For me? Sure. For Jaz? I don't think so. It's never comfortable to think someone wants to kill you."

She had a point. "Has anyone ever tried to kill you?"

She shrugged. "Not like you mean."

"Then how?"

She shook her head. Why? Why had she said that? She could have just said no and he'd have let it go.

"When I aged out of the care system, I was on the streets for a few months. I had to fight for food one time."

And that fight had changed her life. She'd lost and been left bleeding on the street. She still didn't know how she'd gotten to the emergency room, but when she'd woke up in the recovery room, one of the nurses, Jean, had offered her a place to stay while she recovered. Jean's kindness had changed Luna's life.

"One Minute" Survey

You get up to **FOUR books** <u>and</u> a Mystery Gift...

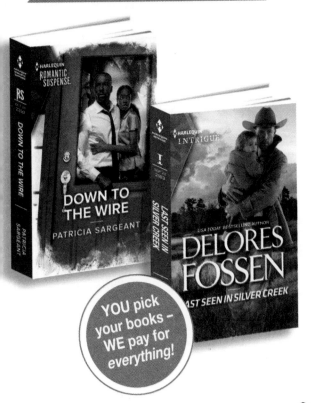

YOU pick your books – WE pay for everything!

See inside for details.

YOU pick your books –
WE pay for everything.
You get up to FOUR new books and a Mystery Gift...
absolutely FREE!
Total retail value: Over $20!

Dear Reader,

Your opinions are important to us. So if you'll participate in our fast and free "One Minute" Survey, YOU can pick up to four wonderful books that WE pay for when you try the Harlequin Reader Service!

As a leading publisher of women's fiction, we'd love to hear from you. That's why we promise to reward you for completing our survey.

IMPORTANT: Please complete the survey and return it. We'll send your Free Books and a Free Mystery Gift right away. And we pay for shipping and handling too!

We pay for EVERYTHING!

Try **Harlequin® Romantic Suspense** and get 2 books featuring heart-racing page-turners with unexpected plot twists and irresistible chemistry that will keep you guessing to the very end.

Try **Harlequin Intrigue® Larger-Print** and get 2 books featuring action-packed stories that will keep you on the edge of your seat. Solve the crime and deliver justice at all costs.

Or TRY BOTH!

Thank you again for participating in our "One Minute" Survey. It really takes just a minute (or less) to complete the survey… and your free books and gift will be well worth it!

If you continue with your subscription, you can look forward to curated monthly shipments of brand-new books from your selected series, always at a discount off the cover price! Plus you can cancel any time. So don't miss out, return your One Minute Survey today to get your Free books.

Pam Powers

"One Minute" Survey

GET YOUR FREE BOOKS AND A FREE GIFT!

✓ Complete this Survey   ✓ Return this survey

1 Do you try to find time to read every day?

☐ YES   ☐ NO

2 Do you prefer stories with suspenful storylines?

☐ YES   ☐ NO

3 Do you enjoy having books delivered to your home?

☐ YES   ☐ NO

4 Do you share your favorite books with friends?

☐ YES   ☐ NO

YES! I have completed the above "One Minute" Survey. Please send me my Free Books and a Free Mystery Gift (worth over $20 retail). I understand that I am under no obligation to buy anything, as explained on the back of this card.

☐ **Harlequin® Romantic Suspense**
240/340 CTI G2AD

☐ **Harlequin Intrigue® Larger-Print**
199/399 CTI G2AD

☐ **BOTH**
240/340 & 199/399 CTI G2AE

FIRST NAME | LAST NAME

ADDRESS

APT.# | CITY

STATE/PROV. | ZIP/POSTAL CODE

EMAIL ☐ Please check this box if you would like to receive newsletters and promotional emails from Harlequin Enterprises ULC and its affiliates. You can unsubscribe anytime.

HI/HRS-1123-OM

Jean had let her stay until Luna had a job and money for an apartment. That one fight, that brush with death, had changed her. It had made her stronger, but it was very different from Nick's brush with death. Someone had been stalking him his entire life and, instead of making him afraid or forcing him into hiding, Nick had lived his life in the spotlight, taking chances and risks that others might not.

Because he thought he was unbreakable.

And, honestly, she could see why. He had survived things that many others wouldn't have.

"What happened?" he asked.

She shook her head. "I fought, I lost, and then someone was kind to me. It changed me. As I imagine your survival after all the 'accidents' in your past did to you."

He nodded at her. "They did. My father wanted me to be protected all the time, but the truth is that no one can protect me. Not even you, Luna. At first, I thought it was fate or the universe, but now that we've seen those letters, I have to accept it's a real person."

"Does that make it easier?" she asked.

"Easier to find them. I mean fate is kind of a nebulous concept. I've never met a person who I couldn't figure out."

"Me either."

Their eyes met and they both smiled at the same time. There was so much to like about Nick DeVere. So much to tempt her into believing he saw her and understood her. But her old fears stirred reminding her that she no one ever really saw her.

Her phone vibrated and she looked down at the screen. "That's Van. He's on his way up with some footage for you to review."

"Great. The sooner we find out who's trying to kill me, the better," he said.

Then she'd be out of his life. The thought came quickly and with a twinge of sadness. She knew it was for the best. She had no place in Nick's Art Deco tower or his life. Not really. But that moment on the stairs, that kiss, made her want a place.

She'd always been so careful to not lust after things that were out of her reach, so why was he different? Why was he calling to her on a soul-deep level? And why was she having such a hard time ignoring it?

"Luna?"

"Yes?"

"Why are you so determined not to admit there is something between us?" he asked. "I could get it if you thought I was a jackass, but you don't, do you?"

She chewed her lower lip between her teeth. Then took a deep breath. "This job is all I have—"

"You've said that."

"I mean that, in my life, everyone leaves. So if I let you in, compromise your security for a few hours in your arms, I'll lose not only my job but everything."

Her honesty turned him on and at the same time made him realize there was still so much to her he didn't know. There was a truth to her Nick both admired and really hated. Now, he couldn't try to tempt her and seduce her into his bed as if she were just another hookup.

Everyone leaves.

She'd put into words a feeling that he'd had all of his life but had never been able to vocalize. Except, for him, everyone didn't leave. He kept people around him with favors and money. Something he'd never really taken the time to acknowledge before.

"I won't let that happen."

"It's not up to you. I don't know why I'm so attracted to you," she admitted.

He quirked an eyebrow. "Thanks for that."

She made and offhand gesture. "Your ego is big enough not to have taken a hit from that. You know what I meant. There is no reason for us to have this attraction."

"Chemistry would be a neat explanation but except it feels like something more."

"Except that," she said.

Luna rubbed her inner wrist in a comforting motion and he knew that he couldn't push any further with her. He'd just exist on cold showers until the person threatening him was found and Luna moved on to her next job.

Because a lot of her objections were based in fact. They weren't going to bump into each other after this job was over. She'd go on to her next client and he'd be back to his life of parties, favors, and board negotiations. The attraction between them would fade as new people came into their lives.

He should just let that be the end of it.

But he couldn't. He didn't want to. He wasn't sure if it was that ego she'd mentioned or something deeper. Yet he didn't want to just walk away from the feelings Luna aroused in him.

"Sometimes I feel the same as you do. That everyone leaves."

"You are literally surrounded with people," she pointed out.

"I know. But they are here because they need something from me," he said.

"I don't need anything from you," she said.

"I'm paying you to be here," he said. "But that doesn't matter. If you live your life from that place of fear, you aren't really living."

"Is that why you aren't canceling the party on Friday?" she asked.

"Partially. I'm not a man to cower or back down. I hear what you're saying, Luna, but the truth is, whatever this is between us is bigger than the both of us. It is strong. You're not really my type, yet all I can think about is how you felt underneath me in the dojo. I know someone is trying to kill me and, in the stairwell, when I would have stayed back and let Jack when he was alive protect me… I jumped in front of you."

She stared at him with those wide brown eyes and he wondered if she was really getting what he was saying.

"It makes no sense for me to do that. But I did it because it was you," he admitted.

"Me? Please don't do this. I'm like the worst person to have a relationship with. I've been left alone for so long; I suck at making anything last…except this job. This job and this sort of family I've cobbled together for myself is all I have."

You could have me.

The thought was in his mind before he could censor it, but he didn't say it out loud. When had he ever been enough for anyone? Even Verity, who'd married him for his contacts and money, had moved on to someone else. He knew what Luna wanted. Secretly, he had always wanted that too. A real family. The kind that TV shows and movies always portrayed but that Nick had never experienced in real life.

Even Finn's and Hazel's families weren't like that.

"I'm not sure what you're searching for exists," he said.

"You're right about that. But I like what I have," Luna said softly. "I think I would like being with you, but the truth is we don't know if you're attracted me because of who I am or if you're attracted to me because we're in danger. And I'm not you, Nick. I have confidence when I'm on the job because I know I'm good at it. But in life... I don't know who I am away from Price Security."

Her words were painfully honest and made him wish he could tell her that she was what he wanted. But she was right. There was no real way of knowing what was true and what was due to the situation. But his gut made him want to believe that what he felt for her was real.

Except, his track record wasn't the best. He couldn't remember a single person he'd felt something this strongly for after they'd left him, and wasn't that the proof he needed that she was right.

"I won't make promises that can't be kept. The only way to know if what is between us is real is to test it out and see if it lasts."

"That's a risk I won't take," she said.

"I will. But only when you're ready," he said.

"What makes you think I will be?" she asked.

They'd had enough soul bearing for this afternoon. "No one can resist me."

She rolled her eyes and shook her head. "We will see."

"We will. So after we meet with Price, it will be time for you to pick out a dress for the VIP event, and I need to go and see Verity's soon-to-be ex."

"What's his address? I want to send someone to check it out before we go over there," she said, switching back into bodyguard mode.

He gave it. He didn't know what his next move with her would be, and that excited him. The unknown had always appealed to him more than following a set path. And with Luna, nothing was as he expected it to be.

Chapter 12

Luna was glad to be around Price, Lee and Kenji. She needed to be in a place where she wasn't alone with Nick and where her expertise was needed. Lee had tied one of the letters Nick's father had received when he was fourteen to one of the deadly incidents, and had uncovered its police report. Though it had been written off as an accident, the officer who'd penned the report had claimed that some of the coincidental facts didn't add up.

"Is Officer Peters still with the force?" Luna asked. "It'd be nice to talk to him."

"He's retired and moved to Arizona. Lee is trying to track him down," Van said. "Nick, what do you remember about the accident? It happened while you were home for the summer?"

Nick leaned back in his chair, straightening his tie as he did so. As much as he might have wanted to track down the person responsible for all of his near misses, it must have been painful to be delving back into his past.

"Yes, I was. My nanny was injured in the accident," he said.

"That's Constance Jones?" Kenji asked as he made notes on the pad in front of him.

Luna listened to the questions they were asking Nick, but she was also comparing the letter to the incident report and two newspaper articles that had run at the same time. A few of the online gossip sites also had some write-ups.

So, she pulled them up on her tablet. She was looking for someone or something that matched the description of the shadowy figure on the security tapes who'd pulled the fire alarm this afternoon. She wasn't sure it could be the same person. The attacker today had been about Nick's age, maybe a few years older. So back when Nick was fourteen, they wouldn't have been old enough...or would they?

What was she missing?

Constance had been driving Nick home from Marina del Rey after he and friends had taken his father's yacht to Catalina Island. Constance had been on the yacht with Nick, and her car had been left in an unsecured parking lot.

Further down on one of the gossip sites, Luna read a statement from a surfer who'd seen someone near Constance's car, and as that area was ripe with thieves looking for wallets in unlocked vehicles left by swimmers and surfers, he hadn't really thought much of it. When he'd gotten closer, the person had walked away and the surfer had forgotten about it until he'd seen the accident on the news.

Not really much to go there. The surfer hadn't been able to identify the person he'd seen; he wasn't even sure of their height or gender.

Luna made a note of it, but that wasn't much. It was weak.

This entire case was weak. The person she'd seen in the stairwell, who Rick had chased, didn't seem old enough to have been stalking him for Nick's entire life.

"Constance could tell you more, but as I remember it, we'd turned off the freeway and onto a curvy road that was also a bit downhill. She pumped the brakes and I know I heard something pop, not sure what, and then she said she couldn't steer almost at the same moment that the car careered off the side of the road," Nick said.

His voice was rougher than she'd heard it before, and, maybe for the first time, Luna truly understood what he'd meant when he'd said he didn't want anyone else to get hurt. These letters were solid proof that Nick's theory about someone trying to kill him was indeed true. But the reality of the people he'd known, the ones who had mattered in his life, being killed or injured, had been with him for a long time.

"The accident report says the car flipped three times before landing on the roof. Were you injured?" she asked.

Constance had suffered multiple injuries—including a spinal fracture that had left her paralyzed from the waist down. She'd been transported to the hospital and treated, according to the police report, but Nick wasn't mentioned.

Possibly because he was a DeVere and police reports were public. Maybe his father had suppressed it.

"Not a scratch. Constance couldn't walk...and I

walked away," Nick said bitterly. "Where is the connection here, Price?"

Van pushed a piece of paper toward Nick and Luna leaned forward to see; it was a copy of the letter Everett had received after the accident.

There's only one woman who is raising your true heir. Too bad the spoiled brat survived. There's always next time…

There was anger and true malice in that letter. How on earth had Everett not thought to share it?

"So?" Nick asked.

Luna remembered something she'd read on the gossip site in the comments section. She started scrolling to find it again as Van mentioned that this "accident" had been specific in targeting not only Nick but his nanny.

Luna found what she was looking for,

"There's also this comment. Might be nothing but… 'The DeVeres have always used their staff and discarded them. Not surprised that the boy was fine but his nanny was paralyzed. Bet they let her go without any compensation.'"

Nick cursed under his breath, shoved his chair back from the table, stood and walked a few feet away. Luna pushed the tablet toward Van so he could look at the comment. The person had posted anonymously but she knew that Lee, with all of her mad computer skills, might be able to trace it.

Luna walked over to Nick and stood there next to him. She wanted to comfort him. That wasn't her job but that didn't stop her from reaching for his shoulder and gently squeezing it.

"We took care of Constance," he said.

"I never thought you wouldn't."

"But others would have. What is the point of this?" he asked. "I don't want to relive every one of these traumas."

"The point is that now that we've confirmed her accident was connected to the letters, there is a chance the attacker left clues that no one was looking for. The point is these clues could leads us to finding Jack's killer and your stalker ."

Nick needed to get away. The letters had put a new spin on his entire life. And, as much as he appreciated the validation of what he'd always suspected in the back of his mind, he honestly hadn't been prepared to deal with it becoming fact.

He wanted to punch something, or someone. He needed to get in his car and drive as fast as he could, and maybe, just maybe, he could outrun the thoughts in his head. How was it that he was always unscathed? He hated that somehow he'd been lucky enough to emerge from all of the attempts without a single injury. Constance hadn't let the loss of her mobility slow her down, but there were times when he'd seen the effect on her.

His father had taken care of Constance. She'd been given a home, and staff to take care of her, and received a generous settlement that assured she'd want for nothing. Nick visited her twice a year, but he knew he did that partially out of guilt. The fun-loving woman Constance had been was still there, but Nick's own feelings overshadowed it. She was fine with who she was now, but part of him always wished that he had been injured instead.

"Can we leave?"

"Not yet," Luna said. "I think we need to still go over the arrangements for the VIP event. Today's incident—"

"Finn can handle that."

She looked as if she was going to argue with him, but then gave him a nod. "Where do you want to go?"

Hell.

He couldn't just leave. He had to make sure Luna and her team checked out any location so that they'd all be safe. Somehow, before Jack's death, it had been easier to just think of himself as really lucky and leave it at that. Sure, there were times when things were uncomfortable, but the truth was, he hadn't really dwelt on any of it and now he had no choice.

"Verity's ex. Can we go see him?" he asked.

Luna glanced over at the table. While the Price team and Finn were all pretending to not be listening to their conversation, he knew they'd heard it all.

Kenji caught Luna's eye and nodded.

"Is my car ready?" he asked the team.

"It will be in a few minutes. I had to get Rick up to Xander's post," Van said, standing and coming over to them.

Nick looked at the other man. There was a toughness to Van that Nick respected, but he saw empathy in the man's eyes and wasn't sure how to deal with that.

"We're going to find the person behind this. Once they're caught, I think… It won't make the past easier, but it might help you to finally move on," Van said.

"What makes you think that?"

"Experience," Van said. "I'd like to go over all of the incidents with you at some point."

"I'll do that," Luna said. "You and the team focus

on tracking down the person who posted the comment I found on the website. I'm willing to bet that's not the only accident people were commenting on. Maybe there's a pattern to be found."

"I'm sure there is. Kenji is also looking into Reddit and other online forums where the DeVere family is discussed."

"People do that?" Nick asked. He knew that there were some online gossip sites that covered his parties and activities, and he used them to monitor what events got the most attention, but he hadn't been aware that there was anything else about his family.

"All the time," Finn added from his seat. "I can send some links. I monitor most of them for unflattering photos and comments. I never thought to look for anything tied to Jack's death."

"I wouldn't have expected you to," Van said to Finn. "Until Everett shared these letters, there was no reason for you to think that the incidents in Nick's past were anything other than freak accidents."

Nick knew he should be angrier with his father but a part of him—the man who'd just had to relive the accident with Constance—almost understood why Everett had kept them hidden. It was easier to just chalk it up to coincidence than to admit that someone had been stalking Nick for his entire life.

"Thanks, Finn. Actually, thank you all for everything you've done today. I'm sorry that you are in this situation."

"That's not really in your control," Luna said. "I'll check in when we are at the location."

Van nodded at her and turned back to the table as Nick led the way out of the room, but not toward the garage. Instead he took the elevator back up to his penthouse.

Without looking at her he went to the bar, pouring himself a large glass of whiskey.

Luna stood at the side of the room and looked around for danger. But the penthouse was Nick's sanctuary, the one place that he let his guard down. The marble floor with the thick Persian rugs spoke of opulence and the kind of breeding he had. The grand piano, right in the center of the room, was set so that whoever was playing would be seen from every angle.

"Why do you have two grand pianos?" she asked. Remembering the one down in the bar and talking about this one up in his penthouse now. She had meant to the first time she'd seen it.

"Because I can," he countered.

Nick was in a mood and she didn't really blame him. He was ticked off that they'd been shot at in the stairwell. She was too. She wanted to go seven rounds with him in a boxing ring and use all of her skills to lay him low and remind him that she was in charge.

But that wasn't an option. No matter how ticked off he made her, she was on the job, and that was the one place she'd always been able to keep her cool. None of her other clients had rattled her the way that Nick did.

And she *was* rattled. He'd been reckless and she wanted to yell at him but couldn't. He was the boss, as he'd succinctly put it. But if he died, no one was going to pay their bills.

"Yeah, you do. You're just arrogant enough to buy two high-price luxury items." She'd said it just to irritate him, but mainly because she knew it wasn't a fight she wanted with him. It was something primal, physical.

Even if he was still doing favors for Verity. A woman Luna admitted she was jealous of and didn't trust.

Even her mind was reluctant to say she wanted sex. But she did. Dirty, late-night-in-a-club sex. The kind that didn't matter or come with emotions. The kind that was just a way of letting off steam.

Except she couldn't do that with Nick. Her feelings for him were already too intense.

And she was stuck in this penthouse with him. Only him and this sexual need that was growing because she'd put him firmly off limits. Why was she so contradictory? She couldn't look to her parents and blame one of them because she had no clue who she came from. She had to only look at herself and own the fact that once she decided not to do something, she had the overwhelming urge to just do it anyway.

Do *him*.

He slammed his whiskey glass down on the counter of the bar and, on his way to the piano bench, threw his suit jacket toward the large sofa that dominated the conversation area. He lifted the black thing that protected the keys—she had no clue what that was called—and sat down. He linked his hands and stretched his arms forward before he started playing. "Toxic" by Britney Spears.

The music suited her mood and the way he played it was slower than the Top 40 radio play version. It was moody and dark, angry and sensual.

It had been a mistake to challenge him. She'd known that but had gone ahead and done it anyway.

She felt like the walls of his gorgeous Art Deco

building were closing in on her. She'd always had the freedom to have a few hours off, a few hours away from a client, but Nick didn't work that way. And this was an important contract, so she wasn't going to mess it up by asking for time away.

If there was one person she'd hold her tongue and do something this restricting for, it was Van. Only him. He wanted this job; he needed to find out what had happened to his friend Jack Ingram.

But Luna knew there was going to come a time when she snapped and either dragged Nick into the boxing ring or the bed. It was a toss-up right now which one she'd enjoy more…well, that was the lie she was going with.

Nick was in a destructive mood. Hell, hadn't he been in one for his entire damned life? It felt that way. It felt like fate was keeping him alive as some sort of cosmic joke that he wasn't in on. Or maybe it was karmic payback for a former life? He didn't believe in that kind of stuff, but that explanation was all he had.

Luna was needling him. She was ticked that he hadn't let her run after the madman shooting at them. And maybe he should have. Then she'd either have caught him or maybe be dead. He got to the tricky fingering in "Toxic" and concentrated for a moment as he played, then he stopped and looked over at her.

"You are the most frustrating woman I've ever met."

"Ditto."

He shook his head, wishing he'd brought his whiskey over with him. Instead, he started playing Rachmaninov's Concerto No. 2. He had to concentrate to remember it and play the notes correctly. It was one of the first pieces he'd mastered. The one he used when he needed to get back to his Zen.

But he wasn't finding it. Jack dead. His father hiding letters from someone who'd been gloating after an incident that had almost killed him. Luna with her damned kissable mouth standing behind him, glaring at him. Making him want to take her. Right here in the middle of the penthouse on that thick Persian rug.

She was justified in being upset with him. He got that he'd hired her to keep him safe. But there weren't words, or he didn't know how to say them out loud, to tell her what it felt like when he watched someone else be shot instead of him.

He was weary. Like, soul-deep fatigued with this life. This was something that had started with his mother's death. His entire life had been in the shadow of someone who hated him and his father. And, at this moment, there was no way out. No way for him to move past this.

"Nick, stop. That song…it's sad."

He stopped abruptly and turned around to face her, swinging his entire body. "You don't like sad."

"Who does?" she asked.

"I don't know. Everyone should. That's life, isn't it?"

"It can be," she said. "But then sometimes, in the middle of something huge like this, you can find peace."

"Yeah, right," he said. "Did you find peace in foster care?"

"I did," she said. "It took me a while because everyone was always talking about finding a permanent family, and one day I decided I didn't need one. I stopped looking at each house as anything but an opportunity to learn."

He crossed his arms over his chest. How had this

beautiful, complex woman never been wanted by a family? "That brought you peace?"

"It did. Find the thing that will bring you peace now," she said.

Her words hung in the air between them.

"Let's go see Verity's ex. If nothing else, it will distract both of us," he said.

He was aware of her following him down to the garage. When they were alone for a split second, where he knew that the security cameras in his building had a blind spot, he was tempted to pull her into his arms. To take what she'd already said she didn't want to give him. But he held himself in check.

In his entire life, this was the first time where he could see that it wasn't fate but an actual person who was forcing his life onto this path. He might have always survived the incidents without a physical injury but his soul had taken multiple hits and he wasn't sure that he could take many more.

He was angry and more determined than ever to find the person responsible and make them pay. Pay for his mother, Constance, his cousins, Jack and…for Luna. Not just the cut on her face, but also the fact that she'd been brought into his life and he couldn't keep her.

Nick was quiet as he drove through the streets of Los Angeles. It just made Luna realize how much of the public man he kept hidden. "Want to talk about it?"

"No."

Watching his profile and sitting close to him in the car, the scent of his cologne was starting to become familiar. That was something that happened with each of her clients, but with Nick it was different. His scent made her pulse race and brought with it the remembered feel of his mouth on hers.

She turned her attention to the mirrors, watching their back as they drove. The house had been cleared and Rick had let Miller know about the shooting. The detective had sent a patrol car to drive by the neighborhood before they arrived. Even she didn't feel great about letting Nick leave his penthouse, but they knew that they couldn't make him stay.

"Tell me about Verity. How'd you two hook up?"

He glanced over at her and sardonically lifted one eyebrow. "Are you sure you want to know about us hooking up?"

She didn't, but she could tell that Nick needed to talk or to do something that would help him mellow out a bit. And, for whatever reason, his ex seemed like something that would be safe to discuss. "Actually, was she ever targeted?"

Nick tipped his head to the side and then shook his head. "We were only married for three months. There wasn't anything at our wedding or on the honeymoon. Jack was my bodyguard then. I'm not sure if he kept any records, but I don't think that anything was going on. Is that weird?"

"Not sure," she said, but took out her notepad and jotted that down. "How old is Verity?"

"Twenty-eight," he said shortly. "She's too young to have rigged Constance's car."

"What about her parents?"

He swerved through traffic and onto the shoulder, bringing the car to a halt as he turned toward her. "East Coast money who don't really care about the DeVere fortune. In fact, they liked me with Verity because I wasn't after her for her money. But please look into them. I'm sure they'd love to know that they are suspects in this."

She knew he was lashing out because he felt so powerless at the moment. She got it. She'd probably have kicked a bunch of dents into the walls of her bedroom if she'd been in his place. "We're more discreet than that. Was her fortune a factor for you in marrying her?"

"No. I like her. She's fun at times."

That wasn't really a reason to marry someone. "Did you love her?"

"Love her? No," he said.

"Then why marriage? It's not as if either of you had to get married," Luna pointed out.

"Dad had his first diagnosis of kidney cancer. So I thought it might be time to think about the future," Nick said.

That made sense. "And then he got better, and you decided you didn't have to?"

He shook his head, resting both wrists on the steering wheel and looking ahead of them, not at her. "Not exactly. Verity is difficult to live with. I know the same could be said of me. We were both too much to be a couple. So we divorced. Dad continued chemo. That's it."

That's it. But it wasn't it. Another relationship where he'd been left alone. She saw the pattern in his life because it so closely mirrored her own. She knew he was being blasé about it, but he must have gotten married for more than the idea of the future. "Did she ask for the divorce?"

"I did. I just wanted— Why does this matter?" he asked her. "This has nothing to do with keeping me safe."

"It does and it doesn't. I think you need to talk, and this is helping. I'm not sure what else to do."

"We could have sex. Right here in the car. That would help," he said.

"I already told you no. I'm not a casual sex person," she said.

Nick rubbed the back of his neck as he turned to look at her. The expression in his eyes filled with heat and questions. "I am."

"I know. It's how you protect yourself."

"And not having sex is how you do it?"

"Sometimes. Mostly, I work and don't have time for a personal life," she said carefully. She hadn't had a relationship in a while. Her job just wasn't one that left time for that, and she liked it that way. Relationships scared her. Sex was complicated for her. The first time she'd done it, it hadn't been great, and she'd realized that sex wasn't really satisfying for her, so she'd stopped seeking it out.

Luna thought it might be different with Nick given that the kisses they'd shared had made her hotter and had been more pleasurable than anything she'd experienced before. But if her past had taught her anything, it was that real life seldom lived up to her expectations.

"And then there's us."

Us.

That was a complication neither of them needed. She wished she could be like Nick said he was. Just have sex and let it mean nothing. But in her heart, she wanted it to mean something. If she was going to get naked, it had to be with someone she trusted. Not someone she was with just to get through something.

"Yeah, I thought we decided there wasn't an us."

"You did," he said, putting the car back into gear and easing back onto the highway.

Nick was quiet for the rest of the drive and this time she left him to his thoughts. She watched their back and kept herself alert to any threat outside the vehicle, ignoring the one that was sitting right next to her.

But then, that threat wasn't on Nick. It was only she herself who was in danger. Because, no matter what Luna had said or wanted to believe, she was becoming more and more compromised when it came to Nick.

Chapter 13

The next two days started to feel almost routine for Luna. She was rested. She'd drawn a line in her mind and put Nick on the other side of it and it seemed, for now, he was he was staying there.

The visit to Verity's ex's house hadn't netted them any more information and a background check on both him and Verity's family had cleared them of any connection to Nick or the threat to his life. In fact all she'd learned was that Nick put on a different persona depending on who he was dealing with. It made her leery of giving into her feelings for him.

Was he only acting like someone she could understand to woo her into his bed?

Which as soon as she had the thought she immediately dismissed. Nick didn't have to work that hard to land a woman in his bed.

She'd also learned more about Nick's life and habits. He started his day early with a workout; she always joined him on the treadmills in another of the rooms in his penthouse. Then he had a quick breakfast smoothie before going on calls all morning. During that time, she observed and listened to his conversations. Thom Newton's name came up several times, and though Nick didn't want to consider him a suspect, Luna did.

She'd discovered that on the day the fire alarm had been pulled and they'd been shot at in the stairwell, Thom had signed in on the building visitor's log, but he hadn't signed out. And he hadn't been in the group of employees and other visitors held outside by the Price team.

She tracked him online and noticed that most of his feed was filled with photos of him with Nick or at events that Nick attended. He seemed to be a low-level influencer with invites to a lot of LA-based events and deals to promote fitness-oriented products like the smoothie Nick had drank that morning.

Nick leaned back in his chair after he hung up the phone and rose. Luna was on her feet and by his side, knowing he liked to pace midmorning and still didn't seem to get that pacing near a window was dangerous.

"I think we can agree that whoever was shooting at me is taking a break," Nick said.

"I don't think we can," she said.

"What were you working on over there?" he asked.

"More digging into your friend Thom Newton."

He shook his head, turning but moving so he wasn't in view or range of the window. "Are you still going on about Thom?"

"Yes. I want to go and talk to him," she said.

"Why? I told you he's harmless."

She scanned the horizon and rooftops then took a quick glance below to make sure that traffic, both vehicular and foot, was moving along. "Really? Then why was he on the visitor's log two days ago when you were shot at and yet he wasn't in the group of people we questioned?"

Nick furrowed his brow and his jaw tightened. "I don't know."

The quiet way he controlled his face reinforced that he wasn't happy with this latest part of the investigation. He considered Thom a friend. He'd known the man most of his life, and though Finn had mentioned that Thom was someone always trying to make it seem that he and Nick were besties, the relationship wasn't that close.

"Let's go talk to him."

"I can't. I have a meeting, and the party is tonight. He'll be there," Nick said. "We can question him then."

"'We'? I think it would be better if it was just me."

"Luckily, I'm in charge," he said, moving back to his desk and clicking something on his computer.

She knew he was trying to definitively end the conversation. But she wasn't done yet. Now that she'd had sleep and a few days to go over everything, patterns were emerging. While Nick thought he was unbreakable and couldn't be harmed, he'd come very close several times and there were only a handful of people who'd been near him for most of those incidents.

Thom Newton was one of them.

"You can either cooperate or I'll go to Van, who will go to Everett—"

"Are you seriously threatening me with my father?"

She hid a smile at the exasperation in his voice. "I didn't want to, but you're kind of pushing me into a corner. I was hired because I'm good at my job. Let me do it."

He rubbed the back of neck and she saw the stress of the last week in him. He did a good job of hiding it most of the time. He was acting as if nothing had changed, and going about his daily routines and life as if someone hadn't killed his lookalike bodyguard and then tried to kill him twice in two days. She appreciated that he was probably nearing his tolerance level.

"Once you meet Thom, you will realize you are barking up the wrong tree."

"Why do you say that?" she asked, moving over to the table she'd used while he was at his desk. She picked up her pen, ready to jot down anything useful Nick said.

"He's weak. He's not the kind of person who could plot this out."

"Okay then, is he someone who could be used?" she asked. Because, as the evidence seemed to suggest, there might be more than one person involved. Or not all of the incidents in Nick's life were connected.

The kidnapping when he was fourteen seemed isolated and traced to a group with a vendetta against Everett DeVere. Also, there hadn't been a letter tied to that event.

"Yes, but would he try to help someone kill me or Jack? I don't think so. He wants to be in my inner circle," Nick said.

"Finn mentioned that as well. What's so special about your inner circle?" she asked.

"I'm in the center of it," he said.

Luna smiled at him. She knew he was deflecting. "I'll ask Finn."

"It's ridiculous, really, but those who are close to me

get offered a lot of luxury perks and deals from big-name brands. I know Thom wants those introductions."

"So why haven't you given them to him?" she asked.

Nick shrugged and looked back down at his computer monitor. "There's something not quite right about him."

That was precisely why Luna needed to talk to him. "I'm questioning him tonight. I'm not asking you, Nick."

"I'll do it with you. If he is in any way responsible for Jack's death, he's going to pay."

The dresses Nick had liked weren't exactly the kinds of dresses that she could move in. They'd compromised, and she'd ended up with a sequined formfitting number made of stretchy material. It had a slit up the side that ended midthigh, and Luna had done several laps around the room to make sure it didn't hamper her movements.

She wasn't entirely certain Nick wanted her to be able to move. He kept trying to protect her even though sometimes that meant putting himself at risk. And this dress…well, it was definitely one that Nick had picked out so she couldn't wear a gun. Reading the incident reports had only sharpened her desire to protect him and find the stalker. Nick had been alone for too long.

Everyone on the Price team, and even Finn, thought that Nick should cancel the VIP event. But Nick wasn't a DeVere for nothing and, of course, had refused. He had surprised her when he'd invited Thom Newton to come early to the reception for a rapper and his entourage Nick was promoting.

But first, they had the red carpet to get through and the screening of all of his guests. Kenji was to be on the red carpet with Rick. Lee was on the metal detector monitors with Van. Xander was at the door, having trained the extra security and bouncers hired for the event.

The Price team was in place and the Art Deco building was as secure as they could make it. She would be by Nick's side all night and, along with questioning Thom, wanted to see who else came out of the woodwork. Since the men of the Price Security team appeared to the public to be the bodyguards, Nick wanted her to be low-key, hence the figure-hugging dress and no gun. He thought, and Van had agreed, that his apparent lack of protection might force the hand of whomever was behind the attacks.

Luna wasn't as sure since her gut was telling her this was an inside job. Someone in Nick's close circle. Finn was nervous, too, and had been in to speak to Nick three times. Finally, he'd left to go downstairs after telling her she looked great.

"You do, by the way," Nick mentioned after Finn closed the door.

She glanced over her shoulder at him. Nick looked delicious in the bespoke tux. Some men were born to wear formal wear and Nick was definitely one of them. The custom-made tux jacket extenuated his muscled shoulders. God, he made Daniel Craig as James Bond look like some dude. Her pulse sped up and her throat felt tight as she fought the urge to drag him back up to the penthouse.

He didn't fiddle with his bow tie or the button on his jacket. He stood there with the same ease as most men did when they were in gym clothes.

"You, too," she said. She'd done a good job of keeping her emotions in check. The investigation was demanding, which had provided the distraction she'd needed, but late at night, when she was alone in her bed, her thoughts always drifted to that kiss in the stairwell.

Seeing him now, dressed to the nines and ready to walk the red carpet and pretend he was chill when someone was trying to kill him…that turned her on. She liked his guts. Liked the way that, even though the facts were telling them someone he knew was trying to kill him, he still wouldn't hide.

It might have made her job easier if Nick had a little bit of natural self-preservation, but Luna admitted to herself she liked that he was willing to face danger head-on. There was so much more to Nick DeVere than even he would admit.

"Thanks," he said with a wink. "So, for tonight, I want you on my right side. We'll be meeting everyone who comes up the red carpet. The photographers that your team vetted and Getty Images will be there. Once we've greeted everyone and gone inside, I'll say a few words and we will have a toast. Then the general invitees will start to trickle in."

"We've been over this," she said. "I'll be on your left and you will stay slightly behind me so I can protect you at all times."

He looked as if he was going to argue but she simply held up her hand to stop him. "It's that or I change into my suit and carry my weapon."

"Fine," he said. "I don't want Lil' M to know you're my bodyguard. He likes his women, so be on your guard."

"He won't know I'm your bodyguard unless he gets handsy, and then he'll definitely suspect something's up," she said, a clear edge in her voice.

"He's not handsy with someone else's woman."

"It's hard to believe you live in the twenty-first century," she said sarcastically.

"I didn't make this world, I just live in it," he said.

"Fair point," she said, putting her mind back to Thom, whom they were both interested in talking to. "I guess we'll know if Thom was the one shooting at you by how he reacts to me."

"We will. I've asked him to come early, but he was vague if he could. Which… I hate to admit it, but that's odd. He's always trying to get into the VIP room here," Nick said.

"That's good. Means we are on the right track. I'll talk to him. I'm really good at finding out things that people want to hide," she said. She thought it was her face; she looked like someone everyone knew, and they trusted her.

"Great. Hope someone I've known half my life is trying to kill me," he quipped.

"I just want to put an end to this so you can have your life back."

He moved closer. She wondered if he was doing it deliberately; she'd done so well at keeping him physically at bay. But he was right there. She could see his individual eyelashes, so thick and black around that intense gaze of his, and smell the mint of his breath.

"Ready to leave me?"

She wasn't. He was making her question parts of herself she'd never really thought about, and it wasn't comfortable.

"I just want you safe."

That was the truth. She did want him safe. She wanted herself to be protected, also, because Nick had a world of people around him to fall back on and she just had a small circle that she didn't want to let down. She'd forced herself back into her bodyguard role these last two days to maintain that distance.

But standing this close to Nick proved to her that it was all an illusion. She hadn't stopped wanting him. She hadn't stopped reacting to him. She hadn't somehow lost her lust for him.

And even though she knew it put them both in danger, it took all of her willpower not to touch him and tell him that leaving him when the job was over would be one of the hardest things she'd ever do.

Nick had spent the afternoon dwelling on what Luna had said about Thom. Then he'd gone into his meetings before again looking at the letters his father had received. He wondered if there was any way that Thom could be his father's bastard. When Nick dug deeper into Thom's past and his family, the murkier things became.

For the most part, Nick hadn't paid much attention to Thom. He had said he was from a prominent East Coast family, but today's digging had revealed he wasn't. What else had Thom lied about? Thom's mother seemed to have no connection to DeVere Industries or anything that would have brought her into Everett's circle. And, most important, Thom was two months younger than Nick.

Did that mean he wasn't his father's bastard? Nick wasn't sure. But he intended to get some answers tonight. But he had to distract Luna, who also wanted to question Thom.

The cut on her face had started to heal and had been

covered with makeup for tonight's event, but Nick knew it was there. Knew she'd sustained it by protecting him. And it was all good and well that she was his bodyguard, but he didn't like seeing the reminder of his failure to protect her. Didn't want to see anyone hurt in his place, especially not Luna.

Over the last few days as she'd quietly shadowed him everywhere he'd gone, he had started to see beyond the lust that had first attracted him to her to the woman she was. She was intelligent and really good about reading people. She knew when to leave him alone and when he needed to talk. He'd watched her handle Finn and the temporary secretary/assistant Hazel had hired with ease.

Luna was good with people. Something that he guessed she'd had to learn to be when she'd found her peace in not wanting a family. Ironic because he knew that everyone wanted one in some capacity. Hell, he wanted his to be closer even after learning his dad had been lying to him for most of his life.

Nick was good with people in a different way, and her quiet manner had showed him that people responded to her in a way they didn't to him. He thought she might be able to get answers from Thom. Hell, he knew she could. But if Thom was behind the attacks, then there was a pretty good chance that once he realized Luna was on to him, he'd snap. And Nick wasn't going to stand by while she was shot at again.

All of that wasn't doing much to distract him from how good she looked in the red dress he'd selected for her tonight. She'd dug in her heels and had insisted on a slit in the side of the skirt of the formfitting dress so she could move in it. That, he'd easily given in on. The slit revealed her long shapely leg.

The bodice hugged her curves, emphasizing her breasts and the long arc of her neck. He was glad he'd insisted she leave her gun in her room because there was no way she could have hidden it under that dress. And there was no way anyone would look at her and see a bodyguard.

Much like Jack, his doppelganger, had seemed like a friend, Luna looked like she belonged at his side. Like a girlfriend. A partner in crime.

She'd let her hair down only the second time since he'd met her and it curled around her shoulders. Though he'd thought it was dark brown, he realized there were warm rich strands of red running through it.

It looked soft and bouncy, and he wanted to bury his hands in it and kiss her. Kiss her and maybe convince her to stay up here. To stay safe until he talked to Thom, which, logically he knew made no sense.

She'd proved to him time and again that she was great at her job. So he had no excuse for wanting to lock her away, except that, deep inside his soul, he needed her safe.

If Luna were hurt, it was one scar that might not ever heal. And that was a risk he didn't want her to take, but one that he couldn't keep her from. So he was doing everything in his power to keep her out of harm's way.

"Van mentioned earpieces," Nick said. Realizing that he wasn't sure if he was getting one or not.

"I have one that I'll put in. Do you want one?" she asked.

"I think it couldn't hurt for me to have one," he said.

"Okay. Come on, lets go to the security room and get you set up. You know everything you say will be recorded, right?"

"I do," he said. "Maybe you'll be able to pick up on something I miss."

She stopped him with her hand on his arm as he was about to step into the hallway and he moved aside for her to go first. "You don't miss much."

"I try, but I'm not you, Luna."

She flushed and he noticed it because he saw the color spread up her chest to her neck and then her cheeks. Interesting. "I'm very aware of that."

"Good."

They were both fitted with earpieces and it was odd to hear the private communication going on between all of the people on the Price Security team. But he was glad to be a part of it. He knew that they were watching not only for Thom but for anyone else who was suspicious, and this way Nick would be part of his own security and maintain a thread of control.

Something he'd thought he'd wanted from the beginning. He'd had a vague idea of how this would play out, but nothing so far had been what he'd expected. As he scanned the crowds as people arrived and paparazzi took photos, he realized that he was more nervous at this event than he'd been at any other. Ever.

It was easy to say it was either because he planned to confront Thom or because he knew that the chances were strong his attacker would strike again.

But he knew it was because Luna was at his side. And he had no idea how to handle that.

Chapter 14

The deejay in the booth was playing tracks off Lil' M's new album mixed in with classic club tracks from all decades. He was doing a good job of keeping people mingling and dancing, which made certain aspects of security slightly easier. Rick was in the booth with the monitors and, since most of the attendees were dancing, Luna was able to watch the crowd around Nick.

He was approached a lot and she was always tense until Xander came on the comms and verified the person had been cleared. Nick was jovial and charming, as always, but that tension she'd sensed on the red carpet remained.

Nick was good at playing the part of the playboy with no cares. Slipped into the role like he did his Hugo Boss suits each morning when he went to his office.

When they were alone for a minute, she noticed he was scanning the crowd. "Who are you looking for?"

"No one," he said. "Just making sure my guests are happy. By the way, you haven't had a drink all evening."

She knew he was lying and suspected he was watching for Thom Newton who, so far, hadn't showed. "I've noticed you have had a few."

"Yeah, but it's not big deal. I'm a heavy drinker," he said.

"Why?"

"Why do you think?" he asked.

"To be numb?"

"Sometimes. Mostly it's social and this crowd likes to party, so over the years… I started out drinking to be numb, then eventually I was drinking so much that it was normal and I wasn't getting drunk or numb. But things have changed. I know my limits, and tonight we're working."

"I am. You're the host. If you get sloshed, I've got you," she said.

"I don't want to be numb around you, Luna," he said.

Before she could respond, Finn came up to them, looking dashing in a dark navy suit with a white shirt and tie. "So, Verity is here with some hot, young thing and looking a little too pleased with herself."

Nick twisted his head and Luna did the same, spotting his ex standing on the other side of the room on the fringes of the dance floor. She had her blond hair pulled back into a low bun at the nap of her neck. She wore a strapless, white sheath dress that hugged her curves. She was breathtaking, looking like a young Grace Kelly. But the way she smiled told Luna that Verity was aware that every eye in the room was on her. And she liked it.

"That's fine. Have you seen Thom?"

"No. Want me to text him? I'm surprised he's not

here. You know he's got a new business proposal for a music streaming service. Figured he'd want to work the room and use you to help him get investors."

Nick's mouth tightened and he nodded. "Like the world needs another streaming service."

"You're preaching to the choir but Thom…he's always looking for a get-rich-quick idea," Finn said.

Verity and her date headed toward him and Finn grabbed cocktail from the tray held by a passing waiter. "I'm out of here. I'll let you know if I see Thom."

"Thanks," Nick said.

Luna turned so that she faced Nick. "I thought we agreed I would question Thom."

Nick put his hand on the small of her waist, it was big and warm even through the fabric of her dress. "Just because I didn't object doesn't mean I agreed with you."

"I'm not going to let you—"

"Not now. Verity is close enough to hear," Nick said under his breath, brushing a kiss against her cheek.

"Nicky! I didn't realize that…what was your name again?" Verity asked Luna.

"This is Luna," Nick said. "And your date is?"

"Lorenzo Palmieri. Ren, this is Nick and his…date?"

Nick pulled Luna into the curve of his body and a shiver went through her. For a moment, the music seemed muted and the crowd and even Verity disappeared as their eyes met. Her lips parted and he quirked one eyebrow at her. He knew she still wanted him. Hell, it wasn't like she'd been pretending she didn't.

Luna took a deep breath and pulled her training and professionalism around her like a big, cold coat, forcing the heat that Nick generated into her away.

"We are dating," Nick said. "Ren, how do you know Verity?"

"Oh, Nicky, this is the man I'm going to marry once I get free of my horrible husband," Verity said.

Lorenzo put his arm around Verity, seeming to comfort her when the music changed to a Latin beat and Mr. Worldwide came on. "Excuse us, I told Luna we'd dance if this song came on."

"I'm not sure dancing is such a good idea," she said as he led her to the dance floor. "I can't really see the crowd."

"Trust your team," Nick said. "Plus, I need a moment where everyone will leave me alone. Van, can you keep watch?"

"I'm on it," Van said in their earpieces.

It was no surprise to her that Nick used his entire body to dance. His hips easily found the rhythm and Luna, who was pretty much a sway-back-and-forth dancer, wasn't sure how to move with him.

Nick put his hands on her hips. "I've got you."

That was all he said. His words were low and whispered into her ear, the one without the earpiece. And that cold coat she'd mentally donned a few minutes ago melted away. The heat of the music, the passion in Nick's eyes and the way his body brushed hers repeatedly as they moved on the dance floor wiped it all away.

She took a deep breath. Wondering if it was okay to let her guard down for a moment. To take this one dance with the man she wanted almost more than she needed her next breath. But as she did, as she put her hand on his hip, followed his easy steps, swaying her hips along with his, she knew it wasn't okay. That this one dance was going to make it almost impossible for her to stop wanting more of him.

And what she really needed was some kind of alarm to go off, or for Nick to be threatened so her professional armor could return, but that didn't happen, and she was helpless to tear her gaze away from him or to stop the mental images of his naked body moving over hers.

Nick needed the distraction. The one time he wanted Thom at an event, the man hadn't showed up. As much as it hurt to think that the other man might be playing a part in threatening him and killing Jack, he was beginning to believe that had to be the case. Thom would do anything for money and a place in the world. Possibly, this was how he thought he was going to achieve it.

Luna's body under his hands, having a legitimate reason to touch her, knowing they were as safe as they could be in this moment, allowed him to let his guard down.

He couldn't ignore that Verity was up to something. But Nick wasn't really in the mood to deal with her. He wanted Luna.

And he knew she wanted him too. The only time he felt like he had an advantage over her was when he touched her. It was clear that she wasn't sure what to do with him. She'd done a good job the last few days of acting as if she didn't want him, but her quickened breath when he'd pulled her into the curve of his body and the way her eyes kept dropping to his mouth told another story.

He'd always been good at seeing what a person wanted from him. Seeing the way that he could manipulate them into doing what he needed them to do.

For just this once, he didn't want to use those skills to take advantage of Luna. Yet he knew he was going to. He wanted to distract her so that she'd stay out of his way when it came to questioning Thom.

Nick wasn't feeling at all civil—in fact, he was pissed and could end up beating the truth out of Thom if necessary.

"What are you up to?" she asked, leaning into him, her breasts brushing against his chest as she whispered in his ear without the communication device.

"Dancing," he said.

"I'm not going to let you put yourself at risk," she said then bit the lobe of his ear.

A pulse of desire shot down his body and he hardened. He stopped moving for a split second, using his hands on her hips to pull her into direct contact with his erection. "I want you."

Just those words were torn from him. For this moment, in the middle of the chaos that was his life, their eyes met and, for the first time, he was telling her the absolute truth.

She wouldn't be here if Jack hadn't pretended to be him and been killed in his place. She wouldn't be here if he hadn't been shot at in the stairwell and their investigation had led them to Thom Newton as a suspect. She wouldn't be here if he hadn't manipulated her onto the dance floor.

So that didn't feel *exactly* like truth.

But for Nick and his world and his life, this was the most honest he'd allowed himself to be for a long time. Maybe ever.

"I want you, too, but we already decided that wasn't going to happen."

"We did," he said, turning and leaving the dance floor. Maybe the time for games was over.

He heard Luna behind him.

"Nick."

He glanced back at her.

"You can't just leave me like that," she said.

He nodded. He knew he was putting them both in danger. He wanted to punch someone, start a brawl. But instead he noticed Finn up in the roped-off VIP section, talking to Thom Newton.

"Let's go. That's Thom," Nick said, turning on his heel and heading for the stairs that led up to the balcony area.

Luna was hot on his heels, keeping pace with him and trying to get in front of him. But Nick wasn't worried about Finn or Thom. He knew he could physically take the other man and intended to use that to force a confession from Thom.

"How rude," he heard someone say. As he turned, he saw a masked man heading quickly toward him.

He moved to face the man as Luna shoved him hard to the side and stepped in front of him. She let out a low groan and folded in on herself for a second as the man turned and ran.

Luna kicked off her heels and started after him. Nick heard Luna's voice in his earpiece. "Suspect moving toward the southeast corner of the room. Lock it down."

Nick righted himself and followed her. He heard the rest of the Price team giving commands, but was only focused on Luna and the man who'd tried to approach him. He caught up to them as the man disappeared into the crowd.

"Where did he go?" Luna asked.

"I'm not sure, possibly that way," he said, gesturing to the stairs on the other side of the club that led to the dessert buffet.

"I'll go up," she said.

"I'm coming with you."

She shook her head. "Stay behind me. He has a knife."

He followed her up the stairs, spying a pattern on the side of her dress that he hadn't seen earlier. It was like a drip of…

Luna had been stabbed.

And she was still going after the man.

His heart raced, and not with fear for himself but fear for her. This had gone on long enough. After tonight, he was getting rid of Luna and Price Security. He had made a promise to himself that no one else would be hurt in his place and it was time to deliver on that.

The pain from the knife wound in her side was numbed by adrenaline as she moved through the crowd. She heard Nick behind her and was thankful the Price Security team was watching out for him. She wasn't going to let the attacker get away. But the crowd at the top of the stairs was thick and Luna was struggling to keep her eye on the blue-suited man.

Nick brushed past her. "I'll go to the left."

She wanted to stop him, but he was gone too quickly. She turned to follow him as the masked man emerged from the crowd, running straight toward Nick. The man raised his knife and Luna ran as hard as she could, trying to get between them, but the attacker brought his arm down, slashing Nick as Nick punched him hard in the stomach.

Nick balled his fists and punched the attacker again

as he spun for the stairs. Luna raced after him, her heart practically beating out of her chest.

Catching the bottom of his jacket, she felt a piece of paper under her fingers. As the attacker pivoted his body and turned, the jacket tore free of her, leaving her holding the paper, which she gripped tightly as she sprinted after him. But he was down the stairs in two leaps and into the crowd.

"He's on the dance floor," Luna said.

"House lights on now," Van said in her earpiece.

Nick was behind her as the house lights came up and the music stopped, Kenji taking over the deejay station. "Everyone stay where you are. We've had an emergency. Remain calm."

Everyone looked around and Luna heard a cry of shock as someone looked at Nick and saw the gash on his left arm. The fabric of his suit had been cut and a nasty knife wound was visible. Some of the partygoers close to them were looking panicked and then Van's words came over the loudspeaker.

"Be calm. Everything is under control." His voice was loud and calming while still putting the fear of God into everyone to make them obey him.

"I just said that," Kenji complained in their earpieces.

"Yeah, but you didn't say it like the boss," Rick said. "I've found the mask near the side door."

"Which side door?" Luna asked, putting her hand on Nick's uninjured arm and propelling him off the dance floor and into a corner where she could keep him protected.

"The one behind the stage. Xander, did anyone leave that way?"

"That camera…the image is static. Damn, I didn't realize it. That's on me," Xander said.

"We'll regroup after we've searched all the people still in the club."

"My guests aren't criminals," Nick said. "Please treat them with respect."

"We will," Van said, coming over to them. "I'm going to ask everyone to leave in an orderly fashion. Kenji and Rick, you watch them. Luna, you keep Nick out of the way."

"It's my—"

"Enough," Luna interrupted him. "Enough of this. You've been injured and the guy got away. We need to patch you up and then regroup. Sorry if your circle of pampered partygoers doesn't get a goody bag on the way out, but the night is over and you're staying put."

Nick looked at her like he was going to argue.

But she was done with him pushing her boundaries and doing things his way. Now that the threat had passed, she couldn't stop reliving the moment when the assailant had rushed Nick with that knife in his hand. Nick was lucky that he'd turned and had taken the blow on his arm.

Luna knew the knife had a thick hunting blade. She had to examine his wound and make sure he didn't need to be transported to the hospital.

"I still want to talk to Thom," Nick said.

"We'll bring him to you. Finn isn't leaving, either," Van said.

"That's fine," Nick said.

"We need a first-aid kit. I'm not sure how deep the cut on Nick's arm is," Luna said.

"On my way," Xander said. "Lee's checking the static feed from the camera."

"Luna's injured, too," Nick said.

"Are you good, Luna?" Van asked.

"I'm okay. We'll take care of Nick first," she said.

Nick moved around in front of her as the last of the partygoers left. "No, we won't. Your dress is soaked around the wound…are you okay?"

"I'm fine. It burned at first," she said, trying to get at Nick's wound. As she lifted her hand, she realized she still had that paper in it. She looked down at it.

"What's that?" Nick asked as he shrugged out of his jacket.

She read it. "Dry-cleaning tag. I ripped it from the attacker's jacket."

"Good. We'll track it down," Van said, as Xander, Finn and Thom arrived.

Nick turned to Thom. The man was visibly white as a sheet, and Finn looked like he was about to have a panic attack, but was holding it together focusing on Nick's injuries. Finn took the first-aid kit from Van and went over to Nick.

"Take your shirt off," Finn said.

Nick unbuttoned quickly and shrugged out of it.

Luna couldn't help herself. Her eyes widened at seeing his naked chest for the first time. He was in shape, no shock there, but his muscles weren't overly developed. She had to turn away, seeing him half naked with an open wound nearly put her in emotional overload.

She wanted him, so lust was coursing through her like oxygen through her lungs, but she had let him down. He'd been hurt on her watch. He'd almost died.

"Thom, we have some questions for you," Luna said, turning her attention to the job.

Van stepped in front of her. "The questions can wait. Go upstairs and clean your wound and come back."

"I'm fine," she said.

She knew she wasn't at her best. It was nerves and determination keeping her on her feet at this moment. Her side ached and her soul felt battered and weary, but she wasn't leaving Nick alone. She wouldn't leave him vulnerable again.

Chapter 15

Luna went into the club bathroom already cleared by the Price team and took off the sequined dress. The wound on her side was worse than she'd thought. She reached for the antiseptic wipes in the first-aid kit when the door opened partially.

"Okay to come in?" Lee called.

"Yes, I could use a hand."

Lee wasn't a fancy person by nature and Luna smiled to see her friend dressed in a cocktail dress. Her short salt-and-pepper hair had been styled into a fancy updo. Lee's eyes went straight to Luna's wound.

"That's pretty bad. I have a compression bandage. Is your tetanus up to date?" Lee asked.

"Yes. Is Nick's?"

"Finn said it was," Lee said, coming closer and taking over attending to Luna's wound, which wasn't deep enough to need stitches.

The bandages Lee used to close the wound seemed to do the job and Luna turned toward the full-length mirror to check it out when her friend was done.

"What happened out there?" Lee asked. "I mean I heard it in my earpiece, but I couldn't get a clear shot of you or the attacker on the monitors."

"I'm not sure. We spotted Thom and were heading that way when the attacker came out of the crowd with the knife," Luna said, replaying the incident in her mind. She couldn't figure out how he'd gotten past the metal detectors with that hunting knife. In fact, Xander would have made sure they'd been installed in a way that no one could sneak anything in.

"The knife had to already be here," she said.

"That's my thought, too," Lee said.

"Enough discussing this without the entire group," Van said through their earpieces. "Luna, you good?"

"Yeah, Lee patched me up. We're on our way back to you," Luna said after she put her dress back on, she led the way out of the bathroom, but Lee stopped her.

Lee took her earpiece out and Luna did the same.

"Nick's reckless. You didn't do anything wrong."

"He is, but I should have anticipated it," she said. She knew what Nick was like. He'd been ready for a fight all evening and despite all of that, she'd gone out on the dance floor and had that moment where she—

"Stop beating yourself up. Nothing went perfect tonight," Lee said. "Nothing ever does. Xander and I double-checked every feed on the security cameras before the first guest arrived. So how did that one go static?"

"Someone knew what we were planning?" Luna asked.

The bathroom door opened and Van walked in. "Ladies, I want to do this as a team. I'm going to assume you took your earpieces out to have girl chat."

"What's girl chat?" Lee asked. "Just so we know if that's what we were doing."

Van came as close to looking chagrined as he ever did. "Two of my favorite girls. Chatting."

"Nice save, boss," Luna said. She couldn't help but feel a little better about the evening even though the blood on her dress was crusting over her irritated side and her feet ached from wearing heels. "Shall we go join everyone else?"

"I told them if I didn't come out in two minutes to come and join us," Van said in that gravelly voice of his before winking at them.

Luna followed Van and Lee out of the bathroom and saw that some chairs had been drawn into a circle where she'd left Nick. She avoided looking at him, save for one glance where she noticed he'd put his dress shirt back on but hadn't buttoned it. Finn was right next to him, biting his nails and watching Nick with a closed expression.

Thom Newton had been slightly drunk when they'd stopped him and was slumped in his chair next to Rick, who was trying to convince the man to drink a Fanta Orange drink.

"Okay, now that we are all here, let's get started," Van said as they all took their seats.

Nick reached behind him for his jacket and handed it to Luna. "You look cold."

She was, but had a feeling it was the combination of shock and exhaustion. She slipped her arms into the jacket, briefly inhaling the smell of Nick and his aftershave. But then she turned her attention back to the group.

"Thom, we have a few questions about the night of Jack's murder. You were at the party, right?" Van asked.

"I was. I go to most of Nick's events," Thom said.

"Even those you aren't invited to," Nick said. "What were you doing there?"

"It was your birthday... I always crash, you know that."

Nick nodded. "Why is that?"

"Why are you questioning me?"

"Until I got stabbed tonight, I thought you might have been the one to kill Jack," Nick said.

"What the f—"

"Don't get offended. We both know you've always been loose with the truth," Nick said.

"And we would like to know what you saw the night of the party," Van said, taking over the questioning.

Luna sat back, observing the dynamics between everyone in the circle. Not her team—she knew them, trusted them—but more Finn, Thom and Nick. Nick was in the center of the two men and it was clear that he was important to both of them. Finn's response was more emotional. He wasn't trying to maneuver himself into seeming to have a closer relationship with Nick, the way that Thom was.

"Thom, do you know anyone who hates Nick?" Luna asked.

"A few people don't love him. But hate? I don't think so," Thom answered.

He looked around the room before turning to Nick. "I know it seems like all I'm after is your connections and investment in my business deals, but I always thought we were friends. I'd never do anything to hurt you, Nick. And if I heard someone else wanted to, I'd let you know."

Nick reached over with his uninjured arm and clapped Thom on the shoulder. "Thanks, Thom."

"Rick, take Thom home. The rest of us will debrief the evening," Van said.

As they got up to leave, Luna remembered the dry-cleaning paper she'd torn from the attacker's coat. She found it on the small table where the mask was still laying and brought it back. "Do we know where this cleaner is?"

Thom glanced over. "Is that Gold Cleaners? They are just up the street from this building. I use them."

Van looked at Rick, who put his hand on Thom's shoulder and had him sit back down. They'd almost cleared Thom, but that had put him right back in the center of their investigation.

Nick didn't believe in coincidence. Fate, he'd always believed in. But it seemed to him that someone was trying awfully hard to paint Thom as the mastermind behind the attacks. It probably would have been more believable if Thom hadn't been drunk and crying and telling Nick how much he loved him before turning and throwing up all over the floor.

Even Van seemed to come to a similar conclusion and once more ordered Rick to take the other man home. Nick glanced at Finn, and his assistant rolled his eyes before getting to his feet. "I'll go with you."

Thom slung his arm around Finn's shoulders and as Nick watched two of his boarding school friends head out the door, he realized he might never be able to figure out who was threatening him. This thing with Thom had felt wrong from the first time Van and Luna had brought him up. Boarding school had been a different world, and no matter that most of the boys who'd been sent there came from a privileged background, they'd all been dealing with a lot of stuff.

Their own stuff. Too much of their own life to try to ruin his.

"Okay, so the dry cleaner seems a bit too obvious," Nick said. "So who else knew we were looking at Thom?"

Nick was tired. He wanted nothing more than a hot shower, and to be alone with Luna. He needed to make sure she was okay. To make sure they were okay. She hadn't met his eyes once since she'd reentered the room. And seeing her over there, her hair mussed, wearing his jacket, which made her look smaller than she actually was, made it damned hard for him to remember she was his bodyguard.

"I'm not sure," Luna said. "The board was questioned and we had a few discussions around them. Someone could have overheard."

"That's true. The board all seemed to check out," Van said. "Lee—"

"I'll go over them again," she said. "Also their assistants or people in their offices. There is a chance they talked once they got back."

"Good call. Xander, what about the construction staff and bouncers?" Van asked.

"Most of them were out of earshot when you were interrogating the board, but that doesn't mean someone didn't overhear Newton's name," he said. "My gut doesn't think it was the construction crew, but I'll run their names past Lee."

Nick listened to them all trying to find connections. What about his father? He hadn't spoken to Everett since he'd turned over the letters. Nick pulled his phone out and texted his father and Aldo to see if another letter had arrived.

Nothing new, Aldo texted back.

"Is there something you want to share with the group?" Van asked him.

"My father hasn't received any more letters," Nick said. "Do you think that means the attacker knows that he turned them over to me? That I know there is one person who is behind all my accidents?"

Van leaned back in his chair, crossing his massive arms over his chest as he took a moment to digest what Nick had said.

"It's probably a good theory and points us back to this building. All of the information has been discussed here. The letters, Thom as a suspect, the setup for the party..."

Xander and Lee both got to their feet. Xander looked at Lee, who nodded to him. Nick had no idea how, but it seemed the two of them were communicating. "Xander will sweep for listening devices. I'll go over the video footage from when we were hired and look for a pattern. Okay to leave?" Lee asked Van.

"Yes," he said. "Kenji?"

"I don't like the hunting knife after the high-powered sniper rifle. This attacker is trained in a lot of different disciplines...and the change from cutting the brake wire on his nanny's car to this type of attack makes me think that it's two different people."

"Related?" Luna asked. She pulled her phone out and started taping on the keyboard. Nick knew she liked to take notes.

"Based on the letters, I'd have to say yes," Kenji said. "How was the previous bodyguard killed?"

"Pushed off the balcony. Made to look like he stumbled and fell," Nick said. "So, more similar to my nanny and the yacht accident where my cousins died. There was a gas leak on the yacht."

"So sometime between Jack's death and now, something changed," Van said.

"What?" Nick asked.

"That's the million-dollar question," Van said.

"I've got the money," Nick responded. "I need answers."

"We all do. Let us work on this. Kenji is good with puzzles and this is just a new part of the one we've been trying to solve since you hired us."

Kenji nodded. "I'll get it."

"Is that all for tonight?" Nick asked. "I need a shower."

"Yes. That's it. We will regroup in the morning, hopefully with some answers," Van said.

Nick stood; Luna was on her feet at the same time. She moved next to him as they walked to the elevator and, though the room had been cleared, she was still alert. And as he'd seen tonight, there was no way to order her to stay safe. She was always going to put herself between him and danger.

Luna hadn't felt this tired since she'd landed in LA. But her mind was clearer tonight than it had been then. She wanted to get out of this evening dress and have a shower herself, but a part of her didn't feel safe yet letting Nick out of her sight.

When they got to the penthouse, she didn't head for her room after making a sweep of the apartment, though

Rick had cleared it after the club had been emptied and before they'd all had their confab. Mentally, she knew Nick was safe here. But emotionally she was still reliving the moment when he'd stepped around her to put himself between her and the attacker.

There were two things warring in her mind. Two thoughts that kept circling around. The first scared her more than she was ever going to admit. And it was that, in her entire life, Nick was the first person outside of the security team to try to protect her. She couldn't allow herself to follow that thought any further. It stirred up feelings she didn't know how to process or handle.

The second was that he had been injured on her watch. That she should have anticipated he'd dart around her because his anger at the person who'd kept threatening him drove him. He'd already done it once before.

Her second thought was so much easier to handle.

Nick was pacing in the center of his penthouse, circling past the large sofas set up to form a conversation area around the grand piano on a pedestal in the middle of the room. He had energy that she wasn't sure how to handle and it seemed to be sparking bolts of lightning.

"You can go shower. I'm sure you're ready to get out of that dress," he said curtly, nodding his head toward her room.

He was mad at her? Maybe he thought the same thing she did. That she'd screwed up tonight. "I don't want to leave you alone," she admitted.

"I'm safe here," he said tightly, gesturing to the entire penthouse. "Your team went over it more than once."

"I know." She wondered if he felt safer knowing that someone other than her had his back. And that made her angry. Anger was so much easier to deal with at this moment than the fear and the other thoughts in her head.

"Luna."

"Nick." She wasn't going to let him push her out of the room. Whatever was on his mind, they needed to clear the air. She remembered the first backstage party with Jaz, when he'd wanted her out because he was doing illegal drugs and sleeping with two groupies, but she had held fast. She had never stood in judgment. She'd been hired to keep her client safe.

That brought her back to Nick.

He breathed in deeply through his nose. It was the first time, she realized, that he was barely holding on to his temper. The tendons in his neck stood out strongly. Clearly visible as he still hadn't buttoned his shirt. Not that she was looking.

"You're mad," she said.

"I am," he said. "I hate that you got hurt tonight. I heard what Lee said. That knife wound was deep."

It had been, but she'd had worse injuries in the line of duty. Somehow, she sensed telling him that wasn't going to diffuse his temper. "The one on your arm isn't anything to laugh at. We both weren't at our best tonight," she said. "I think…the truth is, I've been telling myself if you hadn't tried to get in front of me, I would have been prepared."

He stopped pacing and walked over to her, his open shirt flapping around his strong body. He came so close that she could see the pulse ticking at the base of his neck.

"That's bull," he said, his jaw clenched. "I already told you I'm not letting anyone else get hurt instead of me."

Luna was having a hard time keeping her eyes on his face and not letting it drift lower. Part of her, the most primal female warrior part, needed to strip him naked, examine his wounds and then make love to him so she knew he was safe.

She was already dealing with too much emotional junk involving Nick. She couldn't add something else to the mix. But her body yearned for him. She wasn't sure she was going to survive the battle warring inside her.

"I know what you said, but you hired me to protect you."

"Then maybe I'll think about firing you," he said.

That pissed her off, and she leaned closer until her nose was almost touching his. "I'm not going anywhere until we find the person or persons responsible for this," she said.

He sighed and touched her then, his hand coming to her waist on the uninjured side of her body. His fingers were light when he touched her, and he pulled her ever so slightly toward him. "I don't want you hurt again."

She put her hand on his naked chest. Felt the heat of him and the rapid beating of his heart under her palm. "Me either."

He cleared his throat and seemed to be going to speak again, but Luna knew there were no words that would bring either of them the solace they wanted. She shifted slightly and brushed her lips against his.

He didn't hesitate to pull her into the curve of his body, angling his mouth over hers and deepening the kiss. She stopped thinking, just shut off anything that didn't directly relate to his fiery body under her mouth and her hands.

She needed to affirm they'd both survived and tomorrow would be soon enough to return to her safety zone. For tonight, she was going to celebrate the fact that he was here with her.

Chapter 16

Luna tasted of champagne and something that was unique to her. He deepened the kiss, pulling her more fully into him. Running one hand down the side of her torso until he reached the slit at the top of her thigh. When his fingers touched her bare skin, a tingle went up his arm. He wasn't stopping until she was completely underneath him.

He lifted his head, as much as he didn't want to, realizing he had to make sure she wasn't just kissing him. Did she want this too?

"I need you tonight. I don't know if you are on the same page," he said.

"I am. I don't want to think beyond this moment. I'm afraid if I do, I'll have to walk away."

"Just one more thing. Birth control? Do you want me to use a condom?" he asked.

She chewed her bottom lip between her teeth for a

second and then bobbed her head up and down. "I'm on birth control, so the condom is up to you."

Nick was pretty sure in that moment she'd committed to this. But perhaps she'd made that decision before she'd kissed him. He wasn't going to overanalyze the one good thing that he'd found in his life since Jack had been killed.

He started to feel the panic again that he'd felt when he'd seen her push her way around him to put herself between him and a knife-wielding assailant. Damn.

He wasn't going to be able to breathe properly until he had her naked and made sure that every remaining inch of her was okay. Her hands were on his chest, running over him, the tips of her fingers lingering on his nipples. He stood there for a moment, letting the white-hot heat of lust rule him. He could easily just stay there, but being passive wasn't what he needed.

Nick wanted to prove to himself, at least, that he still had some control over something. And sex was the one place where he always got what he wanted and made sure his partner did too. It was a relief to turn his mind off and let his body take control.

He undid the zipper of her dress and the fabric, which had been skintight a moment earlier, gaped away from her body. With a delicate shrug of her muscled shoulders, the sequined cloth fell to her feet. She stepped out of it and then kicked off the heels she'd put back on when they'd met with the entire group.

He groaned as his cock hardened.

She made a move toward him, but he stopped her. "Not yet."

She tipped her head to the side. "Do you think you're in control here?"

"Aren't I?" he asked, walking slowly around her body. Admiring the feminine strength of it. The muscles of her upper body contained more strength than even he could guess. The curve of her waist and the flare of her hips emphasized the power she held.

The bra she wore was sheer and lacy, so delicate, compared the tough woman who wore it. He used one hand to flick open the fastening. Then stepped up closer behind her, his mouth on the nape of her neck as he slowly drew the straps of the bra down each of her arms and tossed it aside.

Goose bumps spread down her back and arms. Nick cupped her breasts as he pulled her back against him. She was naked except for her panties, and he loved the feel of her like this. He looked over her head down her body, holding both of her breasts in his hands. His thumbs stroking her nipples.

Luna moaned and her hips moved until his cock was nestled between her butt cheeks. She tipped her head back and to the side and he moved his mouth up her neck before leaning forward and taking her mouth in his. She sucked his bottom lip between her teeth and bit him gently.

His erection throbbed with need. It felt good to be alive. He'd had sex before, when it was just something to do. A need that had to be scratched. But after this evening, having Luna in his arms was anything but ordinary.

It was a moment when he realized that all of his near misses had been nothing compared to the one today. Because, for the first time in a long while, he had someone he cared about.

Nick ripped his mouth from hers for a minute to

shove that thought down. He wasn't going to allow himself to care for her that way. People he loved died.

He took one hand from her breast and moved it lower along the center of her body as she shivered in his arms. He traced his fingers around her belly button and felt something...

His fingers were running over a small stud piercing. He toyed with it and felt her hips swiveling against his.

He brought his mouth back to the side of her neck as he trailed his way to her panties. He cupped her through them. Felt the heat of her on his fingers as she rocked her hips into his hand.

His erection was hard, pressed against her back, her pussy hot against his fingers. Nick knew that the moment he took her panties off, he wasn't going to be able to resist tasting her, getting inside her and taking her until they were both exhausted.

He wanted this to last.

Needed something with Luna to feel like it wasn't just happening in the moment.

He continued to finger her through her underwear until she turned in his arms. Her hands went to his neck and she went up on her tiptoes to kiss him full and hard.

He felt her hard nipples brush against his chest as she lifted one thigh so that his cock was rubbing right at her center. The illusion that he'd been trying to build, that he was in control of Luna, their love making, or anything, was shattered.

But as her mouth moved down his chest and her fingers undid his belt, he couldn't really be that upset.

Luna was on fire for Nick. She usually kept herself under tight control when she was working, and she'd been on duty for…well, she couldn't remember the last time she'd had a moment to herself. Coming off tour with Jaz and straight onto working with Nick hadn't been easy.

She knew that there would be repercussions for this night, but she'd already shoved that thought aside and left it buried in the back of her mind. Nick's touch had awakened parts of her that she tried to ignore, had to when she was working because the job came first.

As she bent lower to undo his pants and pushed her hands under the fabric of his underwear, shoving it down his legs, she felt his fingers against her shoulder. She bent to bring his briefs all the way to the floor and, from her stooped position, looked at his cock. It was hard and thick, jutting out from his body.

She slowly ran her fingers up his legs. Taking her time as she watched his cock jump slightly as she got closer to it. But she just drew her fingers across his abdomen while cupping his balls with her other hand.

He groaned and his hand moved down her shoulder to her wrist, took it and placed it on his erection. She wrapped both of her hands around his shaft and stroked it up and down, tightening her grip each time, feeling him getting harder as his hips moved against her motions.

She squeezed his balls and then dropped to her knees and took him in her mouth. He groaned this time. The sound was guttural, almost as if it had been ripped from some place deep inside him. She sucked him until she felt him at the back of her throat, her fingers still moving on his balls. She tasted something salty and delicious.

He pulled his hips back and her mouth away from his cock. He lifted her into his arms, carried her to the sofa across the room and set her down on it. Ripping off her panties, he slid down between her legs. She felt the warmth of his breath against her pussy and then the touch of his tongue.

Luna reached for his cock, needing to touch him while he was touching her. She tried to move so she could take him in her mouth again and he shifted so that she could get his cock in her mouth. She sucked hard on him as she felt his tongue on her clit, just teasing strokes at first and then the edge of his teeth as he nibbled at her most delicate flesh.

Her body clenched and she felt the first fingers of her climax. Her hips were moving frantically as she tried to get his mouth where it felt the best. She tasted more of his cum, swallowing it. Then she felt his finger in her pussy, shoving up and into her deeply.

Everything in her body screamed out as she came hard on his finger and finished sucking him dry. He collapsed against her thighs and she rested her head on his thigh. She looked up his body and their eyes met.

"That wasn't what I'd planned."

"I'm not usually one for breaking a plan, but that worked," she said.

He smiled at her. "I want to be inside you, but I need some time. And I think we could both use a shower."

"Together?" she asked. Still not ready to let him out of her sight.

"Yes. How's your wound?" he asked as he got to his feet and offered her his hand.

She stood next to him, realizing he still wore his shirt. She looked at her side and saw some blood seeping from her bandage. "Fine. Might need to change the bandage. How's yours?"

He took his shirt off, looking down at his arm. The bandage was still clean and nothing seemed to be leaking out of it. She ran her fingers over it and the leaned into kiss it. "I'm sorry you got hurt."

He put his hand under her chin and lifted her face to his, bringing his mouth down on hers in the gentlest kiss she had ever received. "I'm sorry you did."

He didn't say anything else and neither did she. She felt her mind trying to take control and ignored it. She simply slipped her hand into his and walked with him to his bedroom. He took a deep breath as soon as they were in there.

"The bathroom is through there," he said, catching her shoulder and looking closely at her shoulder blade. "I need to shave—you have some beard burn on your back."

"I don't mind," she said, looking over her shoulder at him.

"You don't?" he asked. There was a note in his voice she couldn't place.

"No one will see it but you and I... I guess I like that we have something private," she said, knowing those words were the truth and probably not the wisest thing for her to admit.

He pulled her into his arms and hugged her close. She held him, too, breathing in the scent of sex and Nick. He didn't say anything, but really, what could he say? She was guessing he was aware they were in a bubble that would only last until morning and then reality was going to be back.

But, for tonight, there was only Nick and, for the first time in her life, Luna thought this person was hers.

Only for tonight.

* * *

Nick shaved while Luna showered and then he joined her. He saw that the wound on her side was slightly bloody, but when he checked the bandage, he thought it might be just dried blood that was being washed off the wound.

He caressed her as he washed her and then took her standing up in the shower. She dug her nails into his back as she came and he used his hand on the wall to support himself after he did. They washed off and got dry, and he saw Luna's expression shift back into bodyguard mode and shook his head.

"I get Luna the Lover until morning. Then you can be my bodyguard again," he said as he took one of his monogrammed bathrobes and wrapped her in.

In the back of his mind, he knew he wasn't sure he could let her continue to be his bodyguard. It would be smarter if he switched to Kenji. He was the one who everyone had thought Nick should have chosen from the beginning.

But another part of Nick wasn't ready to give up any part of Luna. Maybe because he knew it was inevitable. To save her, to keep her safe, he was going to have to step away from her.

There was no way he could have her and keep her alive. And the irony of that wasn't lost on him. He'd hired her to keep him safe, but tonight had drawn a line under his belief that he was unbreakable.

She wasn't either.

"I'm not—"

He put his fingers over her mouth. Whatever well-thought-out argument she was going to make, he didn't want to hear it. "It's been a shit day. Let's just have a moment where I can hold you and pretend that I'm not Nick DeVere."

She put her hand on the side of his face and gave him the most tender look he'd ever seen. "I want to be with Nick DeVere."

He hugged her close for this moment, holding her in his arms in his steamy bathroom and knowing that it couldn't last.

He lifted her off her feet and she twisted out of his arms. "You shouldn't be carrying me."

"Why not?"

"Your arm is injured," she said, moving to check it.

Emotions that he didn't want tangled in his throat. Even now, when it was just the two of them, she was still looking out for him. And, yes, it was a little thing, but for him it didn't feel that way.

In a life that had been filled with paid staff and yes-men, he'd found Luna. And her memory would linger long after she was gone. She was changing him, and though he had no way of knowing if that was a good or bad thing, he couldn't deny it.

"I'll be fine," he said, picking her up again.

She didn't argue, just wrapped her arms around his shoulders and rested her head against him. He set her down on his bed and then got in next to her, pulling her to his side.

She nestled close and he heard her sigh.

"What?"

"I can't stay here all night."

"Why not?"

She looked up at him. "Someone will come check on us in the morning. I need to be back in my bed."

"Stay with me."

"I can't, unless you don't want me to be your body-guard anymore," she said.

"I don't."

"Oh." She pulled away from him, sitting up. "Okay, then. I don't blame you."

She didn't?

"Great. I'm thinking you need to get some place safe. Seems like Xander should be in the field and you should be in a room with Lee, monitoring things, so you'll be protected," he said.

That had been easier than he'd anticipated.

"What are you talking about? If I'm off the job, then I'll go. I probably will need to have my actions here reviewed as well."

He shook his head. "No, I just want you somewhere safe, where you can't get hurt."

"Wait, do you want a new bodyguard because I screwed up tonight?"

"No. You did the best in that situation. Even Price said that no one could have handled it better," Nick said. "You're a damned good bodyguard, Luna."

She smiled over at him. "Thanks. But I'm not stepping aside because you think I might get hurt again. I'm not going to pretend that sleeping with you was my best idea, but the truth is, I needed to feel you and touch you after tonight. Had to make sure you were okay."

He wasn't ready to stop talking about replacing her, but he could see she was done with it. Her confession had struck a chord inside him, reminding him of how lonely they'd both always been. How they'd both carved lives that kept them from making contact with too many people.

But now that he'd had her this close, he didn't know if he was going to be able to easily let her go.

Maybe it was the fact that, at this moment, they were completely safe. His attacker had been chased off and, though he hadn't been caught, for this one night he wasn't an immediate threat.

"I needed that, too," he said.

"I know," she admitted, coming closer to him again as he pulled her back into his arms.

"I like holding you."

"I like being held by you," she said. "I don't want to get used to it."

He didn't have to ask why that was. The truth was that they both knew this wasn't going to be something they could sustain while she was working for him. And, once she wasn't, he had no idea what the outcome of this would be.

For tonight, he simply wanted to enjoy holding Luna and not worry about the future. He'd never felt like he had much control over what fate had in store for him and that hadn't changed. But he had.

Chapter 17

Luna was gone when Nick woke the next morning, as he'd expected her to be. He looked at the empty pillow next to his, struggling with emotions he wasn't really sure he wanted to acknowledge. But they were there nonetheless. He liked her.

He headed to the gym for his treadmill run and found Luna waiting for him. It was almost as if the night before hadn't happened. Was she going to pretend like it meant nothing?

He didn't ask her, just ignored how hot she looked in her sports bra and running shorts as she got on the treadmill next to his. Then he noticed the bandage on her side. It had been changed and looked fresh. Nick hadn't changed his bandage this morning as it appeared clean. She must have replaced hers after she'd left his bedroom. For some reason, that pained him.

That reminder of the threat they were facing, and

how real the attacker was, made him decide to stay silent. He turned to the panel on the treadmill and picked a punishing run, hoping it would distract him. To a certain extent, it did, but he wasn't going to be able to let this be.

Nick hit the stop button after a long run. Luna did the same. Sweat was dripping down the side of her neck and his eyes traced that moisture before he felt himself stir. Then he lifted his eyes to hers.

"Are you going to act like last night didn't happen?" he asked. His frustration was evident in his voice. He knew he had to get his emotions under control before he started his day. He was always cool and calm. After last night, he'd noticed that there were a lot of appointments showing up on his calendar today, including a couple of on-air interviews to discuss the events of the night before.

"No. We're both adults, that would be silly," she said, resting her arms on the handles of the treadmill. "There's a lot going on today. Van handled the detective last night, but they want you downtown to fill out a statement this morning. I have a feeling a lot of the partygoers are being asked to do the same…it's for the best that I go back to being your bodyguard and not your lover."

Lover.

What did that mean to her? He'd had more than a few lovers and, of course, an ex-wife. But no one had made him feel the way that Luna did. "Sure. I'm your boss again, right?"

"Sure," she said back to him. "We need to talk about you not following my direction when we are in a dangerous situation."

"Sure," he said again.

"Really? Are we going to do it this way?" she asked.

"I am," he said, keenly aware that he was pushing to see if she cracked; instead, it seemed as if he were the one in danger of crumbling. He cursed and turned his treadmill back on. As usual, talking to Luna was making him more frustrated.

He heard her treadmill start up as well. Listening to the pounding of both of their feet distracted him for a few moments but he kept going through possibilities in his mind of who was threatening him. That gave him a focus. He knew the detective was going to have a lot of questions for them.

Once his run was finished, he stepped off the treadmill and Luna did the same. He took a gym towel to wipe his face and neck and tossed one to her.

He was going to shower, but she stopped him with her hand on his arm. She'd meant her touch to be professional, and it was, but his body reacted as if she were caressing him. "I'm trying to keep you safe. Seeing that wound on your arm, knowing you were hurt last night… I can't let that happen again."

He understood because he felt the same way. "We need to figure out who is attacking me and set a trap."

"Yes to finding out who, but traps don't always work. Let's talk to the detective and then run down to the dry cleaner's and see if we can find someone. Also, I think we should try talking to Thom again today."

He liked the plan she had laid out. They were working together as a team, which suited him right now. Once they had another suspect, he'd be tempted to leave and confront them on his own despite their agreement. He didn't want to let Luna get hurt again.

"Why do you want to talk to Thom again?" he asked as they headed back toward their respective rooms.

"He was drunk last night. Sober, he might remember a detail that he left out last night," she said. "Also, he was at the party the night Jack died, maybe he saw something that he didn't realize was important."

"I hadn't thought of that. Are you just going to question him?" Nick asked, seeing a different side to Luna than the physical one he was familiar with. She was very good at her job as a bodyguard but now he saw her analytical mind.

"I imagine that Rick will be the one to do it. He's really good at interrogation...that word always sounds sort of negative to me, but he just talks and get them thinking and leads them back through events. I've never seen anyone as good as he is at getting someone to open up," Luna said.

"When I first saw him, I thought he was a stoner."

Luna gave Nick a half smile. "He does give off that vibe sometimes. You caught him on a bad day."

"I don't think so. I saw him move, and once he went after the shooter, it was like a different man. You're not like that," he said suddenly. Luna was the same all the time. She didn't switch on when she was guarding him and switch off.

"I'm not," she admitted. "I think it's because I define myself as kickass woman all the time."

He smiled at that. "As you should. What does Rick do?"

"If I had to guess, he switches into cop mode when he's working. His job was tough. He was undercover for a lot of years, so, for him, personal and work are two very different modes."

Nick tucked that piece of knowledge away. It made him realize how grateful he was to have Price Security working for him. It seemed to Nick they had all bases covered.

Luna had to talk to Van and let him know about last night. But a part of her wanted to keep that for herself a little bit longer. Van wasn't an idiot, and he had probably already put two and two together. But she wanted to tell him so he could take whatever action was needed, so she didn't lose his respect or trust.

For this morning, as she stood next to Nick, waiting to be called in to talk to Detective Miller, she was good. She noticed a few people from the night before and knew from Finn, who'd been leaving as they arrived, that Verity was in with the detective now.

Finn and Nick were going over his schedule and Luna just kept alert, watching the surroundings and running over everything in her head. She was fairly certain Nick wasn't going to be attacked at the police station. That left her free to go back to the beginning. Her team had started taking over security for Nick's event from the first day they'd been hired.

There had been a lot of outside vendors hired for the event and Price Security had talked to and vetted all of them. Van and Kenji were interviewing them again today. So the vendors, like the caterers, bartenders and the outside bouncers Nick had hired, were all covered.

Who else had known any details of the event beforehand?

Finn. Luna looked over at him and Nick as they talked. The bond between the two of them was strong and more than employer and employee. Her gut really thought Finn was harmless. Last night, watching his face after Nick had been stabbed, had been telling.

Unless Finn was a really good actor.

Both men glanced over at her and she smiled at them. "What?"

"I want to go to see my dad later today. Can you let Price know? I don't want to take a chance of bringing last night's intruder to his house."

Luna nodded and texted Lee to let her know.

"As if this didn't start with him," Finn said.

"Letters, yes. But a guy with a knife or gun? He's old and frail."

Finn snorted.

"You know what I mean. He wouldn't stand a chance against that guy from last night."

"He won't have to," Luna said. "Aldo would protect him."

Nick looked over at her. "You're right, he would. But if we can take steps to keep that from happening, all the better."

"I agree," Luna said.

Finn left a few minutes later. Nick gestured to the free seat next to him, but she shook her head. Standing, she had a better view of the hall and the room. Nick just shrugged and went back to his phone before pocketing it.

She loved the easy way his body moved and it was hard to keep from remembering the touch of his hands on her body the night before.

"How much longer do you think they'll be? I have to be at the TV station KTLA at one."

"I'm not sure," she said. "I'll text Van, so he knows your schedule."

She sent the message.

"How will that help?"

"Van's in there with the detective," Luna said.

"I hadn't realized they were working together," Nick said.

"She agreed to it this time, and sometimes it's better to have more than one set of eyes on a person as they talk and give their statement," Luna explained.

"Are you good at reading people?" he asked her.

"Sometimes. Most of the time. You are too."

He shrugged again. She noticed he was doing that a lot today. At first, she'd thought he was just chill because the danger from the night before had passed, but now she wondered if he wasn't trying to project that image to her.

"What do you see in me?" she asked him, trying to get him talking so she could figure out what, if anything, he was hiding.

Luna remembered his anger this morning and it would take a lot of self-control to hide that. If she'd learned anything during her time as Nick's bodyguard, it was that he didn't give anything away when it came to his feelings. He only let everyone see what he wanted them to.

"That your job means everything to you," he said. "I know that I threaten that, so you're not sure what to do with me."

Fair point. But then, she'd pretty much told him that. "Nothing beyond the stuff I told you."

"You like blending into the background, you're always watching and anticipating, and even when something doesn't turn into a threat, you stay tense and alert," he said. "I see it in your eyes. Even when you were dancing with me last night and I was turning you on, you still had an eye on the crowd."

He was spot-on with his read of her and, as he talked, that chill vibe ebbed—but then it was back. Maybe he was just trying to be… That was it. He was *trying* to get to a place where he could just go with the flow, and not succeeding. Just like her.

"What about me?" he asked her.

"You like to stand out and want all eyes on you. You do genuinely care about people and listen to them when they talk to you. You seem to cultivate relationships, and though you told me you deal in favors, I notice that you rarely ask anyone in your circle for a favor in return."

"You're right. I seldom need anything from them," he admitted. "But that doesn't mean I wouldn't."

"I know. You're tougher than you want anyone to see you are," she said, remembering last night when he'd tried to protect her against that hunting blade.

"I've had to be," he said.

That was something he kept from the world. So, if his attacker knew him, knew that he'd lay down his life for the right person against his playboy persona, then that might give them an advantage.

Luna waited outside while Nick went in to give his statement. Verity watched him leave the waiting area and then turned to Luna. Today, his ex had bloodshot eyes. She was still slightly tearing up as she watched Nick enter the conference room where the interviews were being conducted.

"Nicky's the best," she said to Luna.

"He is," Luna agreed. "You two seem to have a close relationship."

Though everyone had told her that Verity was harmless, Luna hadn't really had a chance to spend time with her the way she had with Finn. While Finn's loyalty to Nick seemed clear, Verity's was still foggy.

"We do. I shouldn't have ever divorced him," she said, dropping down onto one of the chairs.

Luna followed her. "Why did you?"

"Well...the truth is, despite all of his upbringing, Nicky is a bit much sometimes. I thought we would be jetting around the world all the time, but he just works and hangs out here in LA."

"And you wanted more?"

"I did. But now...well, of course, I have Lorenzo, and it's probably better that Nick and I are friends, but there are times when I miss him," Verity said.

Jealousy stirred inside Luna, and though she'd drawn a line between the night she'd spent in Nick's arms and today, she couldn't help that. How could Nick be attracted to both her and to Verity? she wondered. The woman was nothing like her. Maybe, she worried, Verity was truly the kind of woman he needed by his side. Verity understood Nick's lifestyle in a way Luna never could.

That didn't matter because she had only been in his bed one night, and she was going to do her damnedest to stay out of it.

"You seem to spend a lot of time around him. Is there anyone you noticed who might be trying to kill him?" Luna asked. She'd observed that Verity liked to talk about herself and just making a statement like that might lead her to saying something they could use in the investigation.

"Well, I mean...on the surface, I would have to say

no. But there are people who try to get close to me to get to him."

"Why would they do that? He seems pretty open," Luna said.

"To certain people, he totally is, but there are others who'd used those of us close to him to get access to Nick before. Finn, Thom, Hazel and me have all had people come at us for that connection," Verity said, putting her tissue into the big designer bag she was carrying. "I guess I'm the biggest target for that."

Luna hadn't realized that Thom and Hazel were part of Nick's inner circle. In fact, she was pretty sure this was just Verity's impression since Thom didn't feel a part of it and Nick didn't consider him a close friend. And Hazel was his admin assistant, not someone he socialized with.

"Why are you the biggest target?"

"I mean everyone knows I'm the most social, and that Nicky trusts me. That's why I'm his beneficiary. I guess he could have changed it to Finn when we got divorced, but he didn't. I know that pisses Finn off."

That was news. "What do you mean by that?"

"What do you think I mean? If Nicky dies, I get everything. But, honestly, I never think about it. I don't know what the world would be like without him."

"How did you meet him?" Luna asked, her mind trying to process everything that this could mean. Verity had seemed too self-absorbed and, frankly, too wealthy to be concerned about Nick's fortune, but maybe Luna had written her off too easily. She had seemed to be around whenever these recent attempts on Nick had been made.

"I skied into him in Switzerland. We had a laugh after he saved me, and more. We just connected."

Interesting.

The door opened before she could ask Verity another question and the other woman rushed to Nick's side. Luna followed, watching the woman's hands, but his ex just threw her arms around Nick and hung on to him as she kissed his cheek. She noticed that Nick didn't pull Verity close but loosely hugged her back.

"Sorry about that. I'm just so happy you're okay," Verity said. "I was rushed out last night and only heard from the detective you were hurt."

"I'm fine," Nick said. "I have a very busy day, so I have to go now. But we'll catch up soon."

"That sounds fab. I've sent Finn all the arrangements for Jack's funeral. The viewing and services start tomorrow night."

"He's informed me," Nick said, looking at Luna. "I think they are ready for you to give your statement."

"Okay. I'm just waiting for Kenji."

"I'm here," he said, stepping up behind her. "Sorry, parking is a bitch and I couldn't find a spot. Go on, I've got your boy."

"Thanks," she said.

Luna walked into the conference room and pulled out her notebook before she sat down. She had already gone over the previous night a few times on her own, but hoped that maybe when she added her observations, it would reveal something that they were all missing.

"Before we start, I just learned that Verity stands to inherit everything if Nick dies," she said. "Not sure that's important, but I think we should look into it."

"We will," Van said.

"We've investigated her already," Detective Miller said. "So far, she seems clean."

"We'll just double check," Van said.

"Fine. Keep me in the loop. Now, Luna, take me through the night from the time you stepped on the red carpet."

Luna pulled her notepad closer to her and started walking through the previous night. She hoped that the detective and the Price team found something helpful in her account. Luna couldn't help feeling like everything was happening more and more quickly.

Chapter 18

Nick seemed more tense than he'd been the last time they'd gone to see his father, which felt like a lifetime ago but had only been a few days. His hands were glued to the steering wheel and he drove fast, expertly weaving in and out of traffic as he hurried toward Malibu.

Luna kept an eye on their back, but no one was following them. "Do you want to talk about it?"

"Which 'it' are you referring to?" he asked sarcastically. "There's so much messed up in my life right now."

"I meant…what do you want to talk about?" she asked, sensing there was something on his mind.

"Nothing. I don't want to discuss anything that will simply lead us to more questions," he said.

She kept her gaze to the mirrors but turned briefly to look at him. Her breath caught in her chest at the heated feelings he stirred in her. She wished she were more comfortable in her own skin so she could admit to herself, and maybe to him, how much she liked him. But she couldn't do that. So, the bodyguard in her leaned deeper into the seat and started doing what she did best. "Questions are what lead us to the big discoveries."

"Like what? That someone I know is trying to kill me? That someone who's been in my building really doesn't like me?"

"Nick."

"Sorry. I'm in a nasty mood. It doesn't help that Jack's viewing is tonight. I haven't spoken to his mother since Finn and I called to let her know he'd been killed… I'm not ready to deal with relatives."

She reached over, putting her hand on his thigh and squeezing to give him some comfort. He put his hand over hers, rubbing his thumb against her knuckles. "Surely you've done it before."

He gave a harsh laugh. "That doesn't make it easier. His mom…she was heartbroken, but didn't blame me. I had a huge life insurance policy on Jack just in case, so she was compensated, but I know it's not money she wants."

It wouldn't be, Luna thought. "Why is Verity still the beneficiary of your policy?"

"I just never got around to changing it. I have more than one policy, by the way. Finn has one, Aldo has another. I just want to take care of the people around me."

"What about Hazel, your assistant? Does she have one?"

"No. She's only part of my work life. The others are more like family," he said.

And family mattered. She got that. It was interesting that he said he wasn't close to anyone but did so much for those three alone. Verity now seemed an unlikely prospect. "We haven't really looked into Aldo. He's been with your father all along."

"Aldo? Are you kidding me? Do you think that old man was the one with the knife?" Nick asked as he took the exit from the freeway leading toward his father's Malibu estate.

"I'm not ruling it out. I think we should just ask where he was last night," she said. If she'd known about the life insurance policy that Nick had just mentioned, she would have put him on her list earlier.

"Are you kidding me? Aldo is my father's closest—I don't know what to call him—friend, I guess. He was the one to take and pick me up from boarding school. I just can't believe it would be him," Nick said.

"Did he hire the nanny who was injured?" she asked.

Nick clenched his jaw but didn't answer, which meant that Aldo had. She really didn't want to believe that the man who'd been watching over Everett and keeping him alive and safe all these years had been secretly plotting against Nick.

"Logically, I understand what you're trying to do. But Aldo? I don't buy it. Also, the letters specifically mention Dad's true heir. Aldo still isn't able to give birth," Nick said.

She smiled at the last sardonic statement. That was a wrinkle. "Does he have a lover perhaps?"

"No. The guy is always with my father. When I was younger, he'd come to fetch me and then take me to my dad and stay with him. I have never really seen him with someone romantically. I think we can rule him out."

"Possibly," Luna said. She wasn't crossing anyone off her mental list until she had solid proof they weren't involved with the attacks. She was still considering how a criminal partnership would work for any of their suspects. Even so, Nick had valid points about Aldo.

The older man didn't appear to have a child who could be thought of as Everett's secret heir. He also seemed very loyal to, and genuinely cared for, Everett. It made no sense that he'd try to kill Nick now. Was there any reason he'd be working with someone?

"Luna, I don't want you grilling Aldo when we get there. I'll bring up last night and find out where he was. If he was with my father, we drop this," Nick said. "I know you are trying to conduct your investigation, but I am drawing a line here. Agree?"

She could see that this was important to him. Learning that someone close to him was probably behind the attacks was a difficult thing for Nick. Hearing it might be the man who was his father's companion was too much. She got that. Nick was on a knife's edge, waiting to see when the next attack would come.

She was running possibilities and trying to rule out as many people as she could so they could figure this out. But telling Nick that very thing wasn't going to make him less tense or get them closer to the truth.

Nick waited for Luna this time before walking up to the front door of his father's mansion. He wasn't sure what he expected from this visit, but he needed more information about his father's past. He wasn't going to allow himself to entertain the possibility that Aldo might have anything to do with the attacks. That would be a betrayal he might never recover from.

Of the two older men in his life, it was Aldo who'd been the one to comfort him and to spoil him when his father had been distant and cold. To lose the man he'd always, deep inside, thought of as his father, would hurt almost as much as losing Jack had.

He knew Luna was just doing her job. And it felt like they were running out of time. The attacks had come closer together for a reason. Did someone know more about his father's condition?

Actually, wait a minute.

He stopped before he knocked on the door, turning to Luna, who was scanning the yard and driveway.

"It can't be someone who would benefit from my death."

"What? Why not?" she asked.

"The urgency has been coming from my father. He's the one who only has a few months to live. It's his will that the letters are demanding be altered. So, my death wouldn't get them anything. It only serves to force my father's hand," Nick said.

Luna nodded, her face grim. "You're right. We need to know if anyone other than you benefits from his death."

"Great. So Aldo will still be on the list," Nick said.

"Are you sure?"

"Yes. Dad wouldn't stiff him after all those years of service," Nick said as he raised his hand to knock on the door. "But it does widen the search."

"We want to narrow it. Maybe there will be a connection we haven't seen before," Luna said. "I'll have Lee run a search once we speak to your father. You know I have to come in this time."

"After last night and all the safety measures I thought we had in place, I'm not going to argue with you on that," he said.

The door was opened not by Aldo but by his father's housekeeper, Mrs. Prentice. That wasn't all that surprising. Aldo was really his father's butler and valet and mostly needed at Everett's side.

"Hello, Nicholas. Lovely to see you. Was your father expecting you today?" Mrs. Prentice asked, stepping back to let them enter.

"No, he wasn't. But I need to speak to him," Nick said. It was an old habit left over from childhood, trying to justify coming to talk to his father. He knew that Mrs. Prentice wasn't gatekeeping him alone. Her job was to keep everyone from Everett.

"I'm sure he'll be glad to see you," she said. "He's in the solarium, and I'll be serving lunch soon. Will you and your guest be joining him?"

"We might be," Nick said. "Let me talk to him first."

"Very well. You have about fifteen minutes until he has to eat. I'll leave you alone for twelve minutes," she said. "It takes some time to set his spot and get him ready to eat."

"That should be good," Nick said.

"What's her name?" Luna asked as they left the foyer and Nick led the way to the sunroom.

"Ramona Prentice," Nick said. "Adding her to your list of suspects?"

"I am. She's a woman and she's very protective of your father and his schedule. Also, she looks old enough to have a child your age or slightly older."

She wasn't wrong, except that he'd met her family on numerous occasions and she and his father...well, he couldn't rule out that they'd never been lovers. "Fine. We'll ask my father about her too."

He entered the solarium, which was a large glass-enclosed room with Spanish tiles on the floor. There was a round table that seated six in the middle, and a love seat and arm chairs off to one side in a conversation area. His father, seated in one of the armchairs, looked up when they entered.

"Nicholas, I wasn't expecting you today, was I?"

"No, sir. Did you see the news from last night?" he asked his father, going over to the love seat to sit close to him.

He was aware of Luna's frown as she took in all of the open space around them. She started to speak and Nick raised his hand to stop her.

"We're safe here. There's a cliff drop at the end of the garden to the beach below and two, high, security fences on either side. You have a clear view of the yard," he said.

She just shook her head and found a position to watch the entire backyard, scanning constantly by turning her head from side to side.

If someone were to fire at them, Luna would use her body to protect him. He'd talk fast so they could get out of there.

"I didn't. Aldo left a note that there was an incident at your club," his father said.

Nick quickly brought his father up to date on the attack and Emmett reached over and took Nick's hand. "You were stabbed?"

"Just a scratch. Luna's wound was deeper," Nick reassured his father. "Where is Aldo, by the way?"

"He asked for the day off to go and meet a woman," Everett said.

"Was he home last night?"

"He was. We played cribbage until eleven, when I take my last dose of medicine, and then he helped me to bed," his father said. "Why?"

"Just covering all the bases. I'm afraid I have to

ask you something that I really don't want to." Just the thought of asking about his father's love life and possible partners who would want him dead wasn't something he'd ever thought he'd do.

"I think you better stay for lunch, if that's the case. Luna, will you join us?"

"Only if you are eating in a room that's not as exposed as this one is."

"We can eat in the formal dining room," Everett said.

Nick helped his father up and led them to the room with only one window that Luna could easily see from the table.

Luna wished she'd brought someone else from the team with her. Watching the dynamic between Everett, Nick and Mrs. Prentice was interesting, and she observed as much as she could in between scanning the surroundings. The window here overlooked the backyard that led to the cliff and the ocean. So, she felt better about protecting Nick in this room. She knew he'd probably try to shelter his father in the event of another attack and factored that into her own preparations.

Mrs. Prentice was friendly but not overly so toward Everett, and when Nick saw her watching the older woman, he all but rolled his eyes.

"How's James doing?" he asked the housekeeper as she set a plate down in front of him.

"Oh, very well. He's out on the boat today with Mr. P and our grandkids. I'm so happy he's back on the West Coast."

Nick asked a few more questions about her husband and family, and Luna acknowledged that she could probably rule Mrs. Prentice out as a suspect. She would still have Lee run a check on her, but it seemed less likely that she would think her son was Everett's given how she talked about him and her husband.

After the housekeeper left, Everett turned to Nick. "What was that about?"

"Luna and I are trying to rule out possible women who work with you, or know you, who might be behind the letters," Nick said. "Mrs. P is the right age."

"She is. But she's never been interested in me that way," Everett said.

"We're going to need to know who was," Luna said when it seemed that Nick wasn't going to.

"Who was what?"

"Your romantic partner," Nick said succinctly.

"Ah, Aldo and I have been tracking them down. I thought he sent you the information. None of them had a child that was mine," Everett said.

"He did send the dates you had…affairs. We need the names, so we can check into the individuals. One of the avenues we are investigating is whether someone has a life insurance policy on you. We know they want you to change your will, but perhaps there are other areas that you and Aldo didn't consider," Luna said.

Everett didn't say anything, just continued eating his meal, and with the dose of medicine he was on, she understood he had to eat. But she also had a feeling he was stalling.

Nick sighed and put his cutlery down. "Father, I need this information. The attack last night… I can't keep living like this. Luna and Price Security are the best in the business. You know that, you were the one who hired them. They think this is a good way to find something that we might be overlooking."

"I know, son. I will give you a list. It's just that I don't want to believe someone who I was close to would have been scheming to kill you."

"No one wants to believe that," Luna said. "The person behind these attacks on Nick and the letters you received seems to be someone who has a lot of knowledge of the two of you."

Nick pushed his plate away, rubbing the back of his neck again. "You're right. When my cousins and uncle were killed on the yacht, I became Dad's sole heir. Only a handful of people could have known we'd all be there together."

"That's right. I'll have Aldo go back through my calendar and find out who was working for me then. I wonder if there's a connection we missed," Everett said.

"Possibly. We also need to find out more about the car crash with the nanny," Luna mentioned. "Would it be possibly for me to have Lee Oscar from Price Security get in touch with you? She's an expert at doing a deep dive on people."

Everett took the last bite of his lunch and pushed his plate away. She could tell he didn't want to talk to anyone about this, other than perhaps Nick, but they didn't have much time left. They needed answers and the sooner, the better.

"Of course," he said at last.

"Thanks, Dad," Nick said.

A look was exchanged between the two of them but Luna couldn't read it. It was clear their relationship was complex and more nuanced that she'd suspected the last time. She'd seen the distance between the two of them, but there was also a closeness, perhaps brought on by tragedy or personality, that she suspected wasn't comfortable for either for them. They were both very strong, dominate men used to getting their way.

They kept secrets from each other and, for the first time in Nick's life, there couldn't be any. It seemed that they were both trying to figure out how to deal with it. She messaged Lee to get in touch with Everett about staff and people he'd dated. Lee texted back that she was on it.

Lee also mentioned that they'd checked out the dry cleaner. The suit the tag had come from had been delivered to Nick's building four days earlier.

Nick said goodbye to his father and, when they were in the car, Luna mentioned the dry cleaner.

"Was that your suit?"

He shrugged. "I don't think so. But it might have been Jack's. I can try to get in touch with Hazel when we get back. I think she probably received the suits. We know it wasn't Finn's."

"I don't think it was Finn who attacked you. The other man was three inches taller than he was."

"Yeah, the other guy was my height and build," Nick said.

Her mind was adding more possibilities to the suspects list. Could it have been someone from Jack's past?

They'd already ruled that out, but Luna felt like they had too much information and hadn't found the right connections. Tonight, while Nick and Van were at Jack's funeral, she was going to put the pieces of this puzzle together before anyone could hurt Nick again.

Chapter 19

Funerals weren't ever going to be his favorite thing. Nick had been to so many that he'd developed a routine. Finn was circulating around the room and Kenji had taken over watching him tonight. Fearing another possible attack, Nick hadn't argued. He knew the time had come to get Luna as far away from him as he could.

This afternoon at his father's, they'd operated as a team again, and he couldn't deny that he liked it. Maybe a little too much. There was something about having someone who got him and wasn't always deferring to him. But there was more to his feelings than simple teamwork. He and Finn were also a good team, and while he loved the man like a brother, there was something very different when he was with Luna.

Nick was afraid to name it as love. But it was the only thing that made sense.

"I've checked out the room where the viewing will

be. If you want to have a few moments alone with the deceased, I can offer you some privacy by staying at the back of the room," Kenji said.

Tonight the Japanese American wore a black suit, white shirt and slim tie. He had his thick black hair swept back with a fall of bangs over his left brow. Nick knew he was carrying a gun because Kenji had point-blank told Nick that he never went on the job without one.

And though Nick had been throwing out stipulations left and right at the beginning of this security detail not more than a week earlier, now…he was tired. Constantly being on guard and never knowing when an attack would come had worn him down.

"I'd appreciate that," Nick said, going into the room where the coffin waited at the end. There were chairs and love seats set up around the room to give those who came to grieve a place to sit and talk if they wanted.

Nick also knew there'd be a buffet and drinks, Verity had texted him all the details. But he hadn't wanted to look at them. He hated that Jack was gone, and as he leaned over the casket and looked down at his friend and bodyguard, his heart ached.

Jack had been hired at first because of his likeness to Nick, but over time the two men had become good friends. Jack was nothing like him. He was quiet and introspective, sort of like Luna, always watching everyone and every thing. But, eventually, he'd loosened up, and when they'd gone out he'd been a good wingman and a lot of fun.

For a while, Finn and Jack had had an affair, which had made Nick feel like a third wheel. But that had ended over a year ago. Finn had only said they'd wanted different things. Nick hadn't pushed for more details. But he knew now, more than ever, that loving someone who was a bodyguard was hard.

He'd experienced that with Luna. And they'd only made love once. What would it be like once he was out of this? Could they continue their relationship? How would he feel knowing she was guarding someone else, putting her life in danger for another person?

Nick wasn't sure he could do it.

But he was also very certain that the moment he tried to tell Luna what to do, it would be the end of anything between them. He looked down at Jack, realizing that he'd let his mind drift to get away from grief.

He leaned over and touched Jack's shoulder. He knew his spirit had left Jack's body, but he needed that connection one last time. "I'm sorry. I never meant for you to die for me."

Jack's eyes, of course, stayed peacefully closed, but Nick couldn't help the flash image of the body he'd identified in the morgue. He took a deep breath and blinked so that he didn't cry. One tear seeped out of his right eye, and he reached up to brush it away.

He straightened and fiddled with his tie before turning to find Kenji where he'd said he'd be, at the back of the room, watching the door.

"I'm done."

"Okay. Before we let those in who have come to pay their respects, we need to establish your movements. I think it might be best if you stay in one place and let people come to you," Kenji said.

"I'll try. I'm restless. It's not easy to sit and dwell on what happened."

"Yeah, death sucks. We can move, if you need to,

but it will mean that I'll have to position myself close to you. Your conversations won't be private," Kenji said.

"I'm not hiding anything," Nick said.

"Good, then I guess we're fine. If you want me to interrupt, put your hand in your left pocket," Kenji said before he took another circuit around the room and then spoke into his earpiece to let Price Security know it was okay to let other people in.

Nick hadn't been offered an earpiece tonight, and given that he was holding a viewing for his last bodyguard…he wasn't sure how he felt. Tonight his emotions were all over the place.

As much as he was sure that Luna was safer away from him, he still missed her. He wished she were here, by his side, keeping that silent watch of hers, using her acerbic wit to make him feel lighter than he should. The guilt weighing on him was deserved.

Knowing what he did now, he should have pushed his father harder a long time ago. Should have made sure his theories weren't brushed aside by everyone as the paranoia of a young man with too much money.

He should have…what? He'd told everyone, yet they hadn't listened.

His father's dismissal wasn't surprising. But Aldo should have defended him. He'd known what was going on yet had kept silent.

Nick had always known that Aldo was loyal to his family, but he'd thought that loyalty had extended to him as well. With this investigation, he'd come to accept that nothing was like it had seemed.

Luna sat on the floor of her room in the penthouse with all of her notes spread out around her and her tablet next to her on the floor. Lee sat across from Luna, leaning against the wall, her laptop on a tray on her legs. She was monitoring the comms at the funeral and watching the security cameras here at Nick's building while also helping Luna analyze the information that had been collected so far.

"Kenji says Nick seems edgy and that he doesn't seem to like many of his friends," Lee mentioned.

Luna had declined an earpiece, needing to focus on the information at hand. She felt like she was missing something. She didn't want to believe that sleeping with Nick had taken her edge away, but she knew she was too invested in finding the person behind the attacks on him to be neutral.

Instead of just doing her job, this had become personal. He'd been stabbed—hell, she'd been stabbed, and the wound was a dull ache in her side. That made her even more determined to solve this.

"I don't think they are his friends mostly. I mean Finn is, but otherwise, Nick keeps most people at arm's length. He's just so charming, no one seems to realize what he's doing," Luna said.

Only because she'd been inside his arms could she see now how artificial most of his interactions with other people were. Even with Verity. Nick had treated her the way he had treated Thom and the rapper he'd hosted the event for. She had no doubt most of them thought they were closer to Nick than they actually were.

"Is there anyone on Everett's list who has a connection to this building or to Nick?" Luna asked.

"There is one person on the board who has a very tenuous link to them both," Lee said. " Ben Kovacs."

Luna shifted the papers around on the floor and found the profiles of the board members from DeVere Industries. Kovacs didn't look familiar to her, which meant that she'd never seen him in person. Odd, because most of the board had been here the day she and Nick had been shot at in the stairwell. "He wasn't at the board meeting the other day, was he?"

"Nope. His aunt had an affair with Everett in the eighties," Lee said. "She's on the list that they sent over this afternoon."

This sounded promising. "Is he close to the aunt?"

"I'm not sure," Lee said, her fingers moving over her keyboard quickly.

Luna kept digging through her notes, pulling her tablet close and doing her own search on Ben Kovacs. He was the same age as Nick and had joined the board five years earlier, after the yachting accident that had taken the lives of Nick's cousins and uncle. He'd taken one of the seats vacated by their deaths.

Luna felt like she was on the right track with him. He wasn't married but lived with his girlfriend and her kid.

"Kovacs might be a good lead," Luna said.

"Ah, well, the aunt doesn't have any kids. So she's out as the letter writer. Unless Kovacs is actually her kid," Lee said.

Lee's fingers were still moving and Luna continued her search, ending up on Facebook where Ben's mom had shared a picture of herself pregnant with him in a birthday post.

Ugh.

Every time she got close to something, it slipped away.

"Nope," Luna said, air dropping the link to Lee, who cursed under her breath.

"What am I missing?" she asked her friend and co-worker.

"What are we all missing? I think we need a break," Lee said. "We're focusing too hard."

"You think so?"

"I know so. I'm sort of the expert on these things, even Van says so." Lee tipped her head to the side and then smiled.

"What else did he say?" Luna asked, realizing that Van must have responded in Lee's earpiece.

"That I'm wise beyond my years."

"You are," Luna agreed. "Could you mute for a minute?"

Lee tapped her ear so that their conversation would be isolated. Van and the team would have heard her ask for privacy.

"What's up?" Lee asked.

"I slept with Nick," she said. Just blurted it out.

The worst part wasn't the sex. If it had just been sex, then she wouldn't be feeling like she had to alert the team. But it wasn't *just* sex. It had been more than that. From the moment she'd tackled him to the ground, she'd known he was different.

"He's hot, so I get it, but I'm guessing this isn't a girl-talk thing," Lee said. "What's the problem? You know that these situations can elevate that need to copulate."

"I'd love it if you never used the word *copulate* again," Luna said.

"You're diverting. What's up?"

Luna tried to find a way to put it into words. She had a circle of people she cared for in the Price Security team. There had never been a lover in the past for whom she'd felt anything more than strong affection. Normal feelings. Normal to her.

This was unnerving. Was it deep affection? Could it be love? She had no idea what love felt like.

It was just that she knew she wasn't herself. She wasn't functioning on the job the way she wanted to. She was worried about Nick tonight, and not just his physical safety. It would be hard for him to be at Jack's viewing and essentially be alone.

Finn was there, but he'd be busy making sure Nick was protected socially from those who'd take the viewing as an opportunity to network.

"I think I care for him," Luna said at last. And then immediately wanted to punch something.

She'd tried so hard to define herself in a way that had nothing to do with her past growing up in the foster care system. But this…suppressing her emotions always reminded her she hadn't. She'd never learned how to let her guard down and care for others. That's really where she was right now, and it wasn't a great place.

"I think you do, too," Lee said. "You know, it's okay to fall in love with him."

"No, it's not! I think it's making me sloppy."

"You're not sloppy. If anything, you're more diligent than ever. You just have to give yourself permission to care about him and let him care about you in return," Lee said.

Luna knew that was the truth, but she wasn't sure she was ever going to be able to do that.

"The team is heading back. You good?"

Luna nodded. She wasn't good, but Lee had given her something else to think about. And for now that was enough.

* * *

Nick walked into his building knowing the place that had once been his sanctuary was now another goldfish bowl, but that didn't bother him as much when he saw Luna waiting for him in the living room of his penthouse. She wore a pair of faded jeans and a T-shirt. Her hair was up in its customary ponytail and he felt a mix of lust and affection when he saw her.

Everyone had theories that they wanted to discuss, but he just wanted to take Luna in his arms and into his bed. He needed to just be with her after the long night he'd had. He knew this would be the last time he held her. He'd made the decision to have her removed from guarding him. Seeing Jack's body in the coffin, and talking to those in his circle who were now aware that he was in danger. It had made his vision clear for the first time.

He had to get Luna away from him so she would be safe. Then he needed to go through the people who were close to him again and get justice for everyone in his life who had been hurt. That was his plan.

"Did you two find anything useful?" Van asked from behind Nick.

Nick had almost forgotten the entire team and Finn had come up to the penthouse. Almost.

"We've eliminated another person as a suspect," Luna said.

"Who?"

"Ben Kovacs."

"Why did you suspect him?" Nick asked. Ben was a good guy and had brought a lot of new ideas to the board table.

"Your dad had an affair with his aunt and he got the spot on the board after the yacht incident," Lee said. "Seemed a bit coincidental."

More than a bit if he was looking through the lens that the Price Security team was using. "But he's not a suspect?"

"Well, it seems a bit of a long shot," Luna said. "He's on the maybe-but-not-likely list."

"Who else is on there?" Finn asked.

"You, Verity, Aldo, Hazel," Luna said.

"I guess I'll take comfort in the not-likely bit," Finn said. "I'm not trying to kill him, you know."

"We do," Van said. "That's why Luna said 'not likely.' We can't just decide we like you and cross you off."

"Ah, you like me?" Finn asked, flirting.

Van just gave him a small smile and Nick realized that he hadn't been paying attention to anything but Luna and staying alive. Was there something going on between Finn and Van?

He looked at Finn, who just raised both eyebrows and smiled back at Nick. That was a possible bright spot in all of this.

"So, ruling them out. Who's left?" Nick asked. He didn't think any of those four could possibly be the attacker.

"Staff here. Some of them are temporary or were outsourced for an event. That makes it harder to track," Lee said. "I'm working on it, but it's taking me some time."

"So where do we stand?" Nick asked. "How much longer until we know what's going on?"

"That's hard to say. We won't know until the attacker gets clumsy," Van said.

"That's not encouraging," Nick said.

"We know. Lee and I have a solid list and, now with the names of your dad's former lovers and partners, we should get something soon," Luna said. "For tonight, that's as far as we've progressed."

"I guess that's our cue to leave," Van said, coming over to clap his hand on Nick's shoulder. "Rest assured we'll catch this son of a bitch."

"Thanks," Nick said.

Everyone left the penthouse and he turned to Luna, who watched him with that look in her eyes he'd only seen the night they'd made love.

He shrugged out of his jacket and took off his tie, tossing them on a nearby chair. "I need a drink."

She followed him to the bar area and then, when he went to the piano and sat on the bench, putting his whiskey glass on the top of it, she sat next to him.

She smelled of spring flowers and he took a deep breath, needing to clear out the stench from the funeral home.

"You okay?" she asked.

"No," he said, putting his hands on the keys and starting to play Elton John's "Someone Saved My Life Tonight."

She leaned her head on his shoulder and put her hand on his thigh. His cock hardened, but right now his heart needed *this*. Needed the piano and the music and Luna. Just her body next to his on the bench while he poured out the emotions that he hated feeling.

The senseless loss of Jack's life, the disappointment in his father and Aldo, the affection for Luna that he wasn't sure would last. He played until his hands were almost numb and he had reached a null state. He finished his whiskey and then took Luna's hand and led her to his bedroom.

Chapter 20

Lee hadn't really given her any peace of mind when Luna had told her about sleeping with Nick. This was more than sex to her. And the type of man that Nick was, she knew he cared for her, but this wasn't going anywhere. There was no time, when she looked into her future, to make a traditional home with anyone.

And a man like Nick...

As much as the secret place in her heart wanted it to happen, she had to be realistic.

"It doesn't seem like you're thinking about sex," he said dryly as they entered his bedroom.

"I was thinking about you, does that count?"

"It would if you were ripping my clothes off," he replied.

"I was worried about you tonight," she said, slipping into his arms and hugging him close to her.

This had to be the last time she slept with him. Even

being apart and working on the investigation, Nick had still been on her mind.

"Were you? Don't trust Kenji?"

"Oh, I trust him. He's really the best of us. And that's saying something."

"Then what was it?" he asked, tipping her head back with his finger under her chin. Her lips parted as he did that, wanting his kiss.

"I know you. Tonight was going to be a war between what you want the world to see and the grief and sadness you feel at losing one of the few people you genuinely cared about," she said.

"How do you see me so well?" he asked.

She shrugged. She didn't want to tell him that, for her entire life, her survival had meant watching the people around her and being able to read what they were going to do next. It wasn't a skill born from happy memories. That was why she was so frustrated at not being able to figure out who was threatening him. When she successfully completed a mission, it gave someone else the security she'd never had.

"You can trust me," he said.

"I know."

"So?"

"I've always had to be observant."

"Foster care stuff?"

"Yeah," she said, not wanting to delve back into memories that weren't pleasant. "I just learned to watch how people were when they didn't think they were being observed. I could anticipate their behaviors and protect myself."

His hands slid down her back to cup her butt; she felt the ridge of his erection against her belly.

"So what do you see in me?" he asked.

Too much that she liked. But she wasn't going to say that out loud. "Well, I know that you play the piano when you are trying not to admit you're sad and hurt. I know you like seeing Finn happy and flirting with Van."

"How do you know that?"

"You had the tiniest smile on your face, your lips quirked right here when you watched the two of them," she said, touching his mouth.

He leaned down until his forehead rested against hers. She felt the warmth of his breath against her lips and hers tingled. She would much rather be getting naked than talking to him right now. Saying this stuff out loud only made her want to find a way they could be together.

No matter that every other relationship in her life had proved to her that it probably wouldn't. For just once, she wanted to dream about a future with Nick. Just once, she wanted to think to herself that she could find a relationship that would last. Just once…she wanted to love someone and be worthy of them loving her in return.

Luna didn't have the heart to pretend she wasn't in love with Nick. She might have experienced love before, but she knew what these feelings were this time. She'd kept them hidden inside herself the way she'd tucked away a raggedy old bear in her first foster home.

She turned her head, kissing him, sliding her tongue over his teeth, rubbing against his tongue as he sucked hers deeper into his mouth. His hands cupped her butt and lifted her up onto her toes. She moved her arms, twining them around his shoulders. She sighed and a wave of what felt like sunshine went through her as he pulled her even closer to him.

There was something exciting about being back in his arms. A feeling of coming home. She raised one of her legs and drew it up high, wrapping it around his hip, and felt the ridge of his cock slide against her center. She rubbed her hips against it, enjoying the feel of him.

She wanted him. Emptying and aching as much as she wanted this last time to last, she knew that a quick, hard coupling might be all her impatient body would allow.

She shoved her hand up into his thick hair and bit his tongue as he pulled it out of her mouth. Not hard, just a nip because the emotions he stirred in her were too intense to control.

Luna was horny, wanton, and a little bit angry at life that this could be the last time she had Nick under her body.

He lifted his head and looked down at her. Their eyes met and she wished she could read what was in them. He watched her so intently for a moment, she wondered if he felt the same thing she did.

Wanting something they both knew wasn't going to happen. And the heat between them was off the charts. There was no time to talk or contemplate what might happen later. He walked until she felt the wall against her back and then he brought his lips down on hers again, his mouth plundering hers. Taking things that she didn't know she could give.

His entire body moved against hers in one big caress that sent waves of heat through her. She was moist between her legs, and his cock rubbing against her through their clothes wasn't enough. She tried to wedge her hands between them, but he wasn't having it. Catching her wrists and drawing them up over her head. He held them in one of his as he raised his head and looked down at her again.

This time she had no trouble reading the feelings in his eyes. He'd taken charge, and she was happy to let him for tonight.

Nick wasn't surprised that Luna read him like an open book. There was a connection with her that he hadn't had with anyone else in his life. His friendships with Finn and Jack were deep and genuine, but he felt something different with Luna. And somehow she was stirring dreams of a future he'd never considered before this moment. This woman. In his arms for tonight, and he hoped for the future.

He knew he had to make something happen. Shake the attacker out and make them come for him. Nick had made up his mind when he'd entered the penthouse and seen Luna standing there in jeans and T-shirt like she lived there, and his heart had sped up. Emotions had washed over him. His life wasn't going to be worth living without her by his side.

Having her next to him while he'd played the piano had simply helped him to form his plan. He knew what he wanted. What he'd always wanted. But he'd been too afraid to push fate, to tempt it, by allowing himself to love. Or maybe he hadn't been ready to find love until she'd jumped across the room, covering him with her body as a gunshot hit the glass window of his conference room.

Maybe.

He didn't care why or how. He loved this woman.

He was going to do everything in his power, use all of his luck, to keep her safe and put an end to the threat he was living under so he could find a way to make a life with her.

Holding her against the wall, her hands in his, her body pressed against his. The time for thinking was over. He held her wrists loosely with one hand while he pushed her T-shirt up. His hand moving over her until he could cup her breasts through the fabric of her bra. He undid the clasp at the back and then pushed the fabric off her breast and lowered his head to take her nipple in his mouth, sucking deeply on it.

Her hands slipped free of his grasp. They moved to the buttons of his shirt, undoing them, and then her fingers were on his chest. They were a little cold, but he didn't mind as she caressed him, moving her hands lower on his body, her fingers dancing around his belly button and then lower still.

He lifted his head, toeing off his shoes as he undid his pants and shoved them down his legs with his underwear. Luna did the same with her jeans and panties before she tossed her shirt and bra onto the floor.

He shrugged out of his shirt. He pulled her back into his arms, savoring the feel of her naked body against his. He groaned, shifting his hips until he could get himself between her legs and then lifted her, slightly adjusting his stance until he felt the tip of his erection against the warmth of her body.

Nick drove himself up into her in one long thrust and she wrapped her legs around his hips. Her head fell back and he brought his mouth down on her neck, suckling against her as she clung to him.

He had forgotten how perfectly she felt around him,

and he knew there would be time later to go slow, but right now, he needed her. Needed to drive himself harder and faster into her until she was calling his name. Her nails digging into his shoulders with her pussy tightening around him.

He wanted to make her come again. His body didn't care about anything pleasuring Luna.

He brought his head down and found her mouth, sucking her tongue deep into his as he drove up into her two more times until she orgasmed, hers triggered his and his body shuddered as his climax took everything from him. He continued thrusting inside her until he was empty. Then he turned, holding her in his arms, her legs still wrapped around him, her pussy still throbbing against his cock. He let the wall support them and just held her.

Wanting to believe that the love he had for her would be strong enough to overcome everything that life and fate could throw at them.

But then he looked down at her. Saw that bandage on her side and remembered the times she'd put herself in between him and danger. And that fear that had always kept him from letting anyone close to him stirred.

Why now, when he'd found the one woman who felt like the missing part of his soul, did he believe he could keep her? That he could keep her safe and never let her go.

His life hadn't changed…he'd changed. And fate might still be taking the people he needed and cared for from him.

He wouldn't let fate and his attacker take another person from him. He'd made up his mind. If fate demanded one of their lives, it would be his. He didn't want to live without Luna. Wouldn't be able to go on if she was killed in his place.

"Nick?"

"Hmm."

"I—"

He turned his head, kissing her to stop whatever she might want to say. He made himself stand back from the wall and carried her to the bathroom, where they showered together, and then he carried her back to the bed, made love to her again, and held her close to him. He wasn't sure if she'd fallen asleep or was simply pretending to be. But that suited him.

He couldn't talk right now. His emotions were too raw and his determination to make sure that Luna stayed safe was too strong. He'd made a decision that he might have been too cowardly to make in the past, and there was nothing that would stop him.

Not fate. Not Luna. Not the attacker who'd been threatening him for his entire life.

The even cadence of Nick's breathing indicated he was sleeping, even though he held his body too still to be convincing. But he wanted her to think he was, so she let him have it. Her mind was whirring too much for her to go to sleep herself.

The easier thing to think about was the investigation. She was reviewing the people and faces that she'd been analyzing with Lee earlier in the night. As much as she tried to make a connection in her mind, she only saw Nick. The way he'd looked when he'd sat down on the piano bench and taken a long swallow of his whiskey, and then the music he'd chosen.

Every song had a touch of angst or melancholy in it.

Frankly, she didn't blame him for that. She knew the pressure he had put on himself for years believing that the accidents around him were more than coincidence. Finally having some validation had only brought more confusion into his world.

Luna wanted to solve this case, find the person attacking him, and give him the peace of mind he'd never had.

But she was too close to him to do it. She turned and put her arm around his stomach, squeezing him closer to her. He wrapped his arm around her, squeezing back for a moment. All the feels she had for him overwhelmed her and she turned her face into the curve of his neck, breathing in the scent of him.

She had to leave. There was no other way to find the attacker before Nick was injured again or someone else was killed. She'd indulged herself for as long as she could.

She felt his hand sweeping down her back as he held her closely and she opened her eyes, looking up at him.

Neither of them was sleeping and both were reluctant to talk. The hard conversations had never been the ones she'd avoided.

Until now.

Until Nick.

She took a deep breath.

"Don't."

"What?"

"Say whatever is on your mind."

"I have to," she said.

He sighed and then shifted away from her, sitting and resting his back against the headboard as he turned on the bedside lamp.

She crossed her legs as she sat up, facing him. She had put her T-shirt on after they'd showered.

"Okay then. What is it?"

"I have to stop being your bodyguard," she said.

"Good."

"What?"

"I can't bear it if you're hurt again," he admitted. "I hate that you were at all. I think you getting as far away from me as you can is the best idea."

She brought her knees up and wrapped her arms around them. "I think so too. But I'm going to stay on the investigation. I know there's still something I'm missing, and I want to solve this myself."

"Whatever it is, I'm not sure you or anyone will find it fast enough," he said.

"What makes you say that?" she asked. She, too, had a feeling in the pit of her stomach that another attack would happen soon. But she couldn't put her finger on why.

"Just my gut. Whatever it is that's kept me alive this long…"

He'd trailed off, and she realized there wasn't anything more for them to say. He'd agreed she should be replaced.

She rolled over and grabbed her phone from the nightstand, surprised to see it was almost six in the morning. The night had felt too short.

She texted Van that she needed to be replaced as Nick's bodyguard and that she'd explain later.

He answered her with a message that said he was sending Kenji to take over.

"That's done. Kenji's on his way. I'll get dressed and stay with you until he arrives," she said.

"You don't have to."

"I do. I can't let anything happen to you," she said.

He just watched her with that level stare of his and she wished there was a way to read his mind. To see what he was thinking. He'd been a little too agreeable for her. He'd been adamant that she not be replaced the last time they'd talked. She didn't blame him for changing his mind, but she didn't like it either.

"Are you sure you're okay?"

"No. Of course, I'm not okay. But as far as my life and this situation is, I think I'm as good as I can be."

She reached out to touch him and he took her hand in his, lacing their fingers together. "I don't want to talk about this. I want to find the bastard who's doing this and make them pay. Then I want to come back and—"

He broke off as they both got the signal that someone was in the penthouse elevator. She got out of bed and grabbed her gun, heading out of the bedroom and into the main area. Nick was behind her, his smartphone in his hand as he accessed the security cameras.

"It's just Kenji."

That was quick. He must have been nearby. She had hoped... For what? she asked herself. More borrowed time with Nick? Before this case and his life swept them apart?

"That's good. When he gets here, I'll get my stuff and leave," she said.

"If you can't pack it all, I'll have Finn send it to you," he said.

"I didn't realize you were in a big rush to get rid of me."

He didn't say anything, and she felt something she hadn't since she'd aged out of foster care at eighteen. Alone. Scared. Uncertain of her emotions and her worth.

Not as a bodyguard, she knew she was still very good at that. But as a woman and a person. She hated this. She should never have let her guard down and let Nick into her heart.

But, really, had there been any way to keep him out? She might be good at guarding everyone else, but she'd never had to protect herself from falling in love before.

Chapter 21

Luna left the penthouse without looking back. Leaving, she had down pat. She knew how to let go no matter how much she really didn't want to. She went back to the Price Tower and her apartment there, avoiding Van and Lee, who she knew from the team tracker app were both in the building.

She showered and then changed into clothing she preferred instead of the black suit that being a bodyguard to a billionaire demanded. Her jeans were faded and butter soft, and the T-shirt was from Inferno Brewing—one of the sponsors on Jaz's tour—and said Own Your Vices.

She'd never thought she had any vices, but Nick was making her rethink that.

Ugh.

She tried to shove all thoughts of him out of her mind and sat on the floor with her back supported by her bed as she spread her notes around her and started to run Nick and Everett's acquaintances through different databases, looking for any place where they overlapped.

While the search was running, she got up and went to make herself a cup of coffee. Seeing herself reflected in the mirror, she noticed she had a hickey on her neck. She touched it, knowing it would fade in time and that the mark from Nick would probably be the last vestige of him in her life.

There was a heavy knock on her door. That had to be Van.

She hurried to answer it, taking a deep breath before she opened the door.

"I'm sorry—"

"We can deal with that later. I just got off the phone with Detective Miller. Aldo Barsotti has been found dead in his car about two miles from the DeVere estate. Get dressed and into the briefing room."

"Has someone told Nick?"

"Kenji's doing it now," Van said.

"This is going to make him even more difficult," Luna said. "He'll take Aldo's death on himself."

"Is that why you asked to be replaced?" Van asked.

She shook her head and then shrugged. "I let it get personal. He needs someone with him who's focused on keeping him safe."

"And you weren't?" Van asked.

"Of course I was. But I was also worried about him for my own selfish reasons. You can't observe the situation while you're trying to make sure the client is emotionally okay, you know?"

Van nodded. "I've been there. For the record, I still don't think you needed to be replaced. I think you care too much about him to take the chance you might risk him somehow."

Luna didn't respond to that. Really, knew she didn't have to. That was the truth. She wanted—no, needed—Nick to be safe. She wasn't as sure of herself as she'd been in the beginning.

"Maybe."

"No maybe about it. Get dressed. I want to get a plan in place before the detective gets to Nick's building."

She closed the door and changed in record time, pulling her hair back into a ponytail. She contemplated covering the hickey with makeup for a split second, but left it. Everyone on her team had either been told or had guessed that she and Nick were together. Luna wasn't someone who liked to hide.

Rick and Luna piled into the back seat of the Hummer while Lee drove and Van kept them updated from the passenger side. She liked this part of the job, being surrounded by her team as they were briefed about a job.

She would risk losing this if she didn't figure out what to do with Nick. Would she still be as close with the Price team if she pursued a future with him? There was a part of her that was terrified to think of trying to make a life with him. She knew how to live on her own, to just make the job the only other part of her life.

But she also had the feeling that the job wasn't going to be enough for her. Not anymore. She wanted more with Nick. Now, if only she could believe that she deserved him, and actually take the risk.

"Kenji informed Nick. He took the news as best as can be expected, and Kenji said he's now in his workout room, waiting for us to get to there."

He'd need to work out, Luna thought. She knew how

he had a hard time controlling that feeling of impotence that came from these deaths.

"Did Everett receive a letter?"

"No. He said normally the letter arrives within eight hours of an incident," Van said.

"Which means we've got a few hours until we get any more information. Detective Miller has a team going over the crime scene. Rick, do you think you could go over there and take a look?"

"I'll do it. Miller won't be happy. She found out I'd been talking to some friends to pull records, and gave me a friendly warning," Rick said.

"I can go," Luna said.

"I need you with Nick. He's going to need someone he can talk to and trusts. You're the only one who he confides in," Van said.

Her boss was right, but she wondered if he expected her to tell him everything Nick had said in confidence. "I can't betray his trust."

"I'm not asking you to. I think you might be our best bet to keep him alive," Van said.

All of a sudden, all the feelings she'd shoved down, pretended she wasn't experiencing, swelled up and she had to turn her head to look out the window instead of at the side profile of her boss.

Nick was reckless. This was going to drive him to do something dangerous. She wasn't sure she could convince him to give them a chance to get a plan in place.

And Van trusted her to keep Nick safe.

The man she loved. She had to do it. She knew herself well enough to accept that she wasn't going to fall for anyone else, and as much as they might not have a future, she needed him safe and alive so they could try.

That was the entire reason why she'd had Kenji replace her. "I'll do it."

"I know you will, kid. Rick, maybe talk to the detective and let her know that we need the information even if it's rough and unverified. We have an entire database of people from Nick's and Everett's lives that we might be able to find a connection with."

"I will," Rick said. "But you know cops don't like it when we tell them we have more sources than they do."

"You'll have to be charming when you do it," Van said.

Rick snorted. "That's not me. Maybe you should send Xander."

"She doesn't know him, she knows you," Van said.

They pulled into the underground garage and all got out of the vehicle and into the elevator to the penthouse. Luna ran the image of the garage through her head. Something was out of place, but she couldn't put her finger on it until they got to the penthouse.

Nick couldn't help but watch Luna leave. He knew she'd be safer away from him, but the minute the door closed, he wished he hadn't let her go.

Kenji noticed him eyeing Luna but said nothing. Instead he walked around the living area in the penthouse, familiarizing himself with it. Nick went to the grand piano and sat down. He started to put his hands on the keys and a flood of memories and emotions from last night washed over him.

He felt Luna's absence keenly and turned away from the keys to find Kenji watching him.

"So, what's your routine?"

"Weekdays, I run from six to seven, shower, breakfast, and at my desk by eight. Stay there until six or so. Then dinner and any social commitments. Tonight I'm quiet."

Kenji didn't sit but kept walking around the room, cataloging the entrances and looking out the windows. "Is there anything that Luna did that you didn't like?"

"No. She's really good at her job. That's not why I asked to have her replaced," Nick said firmly, not wanting anyone to think she hadn't been performing her role.

"I know she is. So I'm not clear on why you axed her," Kenji said, coming closer to Nick, stopping a few feet away and putting his hands under his jacket on his lean hips as he stared Nick down.

He caught a glimpse of Kenji's shoulder holster and the faint outline of a bulletproof vest underneath his dress shirt.

"I'm not sure that concerns you."

That was all he was going to say about it. He was so tired of having to answer to Price Security. While a part of him knew that they were doing their best to keep him safe and alive, another part of him wanted all his yes-men back around him.

Kenji pulled his phone from his pocket, read something on it and then texted back quickly. He pocketed his phone and looked at Nick. There was a quietness to Kenji that hadn't been there before and that was telling because the man was eerily quiet at all times.

Even before the other man spoke, he knew that someone else had been killed. Luna? God, please don't let it be her. Don't let him have waited too long to send her away. He'd wanted one more night with her and he hoped his selfishness hadn't cost her life.

"Luna?"

"She's fine," Kenji said.

Nick felt weak with relief and, for a moment, closed his eyes. Grateful that she was okay. "Who?"

"Aldo Barsotti was found dead in his car. Detective Miller and her team are on their way to the crime scene. He was identified by someone he knew from the neighborhood."

Aldo.

No. Nick's gut churned with the pain of loss and anger that someone else he cared for was dead. The feelings that he'd had in the past stirred in him. A lifetime of grief that he had never been able to protect anyone. "Has someone informed my dad? Where was he found?"

"Detective Miller was going to send someone to speak with him. Aldo was found two miles from your father's estate," Kenji said. "I'll verify he's been informed. Do you want to call him?"

"I want to go and see him," Nick said. This was too close to his father. He knew that Aldo had been on Luna's list of suspects. Nick had never really thought Aldo would threaten him. He'd been too loyal to the DeVere family. And despite the fact that Aldo had never told him about the letters, Nick still loved him like a second father. This loss hurt.

Even more than Jack's had. Aldo was one of the few people who'd been in his world all of his life. Now there was only his father left. And his dad was dying. Whoever was doing this was intentionally chipping away at the people Nick cared about.

He felt isolated and alone.

"Of course. Van is on his way here with the team.

We'll get a plan in place and then take you to see your father," Kenji informed him.

Nick just nodded and realized that merely making plans and regrouping wasn't working. Whoever had killed Aldo was taking a real risk doing it that close to his father's house. There was no time to figure things out. He needed to lose the security detail.

"Sounds good. I need to work out to work through this. I'll be in my dojo," Nick said.

"Let me check the room and then I'll leave you to it."

Kenji did a sweep of the dojo. Nick waited until he'd left before he went to the gun cabinet hidden behind a panel in the corner of the room. He took out the SIG-Sauer P220 that he used at the shooting range. Then he put on a bulletproof vest that had once been Jack's. He covered it with his shirt and jacket and slipped out of the dojo. After checking the hall was clear, he made his way to the stairwell that he and Luna had used during the fire alarm. When she'd been shot at.

Hurrying down the stairs, he entered into his underground garage and got in his Bugatti. He hit the remote to open the exit and roared out onto the street, heading toward Malibu and his father.

He kept saying he wasn't going to let anyone else die in his place. Unless he was with his father, the killer was going to go after Everett next. Nick was the only one who could end this.

Whoever this was, it was time for them to stop with the pithy letters and homicides that took out people around him.

As he got on the freeway, part of him knew that Aldo's death was different. That was why he was concerned. This didn't feel like the other attacks. Whoever that man had been, he was responsible for Aldo's death, and he had some connection to the letters that his father had received. Nick was going to find out who he was and stop him from causing any more pain.

"He's gone," Kenji said as they entered the penthouse.

The Bugatti had been missing from the garage. Damn. That was what had been wrong when they'd entered.

"Thoughts?"

"He was worried about his dad," Kenji said.

"I'll go," Luna said. It wasn't that she didn't trust anyone else to keep Nick safe, but she knew him better than they did and had been to the Malibu estate a couple of times.

"Make sure your tracker is on and put in your earpiece. Do you need a car?"

"I'll take one of Nick's," she said. She was already on her way out the door. Knowing the keys were all kept in a keycoded lock box in the garage. In the elevator, she couldn't help looking at her reflection and blaming herself for this. She'd known that he'd agreed too easily to her being replaced and she shouldn't have gone.

But she'd wanted him safe. Or had she? It wasn't hard to see that she'd also been trying to keep herself safe. And now she was going to have try to catch up to him before he did something reckless.

And he would do precisely that.

Nick felt like he couldn't be killed. It didn't matter that she knew differently and had told him numerous times that he could be hurt. He didn't believe it. Not when he was putting others first.

She took the least conspicuous car in the garage, a classic Mustang stick shift with a heavy-sounding V-8, and drove like Nick always did. Fast, but carefully, toward Malibu.

Her mind needed to focus as she drove so that she didn't think of Nick possibly already dead or in the hands of a killer. These attacks were different from the "accidents" that had happened around Nick when he'd been growing up. Jack's death had been staged to look accidental, but the shot at his building, the knife attack in the club and Aldo's death were clear attempts at murder.

She activated her earpiece. "How was Aldo killed?"

"Gunshot, close range. Like the other person was in the car with him," Lee said.

"Thanks."

Luna pulled off the freeway and drove on the winding roads that led to the DeVere estate. When she got to the gated entrance, she waited for the security guard to clear her in. But the gates didn't budge. She parked the car on the side of the road and got out. She pulled her gun as she made her way to the gate, which she couldn't budge.

Great. She tucked her gun back into the holster and climbed up and over the fence. Her arms ached as she lifted herself over the top, which was what she got for skipping her arm workout since she'd been back in LA. She dropped to the ground, making her stab wound throb as she land in a crouch, and pulled her gun.

Sweeping the area before she headed to the guard booth. She approached cautiously. She saw the outline of a slumped body, blood oozing from a head wound.

Luna rushed into the booth. The security guard was in a heap on the floor. She reached out to find his pulse and it was faint but steady. Unconscious, not dead.

She started to put her gun back into the holster when she heard footsteps behind her. She tensed, waiting until the person was close enough, and then sprang to her feet as she turned, dropped into fighting stance and used a front side kick to stop the other person.

Nick.

It was Nick sneaking up on her. She tried to stop the force of her kick as it connected with his body. He blocked it at the same time. So he wasn't hurt.

"What are you doing?" she asked him. Trying to stay focused on her anger and not her relief that he hadn't been killed.

"Trying to protect my dad. Now that Aldo is gone, he's vulnerable," Nick said. "There wasn't time to discuss it."

"I know. Van, Nick's with me. We are at his father's estate. The security guard is unconscious," she said, knowing Lee would inform Van via their comms.

"I'm going up to the house, I don't care what Price says."

Nick's voice was low with anger. She didn't have to relay that to Van.

Luna would go with Nick and keep him out of danger. Whatever it took.

"Keep me posted. I'm with Detective Miller at the crime scene," Van informed her.

She muted her earpiece after that and turned to Nick. Though it had only been a few hours since she'd seen him, it felt like a lifetime. "I thought you might be dead."

"I'm not. I told you—"

"Please tell me you have something other than fate to protect you," she interrupted.

"A gun, a bulletproof vest, and now you," he said.

"Now you want me by your side?" she asked, trying to get her head into that calm space it needed before they walked up to the house.

"I don't think I can keep you away," he said.

There was something in his voice she wanted to explore but that would have to wait. This was the moment she'd hoped wouldn't come but, as a bodyguard, had known it would. She was ready to put her life on the line for Nick as she had for all of her clients. But with him the stakes were higher.

She wanted the person who'd been torturing him for his entire life, stealing his sense of security and safety, to pay. And she wasn't going to let them get away with it.

"You can't. I'm in charge. You follow me when we get to the house. Is the housekeeper there?"

"She doesn't work every day. Dad's pretty low maintenance. So I'm not sure if she'll be there. Given that she was yesterday… I'm guessing no."

"Okay. We'll plan for her to be there," Luna said. "We'll go through and clear each room on the bottom floor before going up. You will stay where I tell you too, agreed?"

"I'll do what I have to," he said.

"Nick—"

He pulled her close and kissed her hard and quick. "I'm not going to take any chances with my life or yours, Luna."

He started walking toward the house and she moved

quickly to keep pace with him. That embrace had raised questions that she wanted answers to. But later. After they made sure Everett was alive.

Chapter 22

Entering the foyer of his father's house, Nick was very aware that Luna was in charge. He wanted to protect her and his father, and he knew his recklessness could put her in danger, so he held himself in check. She started to clear the rooms downstairs and Nick was impatient, wanting to get up to his dad.

All the security measures his father had put in place and none of it had ever really kept them safe. Not really.

"Is this necessary? Dad could be dead upstairs."

She didn't turn her head from scanning the last of the rooms downstairs. On the walk up to the house, she'd given him an earpiece so he could communicate with the Price team. Van and Kenji were on their way to them, and Rick and Detective Miller were still at Aldo's crime scene waiting for a backup unit before joining.

"Yes. We don't want any surprises. Let's go upstairs.

Stay close to the wall and behind me. Can you use the gun you're carrying?"

"I can."

"Watch our back as we move up, just in case I missed something," Luna said.

He nodded and wanted to kiss her again. Right now his mind and body was a jumble of thoughts and emotions. He was scared, angry, upset, guilty, worried, and the thoughts going through his head were ones that he didn't like. Mainly of his dad dead or injured in his bed. Luna injured again. He had promised himself no one else would be hurt in his place.

Only now did he realize how dumb that promise had been. He had no power to protect anyone. And being on the stairs behind Luna just reinforced that. He could watch their back and he could physically hold his own against someone else. But he couldn't control another person's agenda.

As they neared the top of the stairs, they heard voices coming from his father's room. One of them was a woman's. He started to move by Luna, but she grabbed his arm firmly, jerking him to a stop.

"No. We listen, we take a read of the situation, and then we go in. Aldo was shot, so there's a good chance whoever is in there with your dad has a gun," Luna said.

"All the more reason to get in there and protect him," Nick said in a low tone matching Luna's.

"Naomi, I never slept with you," he heard his father say. Who was Naomi?

"You don't remember. We were in love and you promised—"

"I didn't make promises. I was married and my wife was pregnant. You worked for me."

"I did work for you, and we spent a lot of late nights together," she reminded him.

"We did. But you were pregnant when you started working for me," his father said gently.

"I wasn't. That's just a story you've made up to make yourself feel better about what happened," Naomi said. "Campbell is your son and rightful heir. He was born three weeks before Nicholas."

"Shit, that's Hazel," Nick said, recognizing the way she'd said his name. "What the hell?"

"That's not possible. Nick is my only son, and will remain my heir. You can point that gun at me all day and it's not going to change anything." His father was done coddling Naomi and his tone was firm. Nick knew from experience he meant business.

"Well, you can either change your will or die," Hazel said, "knowing that your son will be killed as well."

"With another accident?" his father said sarcastically. "You don't have a great record when it comes to actually getting Nick."

"I don't. But my son does. He stabbed him in the club the other night," Hazel said.

Nick moved around Luna, toward the bedroom once more. She tried to stop him, but he brushed her hands aside. "She's threatening my dad."

"Give me a second to just make sure there isn't anyone else here," she said, starting for the window at the end of the hall where she'd stood the first day they'd come here. She checked the lawn while he moved up quickly behind her, mimicking the way she held her gun near her shoulder, ready to aim. He'd only ever fired at targets at the shooting range and had no real-world experience with this.

Until this moment, he'd believed he'd be able to defend himself with the handgun. But he was sweating and the thought of firing at another person...unless he knew they were the one who'd killed Jack and Aldo, it would be hard. Could he shoot Hazel? He wasn't sure.

Before Luna got to the end of the landing hallway, a shot was fired and Nick tried to push her out of the way, but she leaped at him, shoving him to the ground. He felt her wince and knew that she'd been hit. He dragged them both back against the wall.

The sweats he'd had a moment ago gone, he lifted his gun, covering their rear. "Are you okay?"

"Yeah, just a graze. It's a good bet whomever is with your father knows we're here," she said. "Let's go."

She got up but stayed in a crouching stance and Nick did the same, following her as she moved down the hallway.

"Luna, you good? What direction were the shots fired from? Kenji and I are on the grounds," Van said. "Kenji spotted someone moving on the grounds."

"I'm fine. The shots came from the southwest. There are some trees."

"Situation in the house?" Van asked.

"It's Hazel."

"Nick's assistant?"

"Yes," Nick confirmed. "Price? Hazel's son is out there. I know he's a SEAL. Proably the sniper"

"She's gone silent," Luna added. "Do you think we're safe going into the bedroom?"

"Kenji and I aren't that far away. Wait until we get the sniper until confronting Hazel."

"Spotted the sniper. Going silent. You're good to move on Hazel. Watch your six."

"We'll be careful. You and Kenji stay safe," she said.

She turned to Nick. "I'll go first when we get to the door, I want to verify it's just Hazel and your father in there before we go in."

She moved toward the open door and Nick knew she was doing her job, but he also loved that woman and wasn't going to let her go in there first.

Luna was listening for the all-clear from Van as she put her head around the corner of the door. Hazel stood next to Everett's bed, holding her gun pointed at the older man. She had a two-way radio in the other hand. Hazel didn't look as calm as she had the other times Luna had met her.

The sweet grandmotherly-looking lady was gone. In her place was a woman wearing sleek, modern clothing and holding a weapon in her hand like she knew how to use it. She stared at Everett, not taking her eyes off the prone man.

Everett looked frustrated and scared out of his wits.

Hazel lifted the radio in her hand and spoke into it. "Campbell? What's going on out there?"

"Watch your six, Mom. Nick and his bodyguard are in the hallway. I shot Luna, upper arm or shoulder. She's not down. Nick has a gun as well," Campbell said.

Luna pulled her head out of the doorway as Campbell made that statement. But she could confirm there were only two people in the room. Hazel was on the left side of the bed and they were on the right. So Luna would have to move past the open doorway to get a good shot at her.

Nick looked furious, moving like he was going to

enter the bedroom. Luna stopped and shook her head firmly no. "Not yet."

He held his gun like he was going to shoot and kill Hazel.

"Nicholas? I want you and your bodyguard to stay out of this room or I'll shoot your father," Hazel said.

"Talk to her," Luna said in a low voice, needing a few minutes to figure out the best way to take out the threat to Everett and keep Nick safe.

"Why are you doing this?" Nick called. "Don't I pay you enough that you don't have to extort my dad?"

"He's the father of my son. Campbell deserves his inheritance. Everyone knows you two have a strained relationship. And you don't deserve DeVere Industries. You are a spoiled playboy," Hazel said, a note of derision in her voice.

Again, Nick tried to move and Luna stopped him. "Please just keep her talking," Luna whispered to Nick. "Try to distract her. I'm going to move to see if I can get a shot at her from here."

"I hate this. I want to confront her."

"We are going to get her. But we don't want your father hurt," Luna said.

"Okay," Nick responded then said to Hazel, "You know I'm more than that. You keep my calendar, and you have helped me set up work with charities. I'm not a bad man, Hazel."

"You're not a good man, either, are you? You lie."

"When did I lie?" he asked her.

Luna saw the way Nick held himself and knew that she was on borrowed time before he did something reckless.

He believed he was indestructible. More than once,

he'd told her he couldn't be killed. That belief was so strong in him that she knew there was nothing he wouldn't do to save his father.

It didn't matter that he'd been upset with his father and Aldo because they'd kept things from him. Nick had only a handful of people he cared about, and Hazel had been responsible for picking them off one by one throughout his life. There was a limit on how long he was going to continue to talk to her.

Luna felt stuck, as well, trying to find a good position to get at Hazel.

"When you said you'd be at the beach house for your birthday..." Hazel said.

Luna body-crawled to the far side of the hall to keep her profile as low as she could. She had a glimpse into the open door of Everett's bedroom, but Hazel wasn't visible. She was going to have move into a better spot. She started to crawl toward the left of the door opening.

"Why did that matter?" Nick asked.

"You made me kill the bodyguard," Hazel said.

Luna wasn't sure their earpieces would pick up that confession, but she was sure that Van would get Hazel to repeat that to Detective Miller. She hoped they almost had Campbell because she could see the tension in Nick, and he wasn't going to wait much longer.

"Did that bitch just admit to killing Jack?" Van asked in the earpiece.

Hazel seemed tense. Her voice was getting tighter with each response to a question Nick asked her. She didn't sound hysterical, just really pissed.

"Jack Ingram. That was his name. I didn't make you kill him," Nick said.

"She confessed, but I don't know that we recorded it," Luna said under her breath.

"So you did that?" Nick asked her.

"I did. Once you walked into the office and I realized I hadn't killed you, I called Campbell and asked for his help," she said.

"So he just found out he's Dad's son?" Nick asked.

"He's not my son," Everett said.

"Shut up," Hazel said and they heard the sound of a punch or hit.

Nick was on his feet rushing into the room before Luna could stop him.

"We're moving in," Luna said, taking two large steps and getting to the doorway as Nick moved through it. Hazel turned toward them, gun raised. She fired a shot and Luna lunged for Nick, using the force of her body to knock him out of the way.

She felt the bullet hit her chest, the force of her lunge interrupted by the blow. God, that hurt. She felt the burning and then fell forward. Blood was running down her shirt. She felt light-headed and knew she was about to pass out. She wasn't going to be able to protect Nick.

That was her last thought as she blacked out.

Dammit. Luna was on the ground, blood gushing from her chest. He blocked out the fear that she might be dead and leaped to his feet, running at Hazel, who seemed surprised and fired again. But the shot went wide. He knew he wasn't going to shoot Hazel. Maybe he could have fired at someone he didn't know, but this woman had sat in the office next to his for the last two years. She'd made him coffee, chatted with him and been a part of his team. This betrayal hurt more than

Nick wanted it to. He put his gun back in his holster as he continued running toward her.

Hazel fired again and this time her bullet hit him in the chest. But he was wearing Jack's bulletproof vest and, while it hurt, making his breath catch, he didn't stop moving forward.

"Are you really going to kill me, Hazel?"

"I want to. You don't deserve—"

"To live?" he asked.

She fired again just as Nick jumped at her and tackled her to the ground.

He grabbed her hand holding the weapon, firmly gripping her wrist and slamming her arm down hard until her fingers opened. The gun fell to the floor. He used their joined hands to knock it away.

Hazel dropped the radio, bringing her leg up between his, kicking him hard in the balls. She reached for his shoulder holster, trying to get his gun. Pain spread up his body, but he was so pissed off, he shoved it aside, twisting his body so that she couldn't reach his gun.

She rolled, crawling away from him toward her own weapon. Grabbing her leg, he yanked her, pulling her off balance, and she fell onto her side, hitting her head hard against his father's solid walnut nightstand. Her body made a sickening thud as she fell to the floor, and he moved closer.

God, had he killed her?

He crawled over and checked her pulse.

"Is she dead?" his dad asked.

"She's still got a pulse, so, no. But she's unconscious," Nick said, standing as he handed his dad the gun. "Keep an eye on her. I want to check on Luna."

"We've got her," Van said, coming into the room.

Glad that the security expert was there, he rushed to Luna's side and was about to lift her into his arms when Kenji dropped down next to him. "Don't move her."

Nick held her hand in his and looked down at her face, tracing his fingers along the curve of her jaw and leaning low over her as Kenji ripped open her button-down blouse. He took a pressure pad from a small bag and put it over the wound.

Nick rubbed his thumb against her knuckles, his heart in his throat. This was what he'd tried to keep from happening. This was the very thing he'd feared would happen to her. And he'd been right.

"Keep pressure on this—9-1-1 is on their way," Kenji said. "Detective Miller arrested the sniper. That's what took us so long to get up here."

"Glad he was arrested. I tackled Hazel. She's out," Nick said.

"Van's watching her. Are you okay?" Kenji asked, his dark eyes watching Nick.

Nick wondered if the other man could see the wildness still roaring through him. Holding Luna's inert body in his arms, keeping pressure on her bullet wound, made him regret not killing Hazel. She'd taken so much from him. And why? He still wasn't sure how she'd thought her son was his dad's.

"Dad, how did you know her?" Nick asked from where he was next to Luna. "How did this happen?"

His father had given his gun to Van and looked like he'd aged ten years since the last time Nick had seen him. "I'm not really sure. She worked for me at the office, but that's it. Aldo can—"

Emmett's voice broke off and Nick saw tears in

his father's eyes. The first time he'd seen him cry. He wanted to go to his father but couldn't leave Luna.

Van put his hand on his father's shoulder and squeezed it. "I'm sorry about Aldo. If it helps, we're pretty sure he had figured out that Naomi was Hazel and confronted her."

"He did?" Nick asked.

"Yes," Van said.

"Will she live?" Nick asked.

"I think so. She's just knocked out. And I want her to pay for killing Jack and Aldo," Van said.

"Me too," Nick agreed.

The EMTs arrived, along with Detective Miller, and Hazel regained consciousness in time and was arrested before being taken to the emergency room. Luna was airlifted to the hospital. Nick wanted to be the one to go with her, but his father wasn't looking too good and Van had sent Kenji with Luna.

Nick couldn't get the image of her out of his mind. Pale, blood-stained clothing, and unconscious. That's what had happened to the woman he loved. And now that Hazel had been caught and had confessed, he should feel free. But he didn't.

He wanted Luna in his life, wanted a future with her. But she needed to survive. And even if she did, would she want to be with him? Her life would have to change, and he knew his would too. He wasn't sure a week with him was enough for her to believe they could have a future.

Nick stayed with his dad after they'd learned from Detective Miller that Naomi/Hazel's husband had been abusive, that after he'd died in a car accident, she'd convinced herself that her baby was actually Everett's.

She'd raised Campbell to believe that he was the bastard son of Everett DeVere and that his "father" wouldn't acknowledge him.

Campbell hated Nick as much as Hazel did, and it was only when Everett was diagnosed with terminal cancer that she'd decided it was time to kill Nick and force Everett to accept Campbell as his heir.

Something that Nick knew his father would never have done. He wasn't the kind of man who could be bowed to pressure. And until this moment, Nick thought he and his father were very different.

Chapter 23

Luna woke up in a hospital room. Her chest felt like someone was sitting on it and she heard the beeping of her heartbeat on a monitor. There was an IV port in the back of her hand and she was thirsty.

She looked around for either a bottle of water or the nurse call button, and the first thing she saw in the darkened room was Nick.

He was slumped over in a chair next to her, sleeping. Staring at him, she felt a wave of love rolling through her. But then she remembered that Hazel had been shooting at them. He was okay. He had to be if he was in the hospital with her.

She heard her heartbeat getting faster and took a few deep breaths to calm herself down. She shifted on the bed and Nick jerked upright. His hair was mussed from the way he'd been sleeping in the chair and stood up on one side. It was the first time she'd ever seen him not looking his best.

Their eyes met, and she realized that, no matter what, she wasn't going to leave him without telling him she loved him.

Just this one time she would take the risk that had always seemed too great for her. She was going to ask someone to stay in her life. She wanted Nick with her now and forever.

"How do you feel?" he asked, getting to his feet and coming over to her. She saw the bloodstains on his shirt and a hole in the center from a bullet.

"Thirsty. Are you okay?"

He was at her bedside now and put his hand on the side of her head, touching her so gently. "I'm fine."

He adjusted her bed so she could sit up and got her some water. She took a sip, slowly swallowing it.

"That looks like a bullet hole," she said, pointing to his shirt. "What happened after I went down?"

Nick told her everything that had happened and, while he was talking, Van poked his head in.

"Our girl is awake? Glad to see you, kid," Van said as he came into the room.

Nick stepped aside as Van walked over. She looked at her boss.

"You scared us," Van said. "I think Nick and I both wanted to kill Hazel for what she did to you."

"And Jack and Aldo," Luna said.

"Yes, but mostly you," Van said. "I'll let the team know you're awake. They are going to want to see you."

"I want to see them, too," Luna said. But she wanted some time alone with Nick. "Can you ask them to wait until the morning?"

"I will," Van said. He leaned over her, the scent of mint and his aftershave was strong. He kissed her forehead. "I'll be outside if you need me."

"Thanks, Van."

He turned on his heel, gave Nick a look that Luna couldn't read, and then walked out of the room. Nick came back to her side and stood there looking down at her as if he had something he wanted to say but wasn't sure.

That was so unlike him, she started to worry. Now that the danger had passed and he had his life back, he might want her gone.

She would, of course, respect that. She wasn't going to try to stay in anyone's life who didn't want her. She never had. But this time she wasn't just walking away.

"I think we need to talk," Nick said.

"I agree," she said but, suddenly, with the moment this close, she knew she needed more time. So she went back over everything at his father's house. "You didn't listen to me."

"I just don't take orders well," he said, sitting down on her bed near her hip. "But you knew that."

"I did. I was scared when I blacked out. Afraid your luck wouldn't hold."

"I was scared you were dead and that she was going to kill my dad," Nick said. "I didn't need luck today, I just had anger and a need for retribution."

"Being ticked off is a dangerous time to attack someone," she said. He had been lucky. Somehow he'd managed to control his emotions enough to get the upper hand with Hazel and take her down. "Don't do it again."

"Considering that Hazel is in jail, I'm hoping I won't have to," he said.

"I hope so, too," she said. "Your safety is important to me."

"As is yours," he said. "Which is what I want to talk to you about."

"Before you go, can I?" she asked. She'd stalled long enough. She had to know if he was the man she thought he was.

"Of course," he said.

"I... I don't want to leave you, Nick. I'm sorry. I know we live in different worlds and that, in reality, we might not work. But for the first time, I think I'm in love. I've never had that before." Crap, she was rambling, but he wasn't saying a single word. Just looking at her from that spot near her hip.

She had decided to take this risk but she felt more exposed than she had when Hazel had lifted her weapon and fired that shot at Nick. This was the one leap that was harder to take than putting herself between him and a bullet.

Luna almost started to call the words back. Tell him never mind, but she didn't. She had waited her entire life to fall in love and find a man who could love her. If it wasn't Nick, she'd be shocked. She'd come too far with him to back down now.

"So, there it is. I'm not sure what you wanted to say, but I love you and I want to spend the rest of my life with you."

She licked her lips and realized that this wasn't the hearts-and-flowers confession he was probably used to, but this was who she was.

She loved him.

He had been afraid to hope that she would. Not because he didn't feel like he deserved love but because

Luna was so strong and so capable, she didn't seem to need anyone. He knew what it had cost her to say she loved him first.

Because he'd been almost afraid to say the words out loud to her. But those feelings had really blossomed once Hazel had been arrested. He'd been afraid to love and to lose Luna. Now he was free.

Hearing Luna say she loved him freed the last part of his soul that had been still chained to the past. He wanted to pull her into his arms, but she was fragile, injured because of the threat to him. They had a lot to discuss.

"I love you, too," he said. "I'm used to dancing through my life with no commitments, but since you jumped across that conference room, everything started to change."

"For me too. I thought you'd be just a typical CEO," she admitted, smiling over at him, but he knew she realized he wasn't jumping straight into a life together.

"I've never been typical." He was trying keep her smile, but the truth was she could sense he was holding back.

"Listen, I want to have that life together that you mentioned, but I'm not sure I'll be able to handle you putting yourself in danger. I don't think I can go through that again," he said.

When she started to speak, he held his hand up to stop her.

"I know I can't ask you to give up your job. I've never been in a situation like this before."

She took his hand in hers, lacing their fingers together. "Me either. This is the first time I've ever asked to stay with someone. I don't know how it will work either. But I do want to try. Do you?"

Nick took a deep breath. His entire life he'd drifted along, trying as a child to have close connections and a family of his own, finally finding that a few friendships were all that he could handle as an adult. "I guess this will be something new for the both of us. But, Luna, I can't see you like this again."

"This is only the second time I've been injured on the job," she said carefully. "So I don't think you have much to worry about."

"What was the first?"

"I twisted my ankle going for a morning jog with an ambassador I'd been hired to guard. I stepped off the curb."

He smiled because she was downplaying the danger of her job and he knew that the woman he had fallen in love with was a bodyguard. That asking her to give up her job wasn't something he could do. He was going to have to figure out how to accept it.

"That doesn't sound like you," he said.

"We were being chased by someone in a vehicle and I did push the ambassador out of the way," she said.

"See, that's what I'm afraid of. You are never going to keep yourself safe and I'll be worried every time you go to work."

She sighed. "I've never been in love before, Nick. I want this to work. Can we try six months of me on an assignment and us dating and see what happens?"

He moved closer to her and he knew that he'd do whatever he had to, to make this work. "Yes, of course we can. I've never loved a woman like I love you, Luna. I'd always thought I had a good life, and I do, but when we're together, I realize what I've been missing. And the thing is, I know I can't find that with anyone but you. We can take as much time as we need to figure this out."

He meant that. He wasn't saying what she needed to hear just to appease her. He would do whatever was needed to keep Luna in his life.

"You know I've never had anyone to come home to, Nick. I think that there were times when I was reckless because of that," she said.

"Me, too, but reckless in a different kind of way. Will you live with me and make a home with me?"

"Yes," she said.

He pulled her into his arms and kissed her gently. He wanted to get her home and make love to her. But for now he was happy holding her.

The nurse came in and checked on her, mentioning that Luna was doing well.

Nick sat next to her bed the rest of the night as she slept and when she woke up the next morning the Price Security team came in, Finn on their heels.

Luna was a like a little sister to everyone on the team. This was her family. He decided that he was going to make it a priority to get to know them all.

"I can't believe it was Hazel," Finn said. "I never suspected her. She and I even talked about how unfair it was that you never got a chance to just enjoy being a DeVere."

"In what way?" Nick asked him.

"Just living the good life without all of the trauma. But that doesn't matter. I'm just glad you're both safe," Finn said.

"Me, too," Luna said as the conversation she was having with Van paused.

Nick went back over to her side and took her hand in

his again. "Luna and I are going to be living together when she goes home."

"Just what I was hoping to hear," Van said. "I think we can get her some assignments closer to home too."

Two days later, Luna was released from the hospital and Nick made love to her in his big bed. Afterward, they talked about the future and what their life might be like together.

Epilogue

The last year had been the best of her life, Luna realized as she stood next to her new husband on the lawn of Everett DeVere's Malibu mansion. It hadn't been all smooth sailing, but the good times outweighed the bad. And no matter what, they were both committed to each other.

Luna DeVere would never get used to seeing her name in the headlines—Bodyguard Tames Billionaire Playboy.

"You've been tamed," she said as she set her tablet down in front of her husband.

"Nice to see something can still surprise me," he said, pulling her off her feet and onto his lap and kissing her. They'd been married last night at his father's bedside with just Finn and the Price Security team around them.

As Luna sat on her husband's lap, she knew she had found something that she'd never expected to. Knowing she didn't have to keep her guard up all the time with Nick had given her a new vision of herself.

Everett was still on chemo and hanging on, but his doctors admitted they weren't sure how much longer he would be with them. He and Nick had gotten closer since Hazel and Campbell had been arrested. The trial had lasted for six weeks last September and had been in all of the headlines. Another scandal for the wealthy DeVere family. But Nick and Everett had ignored them and continued working to make DeVere Industries even stronger.

Finn had taken on the COO role within the company, allowing Nick to have more freedom in his schedule. Price Security kept her busy and, after a three-month bodyguard assignment away from Nick, Luna had decided she was ready to move into a different role.

Lee was tired of working in the office, so she and Luna switched roles. Luna realized that part of the reason she'd always wanted to be on the road for assignments was that she'd hated not having a home. Going home to Nick each night was perfect.

So when he'd asked her to marry him on Christmas Eve, she'd accepted. The wedding had been small and intimate, including only the people they loved.

"What are you smiling about?" Nick asked.

"Just thinking about how you thought it was luck that was protecting you all along, but once I became your bodyguard, you didn't need luck anymore."

"Not sure I agree."

"You don't?"

"I think you're my lucky charm," he said.

"And you're mine. Together we can face headlines, bullets, exes and the future."

"Yes. Together we're unstoppable."

* * * * *

Watch for the next book in the Price Security series, coming soon from author Katherine Garbera and Harlequin Romantic Suspense!

#2255 CSI COLTON AND THE WITNESS
The Coltons of New York • by Linda O. Johnston

When Patrick Colton's fellow CSI investigator Kyra Patel sees a murderer fleeing a scene, he vows to keep the expectant single mom out of the line of fire. But will the culprit be captured before their growing unprofessional feelings tempt them both?

#2256 OPERATION TAKEDOWN
Cutter's Code • by Justine Davis

As a former soldier, Jordan Crockett knows the truth about his best friend's military death. But convincing Emily Bishop, his deceased buddy's sister, exposes them both to a dangerous web of family secrets...and those determined to keep Jordan silenced.

#2257 HOTSHOT HERO FOR THE HOLIDAYS
Hotshot Heroes • by Lisa Childs

Firefighter Trent Miles *stops* fires—not starts them. But when his house burns down and a body is found inside, he becomes Detective Heather Bolton's number one murder suspect. Their undercover dating ruse to flush out the killer may save Trent from jail, but will Heather's heart be collateral damage?

#2258 OLLERO CREEK CONSPIRACY
Fuego, New Mexico • by Amber Leigh Williams

Luella Decker wants to leave her heartbreaking past behind her. Including her secret romance with rancher Ellis Eaton. But when the animals at her home are targeted and a long-buried family cover-up comes to light, Ellis may be the only one she can trust to keep her alive.

Get 3 FREE REWARDS!

We'll send you 2 FREE Books **plus** a FREE Mystery Gift.

FREE
Value Over
$20

Both the **Harlequin Intrigue®** and **Harlequin® Romantic Suspense** series feature compelling novels filled with heart-racing action-packed romance that will keep you on the edge of your seat.

HARLEQUIN
PLUS

Try the best multimedia subscription service for romance readers like you!

Read, Watch and Play.

Experience the easiest way to get the romance content you crave.

Start your **FREE TRIAL** at
<u>www.harlequinplus.com/freetrial</u>.